Blood Shadow

Blood Never Lies

an *Eye of the Storm* companion novel

written by Dianna Hardy

Blood Shadow
Blood Never Lies

Copyright @ 2018, Dianna Hardy
The moral right of the author has been asserted.

Published by Satin Smoke Press, April, 2018
First Edition | ISBN 978-0957540477
This print version updated August, 2023

Written in British English.

This book is set in 11 pt Cormorant Garamond Medium by the Cormorant Project Authors, licensed under the SIL Open Font License, Version 1.1.

A CIP catalogue record for this book is available from the British Library.

Satin Smoke Press
(an imprint of Bitten Fruit Books)
South Hampshire, UK

www.satinsmoke.com

A Brief Recap

Dear Readers,

This section acts as a brief recap for those who have read the *Eye of the Storm* series, and serves as a background to the character of 'Jennifer' for those who have not. While you do not have to read *Eye of the Storm* to enjoy this book, it is highly recommended that you do to gain full understanding of everything the characters have been through to get to this point. If you do wish to read it, do not read the section below beforehand, but come back to this book after you've read the series. If you do NOT wish to read it, the below should help you with *Blood Shadow*.

The following contains huge spoilers for the *Eye of the Storm* series...

Jennifer Warren was previously known as Selena Smith. A female werewolf in the Surrey pack who never underwent her change, she betrayed her pack, including her father, Richard, believing she would be saving lives in the long run by doing so. Blinded by fear, jealousy, and bitterness, her betrayal led her, by accident, into an enforced mating with a Trident called Gabriel. (Tridents were horrendous beasts, genetically engineered with the help of magic, by Dr Evan Trident, over two hundred and fifty years ago. They were monstrous versions of the werewolf, driven by base animal needs and not much else. They craved violence and were steered by lust. All Tridents were finally exterminated five years ago.)

Jennifer (Selena at the time) found herself in the worst situation possible, and was imprisoned in a farmhouse in Kent by the Trident for over two months. At their hands she suffered unthinkable abuse, but also fought for her life, rising to become their 'Alpha' (albeit briefly) in a bid to survive. She had to gain the allegiance of a Trident called Edwin (her mate's right hand man), and murder her brother, Stephen, in order to gain the title. This execution was organised by the leader of the Trident – a human called Bab who came from a long line of mysterious travellers originating in Egypt and steeped in magic. These travellers were also called Human Hands. Human Hands *help* werewolves and are friends of all wolves, but at some point, the line of Human Hands split, some turning away from this alliance, instead choosing to dominate wolves. They aligned themselves with the Trident. Bab was their most recent leader.

Finally, through grit and cunning, Selena escaped both Gabriel and Bab, killing Gabriel in the process. His death put her life in grave danger as female wolves are not known to survive the deaths of their mates very long.

Chased by the police and out of options, Selena jumped three hundred feet into a turbulent, rock-laden sea, not knowing if she'd survive.

She did survive, although had no memory of being pulled out of the water. I have included below, the very last scene in which we left her in *Eye of the Storm*, five years ago. It will lead straight into the prologue of *Blood Shadow*.

Happy reading.

Dianna
March, 2018

~*~

Light was what she noticed first; an awareness of it through her closed eyelids, and then, in almost painful amounts as she blinked her eyes open.

Sounds came next: the beeping of machines, the patter of feet, the quiet chatter of...

Startled, Selena sat up – *tried* to sit up – she couldn't.

Doctors and nurses... She was in a hospital.

Fear pounded her heart.

Everything hurt. *Everything.*

She looked down to find needles and wires protruding from her veins. *Jesus...*

She had to get out of here. Wolves didn't go to hospital – not human hospitals. Not unless they wanted to be tied to a trolley and experimented on once all the blood results had come back. Sure, it didn't *always* happen like that, but it had happened that way often enough throughout history. She didn't know the ins and out, but she knew enough of the dangers from things both Hendrickson and her father had told her over the years.

Her father...

God, what was the last thing she remembered?

Jumping. She'd jumped. Because she'd been chased by police. *Shit.* Another reason to get out of here. But how?

She looked around. Other patients lay in their beds – she wasn't alone. She could go for the 'cause lots of chaos' method of escape, but she didn't even know where she was, or how she'd gotten here. She'd be running blind.

Again.

Fuck.

"Jennifer, you're awake."

Who?

A nurse approached her with a smile.

She kept her mouth shut. The less she said, the better.

"You're in Buckland Hospital."

That meant nothing to her, and obviously the nurse caught on to that fact. "Near Dover," she explained.

Dover. That's where Gabriel had driven her.

The nurse picked up her charts, pulled up a chair, and sat down next to her. She was being super-friendly. Super-nice.

And Selena frowned, because usually, she'd be able to tell if this was an act or not. Wolves, in general, had no problems telling if humans were lying, but right now, she couldn't tell. She reached out with her senses, but ... no, she didn't have a clue. That made her anxious.

"You don't have to worry about a thing. You're going to be just fine. Do you remember what happened? Before you were brought here?"

Breaking her rule – she had no choice – she spoke. "How long have I been here?" Her voice was hoarse.

"Seven days," she smiled. "I left this morning's paper right here for you." She pointed to the newspaper lying atop the wheeled table next to her. **Thousands More Missing Persons Found**, read the headline.

Selena looked away from it, trying to make sense of her pounding mind.

Seven days ... the full moon had been and gone. She looked down at herself, at her hands, at her arms, realising she was looking for signs of turning. Had she become a Trident? She didn't feel like a Trident. But ... she didn't feel *herself* either.

"You have some bruising."

Selena looked at the nurse, surprised. She hadn't even noticed, but now, as she looked down at her body again, sure enough, she could see bruises around her wrists; some on her arms. She knew there'd be more around her ankles, knees, hips, vagina and anus, because they were all from the last time Gabriel had fucked her. He'd been rough – really rough, and he'd fucked her in Trident form. She'd said nothing, and had done nothing, so he'd done any fucking thing he'd wanted to – she'd *had* to play it that way in order to get away. She wasn't going to beat herself up anymore over it. He was dead now. *Good riddance.*

She pushed the vile memory to the back of her head, but couldn't push away the more worrying aspect of what this meant: *why hadn't she healed?* She should have healed completely within twelve hours tops; it had been seven days.

"There was swelling in your brain when you were first brought in, but we got that down straight away. You have bone fractures in a couple of places from the dive you took: your right ankle and collar bone. It's a miracle that's all, to be honest."

Yes, it was. She remembered looking down a three hundred foot stretch into a choppy sea. Maybe her body had done *some* healing because pretty much every bone should be broken. In her mind she calculated the hours: it had been the night *before* the full moon when she'd jumped. That meant she'd still been a wolf for about twenty hours while unconscious. If she had turned, it would have been six nights ago, when, presumably, she'd already been lying here in this bed.

But no one was acting like they'd seen a monster.

She felt bewildered. She'd never had bruises and bone fractures that hadn't healed straight away – no wonder everything hurt.

The nurse stared at her, and then lowered her voice. "We've done a forensic medical examination for sexual assault – a rape kit test."

Selena looked at her, shocked.

"You're clear for STDs so far."

She looked away. Humiliation snaked across her bowels. For someone else to so *obviously* be able to see what had been done to her was...

She blinked back tears. Unsuccessfully.

"And the pregnancy test we did was negative."

More tears fell – this time, of relief. She closed her eyes.

"The police would like to speak with you soon."

And how the fuck am I going to get out of that? Had they found Gabriel's body? Her fingerprints were on that gun. So much for escaping prison.

"The man who pulled you out of the water – he disappeared. The police are looking for him, too."

Selena stared at the nurse.

"He resuscitated you; he saved your life. He's the one who called an ambulance – that's how we know what happened. Do you remember that?"

She leaned back against her pillow, saying nothing. What could she say?

"Do you know who he is? Were you with a friend?"

She could have laughed. She didn't have friends. Whoever the hell had saved her life *wasn't* her friend – that she already knew.

The nurse looked at her, clearly waiting for her to speak.

She pursed her lips. That wouldn't be happening.

The nurse sighed. "Well, anything you can remember would be helpful, Jennifer."

What the fuck...? "How do you know my name?" she whispered. Talking felt vulnerable, like she was exposing herself.

The nurse looked pleased she'd said something. Her eyes brightened, and she smiled wider. "Your valuables are here."

Her valuables?

The nurse reached for a handbag.

It wasn't her handbag, but she took it from her anyway, and opened it. Inside was a whole bunch of shit that didn't belong to her. Normal shit – *human* shit. Tampons, a wallet, a notebook, some make-up...

She brought the wallet out, and opened it. Her attention went straight to the driver's licence in one of the card slots. She pulled it out, and stared at her own image staring back at her: *Jennifer Warren*. That's what it said on the licence. Her address looked like it was a flat in ... *what the hell? Yorkshire?*

Was she supposed to go there? That's where her dad was from. No way was she going there.

Like you have a choice – where the hell else are you going to go? JENNIFER.

The nurse patted her arm.

She flinched, then froze.

The nurse pulled her hand away immediately, and looked at her apologetically. "I'm sorry ... I didn't think. You're safe here, Jennifer. Please know that. I'll give you some space before the doctor takes a look at you." She smiled again, and then left.

Selena rummaged through the bag. She pulled out the notebook. The handwriting in it wasn't hers, and it was made up of menial things: shopping lists, doodles, and numbers for what looked like finances. This was ridiculous; this was a joke.

She rummaged further, and found a hidden pocket inside the back section. Slipping her hand in the pocket, her fingers brushed something. It felt like a slip of paper. She pulled it out. It was folded once. She opened it, observing the typed sentence inside.

Her heart raced as she read it.

You are human now.

She let out a shaky breath. *Holy fuck.*

That's all it said.

But it *couldn't* be true.

She looked down at the needles in her veins again. The

hurt they produced was ... new. She realised this now. The pain was *not* like pain a wolf felt from injuries. It was different.

Her bruises also hurt differently to the bruises Gabriel usually left. Their ache was greater now; she felt raw inside from his penetration – *physically raw*.

She had to swallow back rising vomit. She didn't need his violation to feel so fucking *real*.

But, in other ways, she felt less. Less because the arduous, and continual stabbing in her chest was gone. *No more mating pains.*

She looked out the window at the far side of the ward. It was daylight. But now she could tell that her vision wasn't as sharp as normal, she couldn't hear what the people at the very end of the room were saying, she couldn't smell the flowers in the vase on the windowsill...

When the moon rose, would she feel its pull?

She suspected the answer was no.

She felt knocked sideways. She felt terrified. What did this mean? How was she *human*? Was it true about human blood being somehow stronger? Superior? Had the human aspect of Gabriel's blood, mated with hers – *bonded* with hers (she couldn't believe they'd bonded; it was sickening) – somehow made her human? That seemed ludicrous. Nothing made sense.

She looked at the note again.

Someone knew the answers. Someone had typed this out; someone had created a new ID for her; someone had gotten this handbag together. The same someone who had pulled her out of the water.

She felt breathless; this was too much. Which was ironic given everything she'd been through, but there you go.

I'm human... I don't know the first thing about being human.

She looked at the handbag. But she knew where to start:

her new ID; her new address.

Start... She got to start over. The reality of this was like a wave breaking over her. *I get to start over.*

No mating pains, no dying, and no begging wolves she despised to fuck her ... she could *choose* who she mated.

No – not mated. Humans didn't mate... They fell in love.

"Miss Warren."

She was pulled out of her thoughts. The doctor greeted her as he approached her. "And how are we this morning?"

She folded the piece of paper, and slipped it back into the bag.

"Nurse Bailey told me you were having trouble remembering what happened."

Silence. She still wasn't sure what to say. Stepping into her new life seemed frightening, but it was the only path that lay ahead of her.

The doctor looked at her over his glasses. "Miss Warren?"

She took a breath, and cleared her throat. "Yes," she croaked. "Jennifer Warren. That's me."

Blood Shadow

Prologue

5 years ago...

This was it. This was the building. It didn't look much more than offices from the outside, but this was the address the hospital had given her. This was where she went to *share* her feelings about every fucked-up thing that had happened to her.

If she shared the actual truth, she'd be locked up.

Her upper thighs throbbed dully, as did other parts of her. There was still an awareness of Gabriel's touch; his violence. In her nightmares, he often morphed into Bab. She felt them both. The pain should have faded weeks ago, but the downside to being human was a frustratingly useless body that took forever to heal from any injury. So the pain was on repeat.

Why am I here?

Not 'here' in front of this building, but 'here', still alive. And human.

She'd known there was a chance she might survive, but for the first time in her life, she'd been perfectly willing to die.

Okay, no – not *willing*, exactly. But she'd known her death might be the likely outcome of hurling herself into the stormy sea, and she'd been prepared for that. Anything but further imprisonment.

A friend or foe – she didn't really know which – had brought her back.

A woman hurried past her and up the stairs to the double front doors of the building. She looked back at her, quizzically. "Are you coming in?"

Fuck everything. She didn't want to go in, but she didn't see how she could get out of it. If she didn't show up and put her name on the meeting's register, the hospital would know she hadn't been. Then, there'd be more phone calls, more questions, more prodding, and more from the police, too. They might rescind their decision to discharge her.

She let out a breath, and nodded, taking the door from the woman.

"Are you going up to DV?"

She flinched. Domestic Violence. She could laugh, but she didn't. There'd been nothing 'domestic' about anything she'd been through, and from the literature she'd received, it seemed this meeting was catered to anyone who'd been in any abusive situation from verbal assault to rape, and anything in between. She guessed funds and staff were too low to make these kinds of meetings more focused to the needs of the individual.

You only have to do this once. Show your face, get your name on the register, say as little as possible, then get the hell out.

'You have to get out.'

Her breath snared at Stephen's voice in her head, his final words forever etched in her mind.

Go on ... tell the room full of survivors how you shot your brother. That'll go down well.

They had no bloody idea. "Yeah, that's where I'm headed."

"Great. I'm Pam – I'm one of the counsellors leading the

session."

Wonderful.

"What's your name?"

Jennifer. But the name stuck in her throat, because it wasn't her name – something else she couldn't tell them. Anything she chose to share would be a lie.

Pam nodded at what she must have seen in her face. "I'm gonna go on up and make sure the room's ready. It's the second door on the right once you reach the top of the stairs. I'll see you up there."

No pressure, no over-friendliness, Pam turned and left, leaving her alone at the bottom of the stairs, for which she was grateful.

Maybe it won't be so bad. Maybe they won't make you talk.

Hesitantly, she took the steps one at a time ... quietly – she didn't want to announce her arrival. She seemed to be one of the first here though.

At the top of the stairs, she peeked around the wall, and froze. Her heart hammered in her ears, and she blinked, unsure if she was seeing right.

She swivelled back, hiding behind the wall she was pressed up against.

"Everything that's happening to you now is your fault. But there's a particular kind of pain for a mated wolf that is quite unlike any other... Allow me to demonstrate."

No. She couldn't stop the flashback. And she couldn't do this after all.

"Please, no. No, no ... no, no..."

Those cries belonged to *that* woman. That was *her* ... her screams...

Maggie. Her name was Maggie. She was *here*. The woman Gabriel had dragged out of the cage and...

And raped in front of you because you had refused to give him what he'd wanted.

Shit.

She couldn't breathe.

"I'm pretty sure her mind is gone. She's been losing it for weeks. You tipped her over the edge."

"Me?"

"Yes."

Silence ensued.

She looked back at her imprisoned companion. "I did nothing."

"Exactly."

She knew it was her even though she'd only caught a glimpse: the same haunted look, the vacant stare...

"You're a danger, Selena. You're a hazard to everyone around you. You're chaos personified, and do you want to know why?"

She closed her eyes and shook her head. Selena wasn't her name anymore. And she *couldn't do this*.

She turned and raced back down the steps towards the double doors. Maggie would take one look at her and it would end her. She shouldn't fucking *be* here. She wasn't like the others – she was the one who *caused* the fucking pain.

Outside, the warm September afternoon, tinged by the busy Canterbury traffic, did nothing to ease her suffocation. She *couldn't* be part of this meeting.

Scanning the streets, she spied a beggar less than a hundred yards away – a bedraggled-looking female – on the corner of the pavement she was on. This was another thing she didn't get about human society: were the homeless equivalent to rogue wolves? Had they been thrown out of their families? Why the fuck couldn't people just look after each other? Even as the ruthless bitch she'd been, it would have taken a hell of a lot for her to be *thrown* out of her pack.

She made her way to the female rugged up under her coat, despite the warm weather. *Woman, not female. You can't call them 'females' now.*

Digging into her handbag – the handbag that had been left for her; 'Jennifer's' handbag – she slipped her hand into the hidden compartment and closed her fist around the cash that was nestled in there. Her anonymous rescuer – the one who had pulled her out of the ocean and called the ambulance; the one who had left her that life-changing note telling her she was human now – had made sure she was looked after. A man they'd said – they'd only heard his voice on the phone. She didn't know any man who would care enough to do all that. Except one, but her rescuer definitely wasn't him.

She'd been booked into a B&B in Canterbury while she'd waited to be fully discharged by the doctors and the police who were still investigating her part in the events that took place three weeks ago. Those events had included her putting a bullet through Gabriel's head. She'd been terrified she was going to go down for that, but it turned out her rescuer had taken care of that, too. A bit of Datura had mysteriously found its way into Gabriel's body and he had gone 'poof' – or squelch, to be exact – and the police had found themselves somewhat lacking proof of anything, including her own involvement in his death.

"Hi," she addressed the woman sitting on a pile of blankets on the pavement.

Her eyes widened at her, and her palm stretched up.

"Change, miss?" she pleaded.

"Yes – I have a lot of change. But I need you to do something for me – you have to earn it."

Her eyes grew even wider. Hopefully she was sober. Her hair was brown, not blonde, but it would have to do. She didn't think the counsellors had fucking photos of her with them – all she needed to give was her name. "Earn it? What do I have to do?"

"You see that building down there?" She pointed to where she'd come from. "The one called Arlington House with the double glass doors on the front."

She nodded.

"There's a meeting inside on the first floor – second door on the right. It's for victims of domestic violence, and it's two hours long. They're about to start in five minutes. I want you to go in there, tell them your name is Jennifer Warren, and sit in on the meeting. If they make you talk, make up any shit you want, I don't care, but the name you need to give is Jennifer Warren – got it?"

"Domestic violence? Lie about that? To other women in there? You're sick, I'm not doing that."

Oh, Jesus fucking Christ, you have got to be kidding me. She pulled out a wad of notes from her bag. Not all of them – she wasn't stupid.

The woman's eyes almost popped out of her head now.

"Will you do it for two hundred pounds?" The cash had been left for her by her rescuer, right along with details of a bank account and a credit card. The cash was for meals and petrol so she could get to her flat up in York, something else he'd organised for her. She was supposed to be moving in tomorrow.

Never mind – she'd find another way to pay for food and petrol. She'd squirrel away what she had left and make it work 'cause there was no way on earth she was going to set foot in that meeting with Maggie in the room.

The woman couldn't take her eyes off the money. She nodded, slowly.

"Good. I'll be checking later that you did as I asked, and if I find you didn't, I'll get the police to move you on from your comfy spot here." Her heart twinged with guilt at her bluff – just a little. This woman probably deserved more of a break than she did.

And so does Maggie. Especially Maggie, after what you did to her. She growled inside at the thought. Her choices hadn't exactly been many – it was done now. She wasn't going to apologise for fucking surviving.

The beggar stood up with her large rucksack, her gaze still glued to the cash.

"Come on – I'm walking you to the building." But she wouldn't get too close in case Maggie saw her. Just close enough to make sure this woman didn't go back on her word. "I'm not giving you the money until then."

Conceding, the woman turned and walked up the street, Jennifer following close behind.

"Okay, stop here." They were three buildings away. "What name did I ask you to give?"

"Jennifer Warren," she replied.

"Good. Here." She held out the cash.

The woman took it, holding it like it might disappear in front of her eyes.

"I'll watch you go in. Two hours and that's it, all right? That's all you have to do."

She nodded.

"Go now. Meeting's starting."

She nodded again, half dazed, and Jennifer watched her walk into the building. She waited five minutes, ensuring she didn't walk back out.

Good. That's done. She didn't know if they'd buy it, but as long as they didn't know what Jennifer Warren looked like, she might just get away with it.

She turned away from the building and hurried towards the multi-storey she'd parked her car in. Yep – her rescuer had sorted that out, too: a Mazda 323, and a driver's licence in her new name. Fuck the waiting. She'd head to York tonight. She hadn't wanted to go at first, but seeing Maggie...

"Oh, you care – you care too much. You want to live. But that's not enough – no, no, no – not for you. You don't just want to live, you want to win. That's why you're a hazard. I don't know you from Adam, but I know, from one ill-timed smile, that everything you've ever done in your life is because you want to win. At all costs."

Getting as far away from Kent as possible would be ideal. And from Surrey. This wasn't her home anymore – she had no home. Not as Selena, anyway. Jennifer, though, had a glimmer of a chance left.

She'd take it.

Chapter One

Present day...

W e must stop meeting like this." She laced her fingers together, turned her palms outwards and stretched until she heard the faint crack of her joints. This was something she still wasn't used to – the cracks and clicks of bones and joints, and the hint of discomfort they brought. Her bones had never been so brittle.

"It's your brain, honey. You can stop seeing me any time you want to."

Jennifer blinked, also blinking the sun out of her eyes for a split second before its rays filtered through her eyelashes again. "I can't. I can't stop. I never got to say sorry. I am, you know – about what I did to you."

"I know. You've told me many times in the past five years. In your dreams, anyway."

She closed her eyes again for five seconds more, relieved she couldn't smell the male next to her, yet hating that very same fact. She couldn't smell anything, and not just in the sanctuary of the dream space they shared, but in real life ... whatever 'real' was. Scents used to be so sharp; now they barely existed.

She missed the smell of things, as if she'd lost a limb, or a part of her identity.

You have lost your identity.

Jennifer took a deep breath of the non-air that surrounded her and turned to face the wolf she knew wasn't really there and never could be. "Do you think somewhere between the layers of time and space, you can hear me? You can know I mean it?"

He smiled, his green eyes as forgiving as they always had been. "Sure. Why not?"

"Do you think there's any chance these dream meetings are more than that? Like they were with Rya—"

"No." But his smile remained, even as the word stabbed an old wound which still felt too raw. "Sorry – they're just dreams. The normal, everyday kind. The kind you create as a refuge; where you can fix everything, and nothing has to matter."

He blurred before her eyes as they filled with tears. She blinked again, and turned away, looking directly into the sun that pierced the horizon with its beams. They were sitting at the apex of a large hill. Meadows stretched out below her, blooming with flowers and teeming with life – life not hers; life she wasn't a part of. "Nothing's fixed," she whispered, her voice breaking over the truth she had no idea what to do with. Five years had healed nothing. Five thousand years would heal nothing.

"You've got to talk about it." That was just like him to say something like that.

Relive it all? Hell, no. She brought her knees up to her chest and hugged them to her. And even if she'd wanted to... "There's no one to talk to – not about everything that happened. You're the only one who might have listened. You're the only one who cared."

"Not the only one."

A crumpled piece of paper rustled the blades of grass as it blew her way and landed by her feet. She reached for it; unfolded it and smoothed it out in her hands. **It's time to go – wake up**, *read the typed words across its centre. "I don't even know who sends me these."*

"They know a lot about you, though. They know all the bad

bits. You can talk to them."

"I don't know if I can't trust them." Although her mysterious note-sender, her rescuer, had given her no reason not to trust him.

But he'd also remained hidden. Anyone with something to hide could never be fully trusted.

She turned back to her companion – and despite the falseness of his presence, he was the only being in her life she could consider a companion. "You never hid anything. You were so open. I'm sorry I abused that."

He smiled again, but this time, his eyes looked burdened, the green of them darkening a shade. "I know you are. But it's time to go – it's time to wake up."

"I don't want to." A deer caught her eye in one of the meadows that stretched out below. It grazed on the grass peacefully, its coat gleaming under the sun. Many moons ago, she'd have been able to smell that deer – to smell its contentment. Scent wasn't just scent, it was an extension of an emotion; of feelings. "All the bad things stay away from here."

"That's not true, and you know it. It's all still in your head. And now it's here, too."

The deer started, something frightening it.

Her blood ran cold. "What do you mea—" She screamed as she was knocked right off the ground, the blow nothing she could have ever seen coming.

The deer ran, the thudding of its hooves vibrating through the earth.

Landing hard, she rolled, half crying, half gasping; she was sure she heard her ribs crack. They wouldn't heal – not now she was human.

In shadow, she scrambled to her knees, every inch of her shrieking in pain. The pain grew ever sharper when she realised she was now naked, her clothes torn from her in the attack, and she was torn, too, part of her instinctively rising to fight back; another part *insisting she flee.* Run ... run! Like the deer. RUN.

Paralysed between both urges, she did neither, but turned to face her assailant as she clawed along the ground.

Colours could lie, just like anything else. His *eyes were also green, but of the palest, coldest hue – so pale, they sat, a striking, de-caying 'mint', against his tanned skin. Everything about him was striking, including the fist he'd used to hit her with. He was evil in-carnate. It was* his *shadow that swathed her.*

A quick glance around told her her only friend had gone, right along with the deer, and – so it seemed – the sun. It was the moon that now hung over them.

"Alone again." Bab's voice was like a lance through her middle. "You should have woken up." He took a step towards her.

"Don't touch me," she snapped. But her words trembled as much as she did. Should have run. Should have run like the deer.

He smiled, and it was sinister. "I don't have to." He raised his hand, which raised his shadow. The black tint licked her skin as it swept across her, then it clenched her between her thighs. She gasped in horror, the horror embedded in the mortifying fact the contact aroused her.

"Stop." She fell back – no, she was pushed back by the damned shadow. It passed over her breasts and pinched her nipples which puckered. A soft wail escaped her. "Please stop."

"You stop. I'm not even fucking here." Bab lowered himself onto her.

"Don't!"

"Wake up, then. Go running back to your poor excuse of a life. Did you think you could escape who you are?" The pressure between her legs increased; it drew out her wetness and pulsed against her clit until she couldn't hold back the rock of her hips.

She sobbed as Bab moaned. "I never got the chance to sink my cock into you while I was alive. Think I can do it right now?"

And there it was, hard and thick, seeking entrance.

She bucked and yelled; spat in his face.

He laughed. "You're not even trying to stop me. You like it dark, Selena, don't you? Creamed yourself every time Gabriel raped you. You like it really fucking dark." He plunged into her.

She sat up, screaming, only to realise the scream that echoed in her mind had never made it beyond her lungs – her chest *hurt* with the scream, but it hurt with more than that. It hurt with lustful ache – in her groin, in her breasts, in the core of her ... identity.

Who the fuck am I?

He'd said her name. *He'd said her fucking name.* She never wanted to hear it again, and certainly never from *him*.

He's not real, he's not real, he's not real...

He'd felt far too real.

Terrified and shaking, she looked over to the left side of the bed.

David lay sleeping. His soft and steady breathing went a small way to calming her; grounded her in reality. But her arousal stated a different reality – one she couldn't think about right now. *Ever again.*

She was fucked up. Fucked up in a disturbed way. She *hadn't* bloody escaped it, not really. It was still happening.

In dreams, not in real life.

Which was sometimes worse. In dreams, her mind liked to torture her anew; liked to replay events with twists and new endings – endings in which she screamed and begged.

She closed her eyes, and took a breath in, then another, trying to slow her heart rate. It worked a little, but her arousal still called – even seemed to increase. She didn't want to be aroused; didn't want to feel anything like that. It just reminded her of... "Fuck," she mumbled under her breath.

On trembling legs, she levered herself out of bed, taking

care to arrange the covers back up so David wouldn't get cold and wake.

Maybe you should wake him. He could ... relieve you.

Christ, no, she'd be using him.

You use him anyway.

Sod it – she couldn't think about this right now. Her head was a mass of jumbled crap.

She reached for the ache between her legs, needing to appease it, then yanked her hand back. *No.* She was better than this.

No, you're not.

She made her way out of the bedroom and into the bathroom next to it, shut the door and turned the lock. She leaned over the sink for balance. Or in case she retched. The mirror above the sink seemed to taunt her reflection back at her, her long, strawberry blonde hair, hazel-coloured eyes with their copper gleam, and full, smooth lips belying the monster that lurked within.

Was the monster hers to begin with? Or had it been injected into her veins?

You're human now ... you're human now...

So go wake your human lover and ride his human cock.

She didn't want to orgasm.

But she didn't want the arousal to linger, which it would if she didn't release it. All of tomorrow, at work, she'd be reminded of his trespass into her dreams because of the heaviness in her loins.

She looked at the bathroom wall, picturing her boyfriend lying on the other side. He slept naked.

She used to – she didn't anymore, even if the vest and shorts she wore to bed always bugged her a little. Clothes really weren't comfortable in human skin. She didn't know how people wore them all the time, but she'd learnt, the hard way, what a beautiful screen of protection and privacy they offered – one she'd never take for granted again.

But right now, her sleepwear practically itched.

Take them off. Then, wake David up and slide yourself against—

No. She shook her head and turned back to the mirror. She couldn't be in the same room as David. She didn't think he'd mind if she woke him up for sex – it wouldn't be the first time – but he wasn't the reason behind her need which wasn't fair. She had to stop doing this to him. Not that he knew. Of course he didn't know.

He knew *some* things. He knew shit had happened to her five years ago, but she'd kept it vague – he'd gotten the gist. He'd never once pressured her for intimacy, and he'd accepted the fact it hurt her to talk about her past.

That was true to an extent – it did hurt. It was the whole werewolf issue, though, that kept her from confiding in him properly. That and the fact that...

She let her fingers trail downwards until they grazed her clit through her shorts. She groaned.

Quietening herself with a bite of her lip, she glided them forwards and under the cotton, splitting her labia, delving into the slickness that coated her entrance.

The fact was, she didn't love David. But she tried to. She tried to every day. She tried now as she caught her breath at how close she was to climax: David and his love for her, David and his care of her, David and his warm brown eyes; David with his patience and his sweet, sweet smile.

It should be *easy* to love him.

David's face merged into Gabriel's.

Heat surged under her touch, and she gasped.

Gabriel's face became Bab's – those eyes, that sneer...

She threw herself back, away from the sink and her reflection. She couldn't come this way – not thinking of *him*. God, no. She never had, and she never would.

Trying not to cry, she crept out of the bathroom and down the stairs. For a second, she wasn't sure where to go, but her feet took her into the living room and towards the sliding doors that led to the back garden – if one could call it that. It was a tiny patio with a patch of grass.

Turning the key that sat permanently in the lock, she slid the glass door open, and stepped out into the night air.

For a second, she was her wolf again. It was early October, and the scents and sounds of 3 a.m. which veiled the grass and flowers of the neighbouring gardens and the many fields beyond, rushed at her; the dynamism of her senses, electric – and so, *so* familiar.

Then, they were gone.

The emptiness they left behind was stark.

Pushing the crushing barrenness to one side, she glanced at the moon. It looked larger than usual and hung low, three days from being full. There was a time when the moon would have dictated her arousal every month – agonisingly so. It was one blessing at least that the moon no longer held any reign over her, or any wolf for that matter. That's what her note-sender had told her, anyway. She no longer had any connection to her pack, or even the world in which wolves resided.

So all your pain belongs to just you – can't blame the moon this time.

Her attention turned to the four loose bricks low on the wall that separated her garden from her neighbour's. Crouching down, she jiggled them until they came out, then she reached into the space they'd left and pulled out the small wooden box secreted away in a dip in the ground under those bricks.

It was the only place in her house David didn't know about. She hadn't shown him the notes. She'd have to explain what they meant – she'd have to explain her past.

She opened the box. Relief rushed through her; comfort blanketed her. And also, a faint sense of worry – she didn't know the intentions of her note-sender. She didn't even know, for sure, his gender – she just assumed him a male from what the nurses had told her. Another assumption was that the one who had rescued her from the sea and the one who wrote her the notes were the same person. There was a chance they might not be.

But the notes – fifty of them over the past five years – had been her anchor. More than that, they were the only existing bridge between her last world, and this one, and while half of her would permanently bury anything relating to her past, the other half had to concede that the bridge provided her with a surety she found nowhere else.

She ran her fingers through them, all fifty strips of paper loosely piled into the box – typed words on each piece.

Five years ago, she'd have been able to hold these to her nose and smell their scribe; hunt out the one who had kept her standing and kept her safe.

Whoever it was, they – he – knew she no longer had that ability. He had total control. He had kept his anonymity while midwifing her into her new life. He'd given her her name, but she didn't know his. He'd given her a flat she'd finally sold last year; had pointed her towards the job she now had, warned her of the colleague who had tried to get her fired; of the burglar who had tried to break into her house six months ago (*that* had certainly caused a ruckus in this small village)... The list went on. He'd taught her everything she'd needed to know about being human in the human world.

The only thing her note-sender had never once mentioned was David.

A small pencil and notepad lay nestled in the box under all

the paper. She fished them out and wrote on the top sheet: **Had another nightmare.**

The note-sender knew about the box, and knew she left her own notes in reply every now and then. It was a perplexing mix of creepy and abating. She'd tried to catch him out before – she'd left her messages, then hidden upstairs, peeking out between her curtains into the garden to catch him venturing onto her property and pulling out the bricks.

No such luck. He bested her every time; managed to sneak in after she'd fallen asleep, and that was another thing she despised about being human: how much damned sleep she needed. How the hell anyone got anything done was beyond her.

He always seemed to know when she left a note in the box. Was he watching her now?

Unplanned, her awareness slithered awake, then sparked on an intake of breath from her. It became sexual, her arousal pressing once more, not faded at all in the cold night air, but far too present.

He's watching.

She conjured a male in her head, and though he had no body and no face, he had words. Words she needed. More importantly, there was *only* him, and no one else – no beasts to break her.

As illicit as this felt, this was the only chance she'd get, so while she clenched the note she'd written in her left hand, her right ventured past her shorts once more and found her sex.

Crouched on her shins, she rose to her knees, and leaned on the wall, the note crumpling as her hand fisted around it. "God..." She gasped through the hair fallen across her face. Still swollen, and wet against her fingers, she wasn't far from orgasm. And the mind was a powerful thing, because her conjured man might as well have stood behind her – her skin pricked as if he did.

Out of thin air, she created his voice, deep, husky, close to climax himself and breathing into her ear; raspy moans of want... His hand replaced hers, his touch against her heated nerves that little bit harder, firmer... "Ooh..."

He moved against her, with her, was all around her; his warmth swallowed her cold, inch by inch, until all she was was fire.

He groaned.

She came.

It was blissful. Blissful because in those few, glorious seconds that he consumed her mind, all beasts lay slain.

Blinking against the ecstasy of release, she knew the moment of peace would be fleeting. She'd never done *that* before. She'd never used her note-sender in such a way. Had he seen?

She waited for the guilt – the same that invaded her whenever she climaxed with David thinking of ... well, not David. Not really.

There was no guilt. Perhaps it was because her note-sender was so elusive in the first place.

Glancing at the message she'd written for him, she hoped that if he had borne witness to what she'd just done, he'd understand. She'd mentioned her nightmares before – he knew they were torturous for her.

Gingerly moving from her position, still reeling, she folded the note, hesitated, then gently pressed her still-wet fingers against it. Her scent – it was a mark of thanks. *And if he's not a werewolf, he'll probably find it gross.*

She couldn't seem to muster the energy to care. Instead, she yawned, sleep once more filling the space her nightmare-induced fear had reigned earlier.

She put her note in the box, closed the lid, placed it back in the ground, and jostled the bricks into the wall.

With eyes half closed, and floating on release and relief, she made her way into her house, locked the sliding door, and went upstairs.

David was still sleeping. He hadn't moved; he was in the same position she'd left him in.

Climbing into bed as quietly as possible, she snuggled under the covers, wondering if she should cuddle up to him, and unable to come to a conclusion before she fell fast asleep.

• *Chapter Two*

Clock alarms were the worst. They always hurt – her ears, her head... She groaned. She'd long since lost the ability to wake naturally to the sunrise, her body no longer as attuned to the earth – to nature – in the way it had been.

Jennifer flailed out with an arm and smacked the clock anywhere that might work until she hit the right button.

Her eyes still closed, she felt the bed dip, then sensed David lean into her. She heard his smile in his voice. "Morning, sleepy head."

He dropped a kiss on her mass of tangled hair, nuzzled her a little with his nose, then moved down until he found the side of her cheek and left a kiss there, too. "It's Friday. You can lie in tomorrow."

Right. She had to go to work. Work was dull as fuck, but it wasn't horrendous, so she didn't mind too much. It had done a good job keeping her mind off everything else over the years. "It's six thirty?" she groaned.

"Six thirty-two now. I'll get the coffee going."

"Thank you."

He laughed at her mumbled thanks and passed his fingers through her hair. "By the way, I forgot to say that Tom the butcher called me yesterday. He had your order ready. I went and got the lot. We're well stocked for at least two weeks."

She smiled through her closed lids. Her love for meat was a running joke with David who couldn't understand how she could eat so much of it. "Bacon for breakfast tomorrow, then?" she asked, sleepily.

"Yep – and sausages."

"Yay."

He laughed again. "You know, I reckon you single-handedly keep the butcher shop afloat." He got off the bed and placed another kiss on her cheek. "Right ... coffee coming up."

She heard him leave the room.

Getting up this early was a pig, but she'd chosen to move to the country because living in York city itself had been a little too stifling for the part of her that still needed space and freedom, even if she no longer ran trails through woodland, and splashed through brooks.

The quaint and silent village of Summerbridge provided exactly what she'd been looking for, and although the drive into work now took little over an hour, she lived at the foot of the Yorkshire Dales. From her bedroom, she could see the horizon and rolling slopes of land that stretched and stretched, and it lightened her heart. From outside her front door, a fifteen minute walk was all it took to be in the middle of the lushness – bleak to some extent, but she still responded to the call of the land. Some traits, it seemed, would always be 'wolf'.

David had moved in with her. She hadn't been able to say no – not after she'd crushed him completely by refusing to buy a house together. Having spent her entire life being dependent on others – mostly males – she simply couldn't relinquish the little independence she had now gained. Buying together would have done exactly that, and it wasn't a compromise she'd been willing to make.

Her name had gone on the mortgage alone, and he'd

moved in as a lodger, paying her rent which amounted to half the mortgage and all the bills. She then paid for her half and all the food. It worked out well; they were a good team.

If you loved him, it would be bloody perfect.

She groaned again, and finally opened her eyes and moved herself from the bed if only to be rid of that thought. Love was highly overrated anyway. Love wasn't something she'd ever had any hope of giving or receiving from the start, so the lack of it hardly needed to be a loss.

Right ... as if he feels the same way. He's completely in love with you.

Yeah, he was.

She changed into her clothes, and buried that thought, too. What the hell could she do about it?

Cut him loose. Leave him. It'll devastate him, but he'll be free to find someone who does *love him back.*

That was exactly what she should do, and she knew it, but she was selfish, and she wasn't ready. He was literally the only person she had in her life. Without him, there was just her and fifty notes.

And your occasional nightmares.

The loneliness would feel too crushing, and making friends really wasn't her forte. Scrap that – she was downright awful at it. She didn't *get* most people. Didn't understand why they liked the things they liked, found it tiresome that day-to-day conversations were *so* superficial. How was the latest about what's-his-face cheating on what's-her-name on that reality TV programme important in *any* way at all? What the fuck did it matter what shade of lipstick someone wore to whatever meeting in spring, summer, autumn, and winter? Apparently, matching the seasons was imperative.

It probably didn't help that she worked in a beauty spa – of all the ironies. She'd never cared an iota about her appearance until it mattered for earning a living. Getting by as a wolf was all about how strong you were, the force of that strength naturally embedded in your personal aroma; getting by as a human relied much, much more on how you looked, and although David laughed and said it wasn't like that at all, she couldn't see how it wasn't. Social media, smartphones with cameras – cameras fucking everywhere – filters on every app to make everything look pretty – so pretty they no longer resembled anything real... Models and actresses were the gods of this world, even if they couldn't possibly look the way they did on magazine covers and digitalised film. Yet, they were who everyone aspired to look like.

So, everyone was doomed to fail from the outset.

She found it impossible to get her head around. It was as if everyone walked around thinking they lived a life they actually didn't.

"You need *other* friends," is what David said. "People *aren't* like that."

Maybe he was right. It's not like she had a point of reference for being human.

"You don't like the superficial stuff, so see beyond it."

But she didn't understand why it existed in the first place.

She'd tried to put all her pet peeves aside and join in with her work colleagues, but it turned out she was a shit liar now – even worse than when she'd been a wolf, and most annoyingly, she now also sucked at being able to tell when someone was lying to her, which left her feeling vulnerable most of the time. There were many things about being a wolf she missed. Things she never thought she would.

She'd started working at the spa little over a year ago. After weeks of awkwardness all round, her workmates had quietly left her alone to get on with her job in silence, and that's how it had been ever since. She didn't mind one bit, but coming home to David was the only thing she looked forward to by the end of the day, no matter her missing 'deeper' feelings for him. It was so pathetic, she tried not to think about it.

Yes. *Selfish.* She was far too weak to let him go.

"Coffee's ready!" came his familiar call from downstairs.

She flung on the jeans and top she wore yesterday, and ran a hand through her hair, not bothering with any make-up – it would cut into her coffee time. Her coffee fix was more needed.

"Coming!" she replied. She drew open her bedroom curtains and took in the fabulous view from her window, opened it, and breathed that view in.

The locals around here had been friendly enough, but clearly wary of her as a newcomer. She didn't mind that at all – wolves were like that too – and perhaps that was another reason why this little village made an all right substitute home. This was a human reaction she actually understood.

Heading downstairs, she smiled at her toast and coffee waiting for her on the small breakfast table in the kitchen. "Thank you," she said, smiling at David as he gulped down the last of his own coffee, then picked up his rucksack. He preferred it to a briefcase, though it looked a little odd with his suit pants and shirt.

"You're welcome, darling. I've got to run. See you later."

"See you later."

He pecked her goodbye on the lips, and this was it – this was their weekday routine. "Steak and chips for dinner," he said as he strode down the hallway.

"Okay, sounds good."

He nodded, gave her a last wave, then shut the front door behind him on his way out.

She had fifteen minutes before she needed to leave. Taking a bite of her toast and a sip of her coffee, she took a quick peek at the headlines of the regional newspaper that had already come through the door, automatically looking for news of human abductions and anything that signalled pack activity of wolves, or ... other.

There was nothing.

Why do you do it? Why do you look for it?

She didn't know. It didn't exactly help her leave her history behind.

She suddenly remembered last night's dream and her trip to the garden. Dropping her toast, she made her way into the living room, and back outside through the sliding door.

"Hello, dear."

Oh... She rose to her tiptoes and met the eyes of her neighbour over the fence – an elderly gentleman by the name of Jack.

She inwardly grimaced and hoped *he* hadn't been awake at 3 a.m. watching what he shouldn't have been. He had a clear view into her garden from what she guessed was his bedroom window. "Good morning, Mr Stewart, how are you?"

"Jack, dear ... just Jack."

"Sorry – Jack."

"All good, all good ... back playing up a bit today."

"Sorry to hear that."

"Didn't get much sleep."

Fuck. "Oh."

"Have a good day, love. I'd better get back to my pot of tea."

"Right. Yes – you have a good day, too." She wondered what rumours about her might be flying by the end of the day.

Maybe he saw nothing.

What a fucking bright idea, bringing herself off in her garden in the early hours of the morning.

Well, there was nothing she could do about it now.

Glancing up to make sure Jack wasn't staring from any of the upstairs windows, she knelt down and pulled out the bricks, and then the wooden box. Her heart skipped a beat when she opened it: her note was gone, replaced by a new one.

Already? In just four hours? Was she being watched all the time?

You know you are. He always knows when you need him.

Exhilaration ran through her, which was just sad. *Are you really jonesing for someone you've never met? You* must *have a boring life.*

She picked out the note, then shut the box and put it back, along with the bricks.

She waited until she was back inside with the door shut and locked before opening the treasure he'd left. *Could be a 'she', you know – you know* nothing *about him.*

Everything inside her leapt as if wanting to escape the confines of her skin and chase ... *something.* Just to run.

The words... *God, the words.*

He *had* been watching.

**All dreams can show you something.
And I'm glad I could help.**

~*~

David hadn't realised he'd had a smile on his face until his project partner and long-time friend, Prisha, had brought it to his attention with an eyebrow raise and an inquiring stare – a look he knew very well. She was as skilled at decrypting him as she was at decrypting computer programmes.

Despite their closeness, he hadn't been planning on telling her his news. She wasn't a fan of Jennifer; that was plain to see, even if she tried to put her personal niggles to one side for his sake. She'd always been polite to Jen on the few occasions they had met.

His buoyancy, however, seemed to be a tad difficult for him to contain. He unzipped the side pocket of his rucksack and reached into it for the small velvet box he knew was there.

As Prisha's gaze fell on it, her expression went from bemused to mildly alarmed.

Well, he hadn't expected her to hide her thoughts. He didn't care. He was about as excited as he could get. "I'm going to ask Jen to marry me." He grinned.

She looked up to meet his eyes, her mouth opening and closing like a fish releasing air. "Erm..."

"Go on, you can do it. You can say the word."

"The word?"

"'Congratulations'. I know how much you like her, after all." He opened the box, unwilling to let his colleague's slight grimace pull him down.

She stared at the gold band tucked into the cushion, the sun's rays that streamed through the window literally bouncing off the solitaire diamond. He'd picked gold because he thought it brought out the coppery brown of her eyes perfectly; he'd picked a single diamond because it complimented her hard inner-strength – something he greatly admired, and he told her so, often. After the things she'd been through, he felt it was important that he did. He'd read a lot over the past couple of years about how to best be there for victims of abuse. He'd always wanted to support her but had never wanted to scare or stifle her.

"Jesus, David..." Prisha leaned over on her chair and draped her arms around him in a hug. "Congratulations – I'm saying that because I'm your friend."

"And?" he asked, waiting for the inevitable.

She didn't disappoint. "And I think you're far too good

for her, which I'm also saying because I'm your friend."

"I hadn't expected to see you jumping for joy."

She sighed. "I'm happy for you, I am, I just … you don't even own the house you live in – *she* does. She refused to commit to you over that, what makes you think she'll say yes to this?"

"The commitment's there, she just shows it differently."

"Because of her past?"

"Yes."

"The one she hasn't even told you about?"

"She has."

"Not all of it."

"Enough of it. I don't need the details, and I wouldn't expect that from her. What would you have me do? Ask for a graphic recount of all the horrid things that were done to her?"

"If you're going to spend the rest of your life with her, maybe that's not such a bad idea."

"Thinking about it in that way is a huge trigger for her. Besides, I really don't need to know the past to move into the future – we can create it from the present; from where we are now."

Prisha sat back, raised her hands, took a breath in, then exhaled. "Fine. Fine, I give up. I don't think you've ever seen sense with this woman. David, we've known each other since high school, you know what *I've* been through with marriage. If I couldn't get you to open your eyes two years ago when you met her, I can't get you to open them now. I hope you have many happy decades together." She swivelled back around to face her laptop, and David couldn't deny the sting of her words despite knowing they were coming.

"I love her, Prish."

Her shoulders sagged a little, and her pissed-off

expression eased. She offered him a small smile. "I get that. I just don't think she loves you."

"She does. In her own way, she does."

"Her own way? And that's enough for you? That's okay?" Her voice was getting all tight with frustration again. "That she might hold you at arm's length, never completely letting you in until death do you part? You're *okay* with that?"

"Prisha—"

"Explain something to me," she said, her tone churlish, "'cause I don't know if there's some kind of gender difference here – maybe the way we come at this love thing is biologically different – but is it because she's stunning?"

That pissed him off – she knew it would. He snapped the box shut, zipping it back into his bag before returning to his own laptop. "Maybe it is a gender difference – the bitch thing seems to be exclusive to women, after all," he threw back, annoyance fuelling those words rather than any belief in them. That wasn't the way he thought at all and she damn well knew it. She also knew he wasn't shallow – he'd never choose to be with someone for their looks alone.

"I'm sorry," she whispered. "I didn't mean what I said. I'm trying to be happy for you, but I'd be a shit friend if I lied, and the truth is, I think you're making a huge mistake. I'm sure she's not a horrible person – I'm not saying she's a monster or anything – I'm just saying I think she's got issues that'll last a lifetime and she'll dump them on you, 'cause that's who *you* are. You're the best friend she could possibly have. You're her crutch." Her chair squeaked as she swivelled back around to face him. "You're my best friend, too. I don't want to see you get hurt."

The door to their office opened, and Keith, their project manager, poked his head around it. "Hey, kids." His way of greeting them, even though he was younger than them by two years. "Our meeting this afternoon with Battlehouse Media has been cancelled – they've gone elsewhere."

"What?"

"They've found another contract."

That was shit news. Battlehouse were a huge blue-chip company. They were predicted to be next year's main providers for much of the UK's digital market, and to have gained a contract with them would have pulled their little organisation out of the pond and into the expanse of the sea.

"Why?"

"They cut them a better deal than we could afford."

"Our encryption services are unrivalled."

"You know that; I know that. They don't give a fuck if those services are cheaper elsewhere. So we *need* this contract with Maxahill Solutions. How near are you both to being finished on this baby?"

"Two more days," piped Prisha. "We need to make sure the ciphers are flawless."

"Good. Meeting with Maxahill is arranged for Wednesday next week. It needs to be fuck-up free."

"It will be, boss." She smiled, and Keith couldn't argue with it because Prisha was the best in her field. The best David had ever met, anyway. The woman was not only a whiz at what she did, but passionate about it, too. She had big visions – big 'protecting the world from terrorist hackers' kind of visions.

David was happy just plodding along – a comfy, secure job he found mildly interesting that paid for his leisure and hobbies was more than fine as far as he was concerned. Hobbies were the rainbows of life.

Prisha wanted the gold at the end of them – wanted them so much she had blown her gasket thirteen years ago when her father had refused to pay for her university degree in Mathematics and Computer Sciences, insisting the money was saved as a dowry for her arranged marriage. Her family came from a very traditional Hindu culture. They'd already accepted dowries for her three older brothers.

Months of arguments had ensued; she'd threatened to blacken the family name if they refused to pay for her degree; vowed to be an untameable shrew for whatever man she wed so he'd rue the day he accepted her father's offer – in some ways, it hadn't been hard for her, because Prish was ruthless. She was a tough nut with her head screwed on right, and knew how to manipulate her way out of the cultural mire she'd found herself in. She also knew the art of compromise. After driving her parents, siblings, and extended family (even halfway across the world) to the point of breakdown, she'd taken a deep breath, walked into the house one evening, and gave them an offer they couldn't refuse. She would marry whomever her father wanted without complaint, be the dutiful wife and bear children, *only* on the condition he would pay for her degree. Having exhausted all their energy, she'd done a 180 and called her trump card while they were at their very weakest.

They'd agreed.

A year later, Prish had been accepted into Oxford University, six months after that, she'd been married to a second cousin she'd never met, and three months after that, she had secretly had her fallopian tubes sealed whilst lying about being on a residential with the university for two weeks.

Female sterilisation. David had been shocked. How on earth she'd gotten a doctor to agree to that operation at her young age was anyone's guess, but she'd found a way. She had had no plans of ever bearing children – her career was her life – and as far as David knew no one in her family, not even her husband, had a clue about the procedure. In fact, Prisha was pretty sure he'd already fathered children, in secret, with another woman. She didn't give a fuck – she'd gotten what she wanted.

Ruthless.

And he admired it no end. But no way in hell had he ever wanted to be in the middle of all that drama. A quiet life had always been for him.

Keith left them to it, and Prish turned back to him. "That's us putting in extra hours for the next week, then."

"You don't seem too upset about it."

She shrugged. "I love the work." Then, she lowered her voice. "But ... erm ... I couldn't tell you before now, but I've been offered a new job."

"You have?" That was big news. A wave of sadness washed over him. Working with Prish was fantastic – they'd always made a good team. "Where?"

"Down in London," she dropped her voice to a whisper and grinned, "with MI6. I start in six weeks, and if I tell you more, I'd have to kill you."

"For *real*?"

She nodded, her grin widening. "Not the killing part, of course – well, unless you go and tell anyone." She stuck her tongue out in jest. "I got the job confirmation this morning – interview was last week. My notice for Keith is in my bag, though I can't tell him who it's with, and neither can you or I'll be fired before I start. The new job's at top level entry, too. I can't wait!"

"This is what you've been waiting your whole life for! Come here." He held his arms open.

She got out of her seat and landed on his lap for a hug.

"Congratulations."

"Thank you."

"What does hubby say?"

She snorted. "I haven't told him yet, but like he'd care if I commuted. But I'm already looking for a flat down there. They've already said they might need me on call at all hours."

"He won't move down with you?"

"And leave behind the secret family we both pretend I don't know about? I'd rather he stayed here. I really don't care, and my parents are getting too old to bother putting up a fuss as long as we keep up appearances. It's not like we ever really had a relationship; and certainly not what a marriage should be."

"But you've got your dream job waiting for you now, so it's been worth it, right?"

"It has – we all make sacrifices. It's about picking the ones we can live with. Seriously, I can't wait."

"It's going to be great. I'll miss the hell out of you, though."

Her grin faded a little. "I'll miss you, too. Hey ... congratulations, too. On your engagement, I mean."

He raised a brow. "Look ... I know you're not happy about it. You don't have to lie to me."

"Saying I wish you the best is *not* a lie. I really do. I want you to be happy; I *don't* ever want to see you in a marriage like mine. Just promise me one thing, okay?"

"What?"

"That if you have even a *fraction* of doubt, you'll hold off on the proposal. Waiting would only help if there's doubt."

"I promise."

She smiled, then pulled herself off him and back into her own chair. "Good. Thank you. Because you're her equal, David. You're *not* her rescuer."

⸱Chapter Three

I t was here. He knew it was, even if the area looked a bit different in the dark than it did during the day. But this part of the beach did look exactly the same as the one in his dream, so this was it. He shouldn't be here because he was supposed to be asleep – and he was only five – but he knew the way to the beach. There was only one lane he had to walk down. He wasn't going to get lost.

Roman scrambled down the large rocks until soft sand sank under his feet. Grains sprayed over his sandals and between his toes.

The full moon lay huge and low across the horizon, over the ocean, like a giant crystal ball in the sky. Half of it was in shadow, because something very special was happening. His pa had called it a Blood Moon. He'd said Earth's shadow would completely cover the moon and turn it red, but tonight, it would do it while the moon was closer to Earth than it usually was – that was why it looked so big. Those two things didn't usually happen at the same time. That was also why it had to be tonight that he sneaked out of the house to come here. He'd read about the creatures in his pa's books in secret – books with long, complicated words they all thought he was too young for. While he didn't understand most of it, he understood enough to make sense of the dreams he had.

The beautiful creatures were nearer the surface of the ocean every full moon, and this special full moon meant something important because he had been dreaming of her more and more – every night for the past few days.

A siren – that's what she was. Part human, part fish, and partly made of the elements, water being the main one. All sirens were stunning. But the one he saw in his dreams was something special. Her long, white-blonde hair haloed around her head like flowing light; her voice vibrated his ribcage when she spoke. Sometimes, she sang. When she called his name, he all but melted – the warmth it conjured within him was like nothing he'd ever known. It was home away from home, and his own home didn't always feel like he belonged there. They all thought he was weak.

He let the foam of the next wave wash over his sandals, relishing the cold on his toes.

A rustle behind him brought him out of his surroundings. Bab.

He gritted his teeth. Of course he'd followed him.

Annoyed, he turned, and saw his brother climb over the rocks after him. At fifteen, Bab stood much taller than Roman – almost a man – and those ten years between them made Bab head of the household whenever Pa wasn't around.

It irritated him, but he couldn't be too irritated with Bab because as annoying as he could be, he had always looked out for him and defended him against Pa, and just two months ago, Bab had saved Roman from a demon he'd accidentally conjured trying to prove there was more to him than everyone thought.

Pa had been enraged – he'd never seen him so angry. Bab had calmed him down though – he'd swooped in to clear up the mess Roman had made. Roman had put the whole family in danger. Bab was the one good at magic; Roman wasn't. All he had were pictures in his mind; sometimes they were visions, sometimes they were dreams – his grandmother called it clairvoyance – but most of the time they came in bits and pieces he couldn't make sense of. Bab called it a pansy skill – it was good for nothing. Bab, on the other hand, could create potions that made people do things, or think things. Two weeks ago, he'd finally got a demon to do his bidding.

Pa was so proud of Bab. "If you can control demons, my son, you can control beasts – we must all learn to do that," he'd said the other day as if he'd had a secret only for his eldest son to know. Then, he'd looked scathingly at Roman. "Emotions are unpredictable and wild. Anything wild is a beast that needs to be tempered."

His dad saw him as a beast; a lesser thing.

Roman had tried to be colder and harder like Bab, he really had. But the visions which happened every day and some nights ensured he felt everything that happened in them. Over the past year since the visions had started, he'd felt thousands of feelings that didn't belong to him.

Pa hated feelings because they got in the way of doing magic properly. Bab took after him, soaking up all his lessons.

"Why did you follow me?" he called out, arms crossed over his small chest, trying not to let his irritation show and pretending he wasn't a bit scared now Bab had found him. If he told Pa...

Bab finally caught up to him and smiled, his eyes – pale and green like his great-aunt's were, and like the revered Asenath's had been – glinted silver under the moon. "Because of this." He pulled a notebook out of his jacket pocket – Roman's notebook, or his sketch book to be more precise.

"That's mine!"

"Yeah, and..." He opened it on the last page he'd drawn in. "This is why you're here, isn't it?"

The graphite siren stared at him from the page. That was his other talent: drawing. His pictures rivalled those of adult artists, apparently. Ma called him her little prodigy. Ma often beamed with pride at this talent. Pa considered it a waste of time. "I've been dreaming of her. This is important."

"You're such an idiot, and I followed you because you're an idiot. 'Cause I reckon I'll need to save your life again since you're so stupid," he taunted. "That's a siren. Sending you dreams is what they do – it's their way of calling you – and when you come, they catch *you and keep you for mating."*

He knew about mating because he'd seen cats and dogs do it. He knew it was about making babies. "That's gross. And that's not what she's doing."

"That's exactly what she's doing."

"No, it's not. I'm only five years old."

"So? She'll keep you prisoner 'til your balls drop."

He frowned. He wasn't sure he really knew what that meant.

Bab smirked. "She'll keep you imprisoned for years until you become a man, then she'll use you."

"That's not true!"

"Yes, it is. Does she sing to you in your dreams?"

Roman tightened his lips, refusing to answer. Because the answer was yes. It still didn't mean what Bab thought it did, though. He knew sirens sang to catch men – he'd read about that, even if he didn't completely understand everything in the book – but in his dreams that wasn't what his siren was doing. "It's different."

"Fine. You don't believe me? Call her. Tell her you came. I'll wait out of sight behind the rocks and watch, but I want an apology when I have to jump out and save your life. Again." He sneered and walked away, back towards the rocks they'd both scrambled over.

Roman looked back at the ocean, but just felt angry now. It was ruined. The peaceful feeling of her and his dreams and this beach was gone, and he didn't much feel like meeting the siren knowing Bab was watching. It made something that was supposed to be special, horrible.

He blinked away angry tears. Bab was wrong – about this, anyway. He knew it because he felt the siren's feelings in his dreams. She didn't want to steal him away. But what she did want with him, he didn't know.

He'd just have to sneak out again some other time, and next time, he'd be extra careful.

Roman was about to turn away, when he noticed everything

was almost pitch black, like the lights had gone out. Looking up at the moon, he saw it was nearly completely in shadow. His breath left him when red began to seep across the globe, starting from the bottom-right, making the moon look like it had wounded itself. It looked in pain, but still amazing. "Blood Moon," he whispered. It was beautiful, but his gut knotted at its mysteriousness. It looked spooky as well as beautiful.

A splash in the water had him jerking his head down with a gasp, looking for the source of the sound.

There she was.

She's come! *He held his breath now.*

It was her hair he saw first because it glowed pinkish under the Blood Moon. When she rose from the water, he could see her eyes were also the same as in his dreams: black from edge to edge – no whites and no pupils.

Her chest came into view, her hair hiding most of her breasts. It was her ribs that caught his attention, or rather, what he saw in between them: one slash across her skin under each protruding rib. These were her gills.

He was stunned, wondering what it must be like to be able to breathe under the waves.

Her skin shimmered with tiny opalescent scales.

When she was halfway out of the sea, she stopped. The tip of her tail poked out of the water, and Roman understood this was as far as she could go without legs.

She held out both arms to him.

He heard her voice in his head as clearly as if she'd been speaking the words out loud. 'Come, little dreamer. You can feel the moon bleed.'

He could. It was a deep, aching sadness he didn't have a name for. He took a step towards her.

'You are one of us.'

"Is that why you called me?" he risked asking her.

She smiled, and her teeth were like that of a Piranha fish. It should have scared him, but he found himself entranced. 'Sweet boy, you're the one who called me through the waves of your mind.'

He had?

'It was your call I answered, and I can teach you. I can teach you why it is you feel the pain of all others. It's a gift.'

A gift. Not one of his family had said it was a gift. "Will you teach me how to breathe underwater?" *Excitement bloomed. That seemed like a cool super power.*

Her smile widened. 'Oh, yes.'

He returned her smile, stepped into the froth of the receding wave and started to wade towards her. He faintly heard something whiz past his ear.

Suddenly, a scream like no other filled the space around them. It seemed to come from everywhere – from the ocean; the air itself. It pierced his ears and his middle; twined around his brain and squeezed until he was screaming, too.

The siren fell back into the sea, splashing water as her torso smacked its surface.

Through his own small body, he felt the wound: Bab had shot her with his dart gun.

Face down, her hair spread as it floated on the waves.

More splashing, and Bab tore past him, the sea up to his middle by the time he reached the siren.

"Don't!" *screamed Roman, even though he wasn't sure what he was going to do.*

Bab grabbed the tendrils of her hair in his fist and pulled her body behind him as he walked back to shore, a grin of triumph on his face.

"STOP!"

"Shut up, Roman. Don't be a fucking retard. I just saved your life, though Pa's going to belt your arse for this. Can't save you from that – you deserve it, too." *He dragged her onto the sand, panting* with the effort, then pulled her over so she was lying face up. "Jesus ... look at her."

He wished he wasn't so pathetic – Roman started to cry. He sobbed as Bab moved the siren's hair from her face. "What shall we do with her? Don't think I can drag her all the way home up the lane, but we can't leave her here."

Roman couldn't answer for his sobbing.

"Hey," Bab grinned again. "I should have brought my camera – could've got a photo of me with my prized catch!"

Anger stirred behind the hollow feeling inside him. He hated Bab right now. Hated him.

"I've never seen one before." He trailed his fingers from her hair, down her face, and a weird look glinted across his features. The panting from dragging her out of the water had eased, but he was still breathing heavily, though in an odd way.

His hand went to the dart wedged under one of her ribs – it had probably torn a gill. He pulled it out. "Didn't know the poison would work that quick."

The anger grew. Roman clenched his fists, eyes still streaming.

Bab dropped the dart on the sand. His hand went back to her skin, stroking it. He seemed mesmerised by her almost invisible scales – they grew much larger around her hips before they formed her tail.

Bab passed his hand over one of her breasts and Roman heard him catch his breath. His hand was shaking.

Roman was shaking, too – with a rage that was mounting.

Bab shifted his position to kneeling and looked down the siren's body. His hand went to her hips, his eyes searching her tail, and then his hand was searching her tail, too – pushing and prodding. "How do they do it? The mating? Where's the hole?"

Roman screamed. It was filled with fury. He ran and leapt at Bab who was too transfixed by the siren to realise what he was doing. With arms outstretched, he landed on his brother's head, small hands fixed around his neck as they both fell onto the sand.

Still screaming, he shoved whatever sand he could into Bab's face, then Bab was screaming.

His fist hit Roman's cheek and Roman went flying back, his fall winding him. "You little SHIT! Aaargh!" Bab had his eyes squeezed shut, both hands raking his face to try and get the sand off. "Pa's going to kill you! I'm telling him everything, you little prick!"

Bab blinked furiously, still moaning at the pain of the grit. "He'll send you off to Uncle's for this! You're out the bloody house. I'm telling him now then he'll be the one to get rid of the siren. Maybe he'll cut her up and cook her – you can eat the fucking fish!"

Bab sprinted away, furious, spitting more damning words as he went.

Roman knew he was in for it, but all he cared about at that second was the dead siren on the shore. He whimpered as he got to his feet and went to her. All his anger faded as quickly as it had risen. Tears threatened to run again. "I'm sorry," he cried as he fell beside her.

He lay himself down and nestled his head against the crook of her armpit, just like how he laid with his mother when he wanted a cuddle. "I'm sorry I called you – I didn't know he'd be here. I'm sorry I couldn't stop him killing you. I don't know what to do now." He was sobbing again.

He didn't care.

Eventually, he stopped. He knew it was just a matter of time before Pa showed up, but he couldn't move the siren on his own.

'So much to learn, little dreamer.'

He bolted up and blinked. She'd spoken. Only, she couldn't have because she was still lying there, motionless, with her eyes closed.

'Your blood is in shadow. Like the moon.'

Her voice was in his head, just like in his dreams. He looked up at the moon. It was a deep crimson now, completely eclipsed by the earth. It slipped out of his line of vision as he landed hard on his *back, not understanding what had just happened; not understanding why the siren loomed over him, eyes open and black, mouth wide in a smile full of small, sharp teeth.*

'But blood never lies.'

Every single one of those razor-sharp teeth sank into his right shoulder. He would have screamed again. Instead, his breath left him as he sank, falling ... a strangely peaceful sensation. Above him, the siren melted. Her hair became froth, her skin became salt water sliding down his face and neck, mingling with the wound where her teeth sank in. Everything sank in.

The ocean sank in.

"Wake up."

Roman frowned, Hai's shaking pulling him out of the memory. "I'm not asleep. Did you knock?"

"I knocked three times."

Roman opened his eyes to find his long-time friend and mentor – also his Tai Chi and Sanshou instructor – hovering over him, concern in his dark eyes. Grey and balding, the man was near seventy now. Roman didn't want to worry him. "I was deep in trance." He sat up on his bed, then swung his legs over the edge, ignoring the way he felt light-headed. "Took myself back to that night with the siren. I wondered if there might be anything I missed; anything new that might help."

"And?"

Roman threw him a sideways glance and made for the bottle of mineral water on his chest of drawers, unscrewing the lid. "And nothing. Nothing I didn't already know, anyway." He brought the bottle to his lips and gulped the liquid.

"Given our estimations, I'm not sure it's a good idea to disappear like that, whether in trance, or dream."

"Not dream? I rarely control their onset, you know that."

"But perhaps try – at least until the full moon is over."

He shook his head. "I can't."

"You mean you won't."

"She needs me. She's dreaming more, too, right now."

"It's time to meet. You have to tell her."

"If we meet, she won't listen to a word I say, and you know it."

"Then find another way, but she must know. She can't protect herself if—"

"I'll protect her."

Hai snorted, albeit a gentle snort. The man was never anything but gentle, and maybe that was why Roman had always connected with him. He'd missed him when he'd left. It had been nearly ten years since they'd seen each other, but after that night five years ago, Roman had been forced to find him – Hai was the only one who really knew what happened at the beach; the only one he'd told...

They'd forged a bond soon after meeting, just after Roman had turned six and his father had insisted he'd needed a hobby – some occupation – to keep him from repeatedly putting all their lives in danger. That had been right after his encounter with the siren.

Hai, then one of the best known martial artists from China, had been appointed to teach Roman Sanshou – a combative Chinese martial art based on the structure and principles of traditional Kung Fu. He'd also taught him Tai Chi to counter Sanshou's yang energy and keep his training balanced.

But Hai had become much more than an instructor very quickly – he'd become like a second father to Roman, and he was *only* Roman's. Bab had never taken lessons from Hai. Roman could keep him all to himself, and he did, relishing in their closeness and telling him secrets he'd never tell any other member of his family.

In turn, Hai had aided him in managing, understanding,

and, most of all, accepting his dreams and visions. As a consequence, as he'd grown older, no one other than Hai – not Pa, not Bab – had really grasped the full extent of the skill and experience he had with dream work. His own brand of clairvoyance had foreseen Bab's destruction five years ago and had gotten him out of that mess alive.

It was a mess he'd always regretted being dragged into, but his family ties ran long and deep, spanning generations, and walking away from his father's work and passion, which had then become Bab's work and obsession, had not been an option. The only part of that mess that still existed was...

"Isn't that what she's spent five years escaping? Men dictating her future?"

"That's not what I'm doing," he growled, turning away from the chest of drawers to inspect himself in the wardrobe mirror. He wore no shirt, having taken it off before lying down. Sometimes, after dreaming or trancing, he never quite felt like himself. His eyes immediately went to the faint – very faint – shimmer across his right shoulder. If one got close enough, they would see the smallest opalescent scales dotted in crescent moons across the front and back of that shoulder. Right now, the old wound itched. He refused to scratch it. "If I show her my face, I risk destroying everything she's built since she escaped my brother."

"I see. So, you are planning on hiding forever, yes? As a dragon, or a tiger? Because you are neither."

Roman scowled.

"*Chún-wáng-chǐ-hán.* If the lips are gone, the teeth will grow cold. You must tell her. You do not protect her by hiding."

"Did I ask you to come barging in here, making sense?" He grabbed his shirt from the back of a chair and put it on.

"I did not barge, I knocked. Three times."

Roman grunted.

Hai held out a brown envelope. "I have the information you wanted."

He took the envelope from his friend and ripped it open, pulling out the four sheets inside. His heart beat a little faster. "Is this everything?"

"Everything that I could find. And the alignments and planetary configurations are there. There is nothing more about sirens, though, other than what we already have."

"Which is fuck all," Roman muttered.

"They have always been elusive creatures, and successful with their kills and captures – there were never many left to tell the tale."

Coordinates stared back at him from one of the pages he held open. The coming Supermoon would bring the moon closer to Earth than it had been thirty years ago, and the eclipse... *Damn it.* "It's confirmed then: it'll be a total eclipse – a Blood Moon. On Sunday?"

"Yes," nodded Hai.

Roman sighed, sliding the pages back into the envelope for now.

"If I may, I would like to take my leave for the next few hours before nightfall."

"Of course. Thank you for this."

Hai nodded, then headed towards the door. "Tell her, Roman. You know you must. She can't fight blind."

"She might not have to fight at all."

"Because you'll do it for her?" He stopped at the doorway, looking back. "Not really your decision to make, is it?"

"I don't know what the outcome will be for her – or me. None of this seems to have happened before; there's no record of anything similar to what took place five years ago ... or thirty years ago. And the wolf's still in there, I can feel it."

"That may be so, but the truth remains: you know more than she does. You must tell her." He left it at that and walked out the door, dutifully shutting it behind him.

Roman pulled his collar straight as he stood in front of the mirror. *Fuck it, he's right.* It's not as if he'd never thought he'd have to confront her one day – he'd just...

You ignored it, that's what. Pushed it out of your mind 'cause you didn't want to deal with it. Can't do that now, can you?

He tied his dark brown, shoulder-length hair back, and gave his right shoulder a wriggle to ease the irritating prickle that ran through it.

He hadn't done it on purpose. He hadn't *known* it was happening until it was too late. He'd been *trying* to save her life, that was all.

Quit wallowing – it's done. Now figure out how to fix it for her. Ideally, before you tell her.

He grunted to himself, gathered his wallet and keys, and left his flat. He wasn't sure where he was going exactly, but he knew Jennifer was fine for now – there was no pull of his blood, or his heart, or his mind. She was getting on with her day.

He had to prepare for the Blood Supermoon.

~*~

"Shall I book you in for two weeks' time?"

The client – a regular – nodded absent-mindedly as Jennifer flicked through the diary pages. "Can we make it on Thursday 20th instead of the Wednesday this time?"

"Sure, no problem." Jennifer tapped the date into the screen in front of her, acutely aware of the man sitting in the waiting area who had been staring at her for the past ten minutes. She'd completely ignored him, pretending not to notice, but it was starting to get on her nerves. Being human came with an increase in vulnerability, not just imagined, but very real. Strength was not on her side – not the way she used to have it – and there was no pack to protect her should the worst come to pass. Whoever this guy was, she wanted him out of here before she left for the day. He was waiting for his girlfriend apparently – she was in room two having a Swedish massage. His gaze had better glue to his other half the minute she walked out, and stay there.

"I don't suppose you've changed your mind about my proposal?"

Jennifer smiled. "No, Ms Rowland, thank you." The woman had offered her a modelling contract on the spot the minute she'd set eyes on her six months ago. She owned an agency in London, now with a branch in Leeds, and whenever she was in Leeds she'd come here to the spa on the outskirts of York city.

Ms Rowland made a noise with her lips and teeth, then shut her diary. "Such a waste, my darling."

"It's just not for me. I wouldn't be comfortable." That was completely true. Cameras trained on her; people staring... Even with all good intentions, it reminded her far too much of her imprisonment.

"You're not even wearing make-up; what I could *do* with that face, and your figure is stunning." She shook her head in exasperation. "You'd never be short of work, I guarantee it."

Jennifer let out a soft laugh in politeness, but felt agitated within. The man in the corner could hear the whole conversation without a doubt. She didn't need him thinking about her figure. "That's all done for you, Ms Rowland, and here's the print-out of your receipt and your next appointment."

The woman took the paper from her. "All right. Have it your way. Even with your discomfort the camera would love you, though. There's a certain vulnerability that can be captured with a lens that's quite alluring."

She felt herself stiffen. God, that was something Edwin would have said and Gabriel would have loved. Her stomach lurched, and for a moment she had to grip the sides of her desk to steady herself. She hoped her reaction wasn't obvious.

"But as you wish," she conceded. Ms Rowland was a nice enough person – very business-like; pushy to say the least – but seemed to know when to cut her losses, and Jennifer hoped she'd consider her a loss sooner rather than later. "See you soon."

"Goodbye," Jennifer called after the lady as she opened the glass door of the reception and headed out. She almost wished she'd turn around and come back, because creepy starer was the only one left in the waiting area. It was just him and her.

She continued to ignore him as she opened the screen for tomorrow's bookings, scanning all the times it showed as she scrolled downwards to make sure all the clients had received the automated reminder of their appointments.

The man rose from his seat, and she froze – not because he'd moved, though her warning bell had certainly gone off loud and clear – but because his scent had just wafted her way and she'd *smelled* him. In that *wolf* kind of way that received all the in-between layers of his musk telling her where he'd been and who he'd been with. It had been so long since she'd picked up information that way, she was thrown.

But my wolf's dead. I'm human.

There was no time to figure out the how or why of the oddity – his aroma carried a very specific scent that raised her hackles: fear. Not his. Someone else's. Someone he'd made contact with earlier that day had been scared, and if he was the one who'd made them scared...

On instinct, she stood from her seat, not willing to have him look down on her. She needed to meet his eyes on an even keel. "Your girlfriend's massage is just coming to an end – I'm sure she'll be out soon."

"She's not my girlfriend; we're casual."

She didn't need to be a wolf to know *that* was a lie. "I've a feeling your girlfriend might think differently about that," she shot back, curtly.

He stared right at her; into her ... tried. Her wall went up like a tower of ice, and only at this precise moment did she realise how much of that wall she'd brought down over the past few months.

Amanda, one of her colleagues, walked into the reception from the hallway that led to all the therapy rooms.

Inside, Jennifer sagged with relief. She didn't let her stance change for this male, though.

"Hi ... how's it going?" asked Amanda, a slight lilt to her voice that said she'd just picked up on the tension.

The guy smiled, his blue eyes and blond hair making his smooth features seem even more innocent than they already did. He had the boy-next-door look down to a tee. "I was checking to see when Katie was finished."

"Aah, right. I think I heard her voice when I walked past room two – she'll be out in a minute."

"Wonderful. Could you let her know I'm waiting for her outside, please? I'll be in my car."

"No problem," said Jennifer.

"Well, I wasn't expecting one," he replied with a tight smile.

Dick head.

"Catch you around."

No, you won't.

As if he'd heard her, he stared at her a second longer than

he had to, then turned and walked out.

"Wow," said Amanda, coming to stand beside her. "What was that about?"

"I don't know. He's been staring at me for a quarter of an hour – freaked me out a bit."

"He's not been in before, though Katie has. Katie's nice."

"Katie needs to find herself a new boyfriend," she mumbled.

"Hey, he didn't try anything with you, right?"

"No. But you walked in just as he approached the desk. I don't know if he *would* have tried anything if you hadn't arrived when you did."

Amanda grimaced. "What a git. Best forget about it. I don't think Katie will book in again for a while since she came in with gift vouchers. Listen, I was going to ask ... a bunch of us are going to The Olde Shippe in York for drinks after work. Do you want to come?"

"Oh ... I don't know." In truth, she was more than a little surprised. She hadn't been asked out by her colleagues for well over half a year.

"It's Shauna's birthday. There'll be karaoke."

"What's karaoke?"

Amanda stared at her, shocked. "That's a joke, right?"

"Er..." Awkward was an understatement for what she felt. This was clearly one of those human things she just didn't get.

"Oh, my god, Jennifer ... were you sheltered as a child?"

"Well—"

"I mean, that's what Carly said you told her – that you'd had a reclusive upbringing?"

She racked her brain trying to remember what the fuck she'd said over a year ago when she'd first landed the job here. "Um ... right. Yes."

Amanda leaned back with an elbow on the high, curved

reception desk, clearly intrigued. "We know you're ... introverted. But, you know, it would be good to come out – stretch your boundaries."

Stretch her boundaries. Gabriel taking her from behind flashed into her mind – all beast, no human. Her mouth went dry, and her chest went tight. "Boundaries ... um—"

"Was it religious?"

"What?" She didn't want to noticeably gasp for air, but she was feeling closed in.

"Your upbringing. Was it like, really religious? Traditionally Christian, or something? Or were your parents super strict?"

"No, erm, it was ... we lived out in the woods in the middle of nowhere and didn't venture out much."

"Oh, so was it like off-grid living? Was your family into the whole natural living, hippy thing?"

She didn't really know what Amanda was on about. "Something like that."

"Okay, well, time to spread your wings." She grinned. "Come out tonight. It'll get your mind off creepo, and we'll introduce you to the delights of off-key singing. Can you sing?"

"Sing?"

"The karaoke. You really don't know, do you? It's about taking the stage and singing your favourite songs – most fun when you, and everyone around you is off their face on alcohol."

"I don't drink."

"Jeez, your family must have been a hoot."

"They were allergic to alcohol."

Amanda gave her the weirdest look, clearly not knowing what the hell to think. "Drinking aside, *can* you sing?"

"Nope. Can't hold a note to save my life."

She clapped her hands with glee. "And therein lies the

fun! Say you'll come – bring your boyfriend."

David would love it, she already knew that. Anything that involved her being out and socialising, which he was always trying to encourage, would get a big thumbs up from him. The thought of everything Amanda had just said made her want to run a mile, but suddenly, everything felt just a little too hard. Five years keeping a distance between herself and the world she had to live in seemed excruciatingly difficult. "I'll call him – I guess he could meet me there."

"Excellent! I'll let Shauna know."

She was going to have to get a birthday card and a present – god knew what. She didn't really know the woman even though she'd worked with her for over a year. Shauna had said something about redecorating the living room – maybe she'd get her something for that. A few candles or a statue for a shelf. "Great. Can I take my lunch break now?"

"Yep – I came out to cover you."

"Thank you. See you later." She walked quickly out of the reception area, down the hallway, and into the staff room at the back. She felt a little sick at the thought of mingling so publicly – in a pub, too. She'd never set foot in a pub before – there'd been no point since alcohol was poison to any wolf. She'd tried wine since becoming human, and she still couldn't get to grips with the taste of the stuff, even if she was no longer affected by it. It tasted foul.

She almost turned back to call the whole thing off, but it was the weekend tomorrow, and David would be happy about this little outing for *days*, so maybe a couple of hours of discomfort would be worth it. She felt bad she was such a hermit – he always stayed in with her.

Her mind made up, she reached for her bag and pulled out her phone to text him tonight's plans when something caught her eye – something she didn't remember putting into her bag.

Cautiously, she pulled the handles wider apart, and reached in for the brown coloured envelope. She *hadn't* put this in her bag. She didn't even know what it was.

Relax. One of the girls must have done it – it's a work letter.

She didn't believe that for a second as she ripped the envelope open. She pulled out the folded papers inside it and exhaled in relief when she saw the familiar typed words on the side that faced her: **Please read this, even if you don't understand why.**

It was from her note-sender. How the hell had he gotten this into her bag though, and *when*?

She opened the two folded sheets and frowned. They were photocopies of text that looked like it had come from a book – some kind of reference book. The style of typography looked a little old.

Sirens of Myth and Legend

What in god's name was this about?

Feeling a little disturbed, yet excited to have some connection with her note-sender again, she put the papers and envelope back in her bag before putting on her coat.

Amanda was manning the reception by the time she headed back out.

"Do you want anything from the shops?" she asked her.

"No thanks, I'm good."

"Okay. By the way, has anyone been hanging around the staff room today? Anyone who, I don't know, maybe isn't a customer? But not staff either?"

There was that stare again. Yeah, she was the regular weirdo around here. "No, I don't think so. I've been in and out of there most of the day, and I haven't seen anyone."

"So, no one who's like, say, a handyman, or electrician, or someone like that?"

Amanda let out a little laugh, presumably at her strange questions. "No."

"Okay, then. Well, I'm off to lunch."

"Have a good one," she called after her.

Jennifer scanned the car park as she made her way to her car. The supermarket was a five-minute drive away. She'd probably grab a sandwich and sit in the park nearby, though that didn't seem too appealing if creepy guy was around. *What if your note-sender's there?*

Her stomach somersaulted at that. She couldn't deny that *was* appealing ... and also not. If she suddenly knew who he was, what happened then? He'd been anonymously in her life since her escape from the farm. If that changed now... No, she couldn't risk that. Even if she was dying to know who he was, she didn't want a change she couldn't cope with. She understood David relishing the security and safety of a quiet life in some ways.

Yes, the quiet life is so 'you', isn't it?

She pushed away her inner voice.

As if I'm going anywhere – you can't get rid of me. You're still living your life in chains, only they're there by choice this time.

She reached her car, unlocked it, and got in. After a moment's hesitation, she decided to lock the doors from the inside.

You're imprisoning yourself in your car now?

She pulled out the folded sheets from her bag once more and opened them.

Greek in origin, Sirens were companions of Persephone, sent to watch her by her mother, Demeter. When Persephone was abducted by

Hades into the Underworld and raped, Demeter cursed all Sirens for their neglect in looking out for her daughter. She cursed them with wings, demanding they forever search for her lost daughter; she cursed them with the sweetest voices which became their weapon – they were forced to sing when any man ventured too close to their womanhood and virtue, the song so sweet his ears would bleed, and his heart would stop.

In later popular European mythology from the seventeenth century, the Sirens became creatures of seas and rivers having lost their wings – they were given fish tails instead. An obscure legend of the Greek Isles tells that instead of perishing when Odysseus bested them, Demeter took last-minute pity on the Sirens, changing their wings to fish tails when they fell into the sea, so they could survive, thus, the winged Sirens became creatures of the sea, and associated with the mermaid of modern times. Their physical allure and magic of song remained the same, with the added terror that a storm would follow any song they sang.

Bloody hell.

Her palms were sweaty. That was only a small extract from the two sheets; there was a fair amount of information there, but the words 'abducted' and 'raped' imprinted in her mind, and she really wished they didn't. She couldn't read all this now – it was two whole pages of smallish text, and it looked like it was *all* about sirens. She was stumped as to why the note-sender would give her this.

You need food.

Yes, she did.

Stuffing the papers in her glove compartment, she started her engine. She'd eat, then call David and tell him about tonight. Everything else could wait until tomorrow.

Chapter Four

Friday night in York was probably like Friday night in any city in England. That didn't make Jennifer feel any better about the crowds and the noise as she finally pulled into a parking space down one of the narrow side roads that made up the historic beauty the city was famous for.

She'd been born in this county, not that she remembered it. Her father had left with her and her brother before she was one year old – more opportunities down south, was what he had told her. She never knew if he'd missed it at all – the rolling dales; the rustic charm of the city and the quaintness of the villages. She missed Surrey. The greens were much richer there. Although beautiful in its own right, the majesty of Yorkshire always seemed wrapped in a veil of bleakness.

Or maybe that's just you.

She turned off the engine after parking the car, and reached for her phone. David had texted half an hour ago to say he was leaving work. He should be at The Olde Shippe in about fifteen minutes. She was the first to arrive having left earlier than the others – it hadn't been her turn to lock up and she'd felt too awkward hanging around with her colleagues, waiting.

What should she do? Remain in the car for fifteen minutes, or make her way to the pub on her own?

The thought of being on her own surrounded by bodies had her swaying in her seat. *You're pathetic, you know that? There was a time you'd have walked into any room and owned it.*

Desperate frustration at that simple truth made the decision for her. While the female she had been didn't rank very high in the popularity stakes, she part-loathed the woman she'd become. 'Selena' had been vile, twisted by fear and jealousy, and she'd made bad choices; but 'Jennifer' was stagnant, dampening down *all* her feelings, and she made *no* choices. No matter how hard she tried, she couldn't find a happy middle.

With a soft curse, she grabbed her bag and Shauna's present, and got herself out of her car. *It's just a pub; they're just people.*

Locking her Mazda, she found herself transfixed by the waxing moon haloing the peak of York Cathedral, which she could just about see against the dusking sky. *Wow...* The moon was huge. So huge, it looked too heavy to be suspended in the air. *Any minute now, it'll come crashing down.*

Sounds shrieked.

Shocked, she dropped her keys and bags, her hands flying to her ears to muffle whatever the hell was so loud. But the cacophony was gone in an instant.

Slowly, she brought her hands down, her heart thumping. She couldn't even say what the noise had been – nothing specific – just *noise*. All the usual sounds – people talking, traffic moving, rustling and bustling, but it had all been twenty times louder than...

Than if through human hearing.

Fuck. That's what she'd heard. She'd heard the sounds of the evening through her wolf's ears. It had been so long ... but that was how it all used to sound, wasn't it? Why was this happening now? What was going on?

Your wolf's dead.

But even as she thought it, some part of her denied it – rejected the untruth. Too faintly to know if she was sensing it properly, the she-wolf in her growled.

Jennifer tried to slow her breathing; tried to tow in her alarm. "But I'm human now," she whispered. And riding on the tail of that whisper was the devastating realisation that her note-sender might have lied. She didn't know him at all. She'd painted this picture of a saviour, but what if he meant her harm? What if he'd *always* meant her harm?

With shaking legs, she bent down to pick up everything she'd dropped. The birthday gift – a candle and vase – still appeared to be in one piece, thankfully.

She needed a drink – water. She needed peace and balance. She needed the woods on one side, and the ocean on the other.

Making her way down the street having gathered her things, she vaguely wondered where the thought of needing an ocean had come from – she'd never lived by the sea – when an arm went around her shoulder.

She screamed and turned, disorientated.

"Whoa! It's me." David's grin fell away instantly at the understanding he'd just scared her. "I'm sorry, I thought you'd heard me – I called your name. Shit, I'm sorry, Jen." He took her in his arms, and she sank into them with relief. She was genuinely pleased to see him; to feel him...

"I was far away, I didn't hear you."

"I'm really sorry." Regret was evident in his voice, but he had always been careful not to trigger her memories from a past he only knew bits and pieces of.

"It's okay. I'm okay."

"Are you sure?" He pulled himself back enough to study her face and meet her eyes.

A rush of affection for him and his care took her over,

and she leaned forward and kissed him. "I'm sure. And better now you're here." That wasn't a lie, though a part of her bristled at the thought of any man holding so much power over her reactions. But David, she could trust, so she let herself relax as he brought her in for a last quick hug.

"I got here earlier than I thought I would – the traffic's not so bad today."

"I don't think anyone else is at the pub yet."

"That's fine. It'll give us time to try and find some decent seats and get ourselves settled." He took her free hand in his as they walked. "I'm so glad we're doing this. I love being out with you."

She looked at him and smiled. She wasn't quite at the 'glad' stage yet, but with David now here, she hoped it wouldn't take too long to reach it.

Karaoke was fucking awful. She didn't understand how people enjoyed hearing other people sing badly – and most people sung badly. After fifteen minutes of the horror, she had to conclude it was worse than a piercing dog whistle on repeat.

Shauna and Amanda, and the four other women who had met Shauna here, didn't seem to mind. They were all in their element singing badly, and half of them were well on their way to being drunk.

Jennifer finished off the last of her scampi and chips, and sat back in her seat, wishing her ears didn't twitch every time someone hit a wrong note, which was pretty much on every note. Shauna and Amanda were performing a duet of "Living On A Prayer".

Her temples throbbed, and a headache threatened.

David wasn't singing, and was adamant he wasn't going to, but he was loving the vibe of this place.

Jennifer was having a hard time seeing it as anything other than claustrophobic.

David nudged her with an elbow, aware of what she was thinking. "Shall we give it half an hour more, then head off?"

She nodded with a sigh of relief. *Yes, thank you!*

He laughed, but squeezed her hand under the table. He was obviously just glad she'd come out, and there was a part of her that was happy to have made that small sacrifice seeing how overjoyed it made him.

Drunken applause and whistling ensued as the double act hit their last note.

"Right," she said, getting up from her seat, "I'm going to get a last drink. Do you want one?"

"I'll have another bottle of Cobra."

"Okay, back in a second."

But before she could leave, Amanda and Shauna came bounding to her side. "Jenny! Jenny..."

They never called her Jenny. Nor did she particularly *like* 'Jenny'. *They must be pretty drunk already.*

"Jenny, you have *got* to sing. Come on..."

Her arm was pulled to no avail. She wasn't going anywhere near that microphone.

"It's so much fun!" squeaked Amanda.

"I promise, everyone will leave if I even attempt to sing. Besides, I'm going to get drinks – do you want one?"

It was a poor try at distracting them. She thought it was working for a moment, but then Shauna shook her head, and let out another giggle. "We can do a song together if you like. It's my birthday! Come on – pleeease."

Ugh. The birthday guilt trip. "Let me just go get drinks first."

They clapped in glee, and she hoped they'd swallow the bluff and find themselves someone else to drag up there while she was gone.

She meandered towards the bar. It was crowded, but the throng of people – mostly men – seemed to part for her and she suddenly found herself at the front of the queue, leaning over the counter.

"What can I get you?" asked the guy behind it. He seemed transfixed by her, too, staring openly from her face to her cleavage, which was hardly on show, and then back again.

It got her back up, but she ignored him. "A bottle of Cobra and a pineapple juice, please." She had tried a sip of David's Cobra earlier that night and decided that beer tasted a bit like salty piss.

Her eyes fell to a paper napkin on the counter as the guy prepared her drink. She froze on the spot, unable to look away from the writing scribbled across the napkin: *DO NOT SING.*

She whirled around and scanned the pub. She'd seen his handwriting before. Although most of his notes were typed, four or five of them, he'd written. She knew this was him. *This was him.*

But she had no clue what he looked like, and no one was looking her way.

Actually, that wasn't true. About five men were looking her way from different parts of the room. *Ew, yuck. The whole glaring at women thing – at what point in history did anyone decide that was a becoming trait.* She turned back towards the bar and the napkin on it.

"That's £6.90."

Distracted, she fumbled with her wallet before plucking out a £10 note. She couldn't take her eyes off the writing, but there was something else.

Heat bubbled low in her belly: anger.

Do not sing? Who the fuck did he think he was?

Another dominant male, that's who. Her whole fucking

life was made up of *men* telling her what to do. Granted, most of them hadn't been human, but at least they'd had the decency not to shout out orders anonymously.

Her anger grew.

Throw in her pathetic inability to function without David as a safety net, and she was still living in a prison; the walls were invisible this time, that was the only difference. What was *exactly* the same though, was *men*.

They all still stared – all thought they could; they all still wanted to fuck her. She knew this because she could *smell* it on them – right now. Right here in this room: their pheromones, their lust... *She could smell it.*

Which meant she'd been lied to – she *wasn't* human, at least, not completely.

"Your change?"

She took it from the bartender with what must have been a scowl on her face considering the way he raised her an eyebrow. She bit back a retort, turning away from the bar and the offending napkin, a drink in each hand, and made her way back to the table. Again, the sea of men parted; she felt their gazes burning.

The bubbling in her belly was dialled up to maximum now. She wasn't fucking meat just because she was attractive; just because she was unmated.

The bubbling became an insistent growling that only she could hear, but it was only meant for her – a homecoming call from her wolf.

Not. Fucking. Human.

Which meant fighting for her place; fighting for survival. It meant pain.

He lied to me.

She was still a wolf. Her first reaction was to skim the room for any other wolf, especially male wolves. Being unmated at her age made her a target, and all the testosterone leaking out pheromones created the perfect fighting ground.

Luckily, she couldn't pick up on any other wolves present, but her senses were not what they used to be, her own animal still buried under five years of ... whatever the hell had taken place. She didn't understand it. How could she *not* feel her wolf for five years only to have it come charging back, full force? Without a doubt *some* transformation had occurred because all her blood tests while at the hospital had come back *human*. Her sharp hearing, her impeccable sight, her wolf sense of smell ... they had all disappeared.

All those senses now re-emerged, albeit in an abstract, chaotic fashion, and she didn't know why. Her note-sender knew though, she was sure of that, and it made her blood boil. *He lied.*

And she was the fool who'd spent five years accepting from the hand that fed her, because she'd had no choice.

Thought you'd escaped? Nope – Still. No. Choice.

"Sweetheart?" David took the drinks from her hands, a look of concern on his face.

Her anger faded a fraction. He was innocent – he knew nothing, and he'd never looked at her or thought about her the way other men did. Shit. He should never have been caught up in her life.

"I'm going to sing," she announced, much to the delight of Shauna and Amanda who both squealed and did a little dance on the spot.

David was shocked – she'd never seen such a shocked expression. "Are you serious?"

"Yep." Though in truth, she was shocked herself. It had just come out, partly as a snub to the *order* she'd been given, but also because she'd get a better view of the room on that little stage – her note-sender was in here, watching her, she was certain. She wanted to catch a glimpse of him. And maybe if all the males in here heard how fucking badly she sang they'd avert their lust and project it elsewhere.

She grabbed the pen and paper and wrote down the number of the song she wanted. It was some commercialised version of a folk song her dad used to sing when she'd been very little, and pretty much the only song she knew apart from *Happy Birthday*. He'd told her her mother had sung it to her in the womb.

David suddenly smiled. "That's awesome! Good on you."

She threw him a tight smile, guilty that her motives were hardly pure. With her awareness of her wolf's presence, she leaned forward into David's frame and gave him a hug, then sniffed his neck. Yeah – there was her wolf. She could now detect the layers of David's aroma where she hadn't before. Sadness coiled around the awakening, because their scents were not compatible. She found no pull towards him, and it was gutting, because her heart *did* care about him, even if that elusive thing called love had never bloomed for her.

She had detected layers of scent last night in her garden, hadn't she? Though she hadn't thought too much of it at the time, for a few seconds her wolf had reached the surface. She hadn't seen that moment for what it was – that she still *was* the wolf. But after the way she'd been able to smell the creepy man at the spa, and the way every sound had shrieked as she'd gotten out of her car tonight, it was too obvious to deny.

She had to be careful. While she'd never fully turned into a wolf in her previous life, she'd still had more strength than she had now. Her physical capabilities were at human level, and she could feel human aches in her body. She had no idea why her wolf's strength remained hidden, but it made her feel vulnerable. She wouldn't be able to defend herself should she happen upon any male wolf who got too friendly.

"Wish me luck," she whispered into his ear, pulling herself away from him.

"You won't need it – you're amazing."

How she'd *longed* for this kind of genuine adoration from a mate. How wrenching she'd finally received it from a man she couldn't be with.

"Jen, there's something really important I want to say to you when we get home. Not here in front of everyone. But you *are* amazing, and I love you."

Utterly wrenching.

She pressed her lips to his in response, then picked up her slip of paper with the song on it.

Paying no mind to the excitement from the women she'd come with, she made her way to the guy managing the karaoke. She needed answers.

DO NOT SING

Pfft. If her note-sender was that adamant she shouldn't sing, he'd have to show himself and stop her. Then, she was going to give the coward what for.

~*~

Melody perfected was a song in itself – a ballad between notes that held all notes together. It was emotion unfurled and impeccably orchestrated, and if it did its job right, it would have no sense of itself. Melody became the story; its song and the singer, one force.

The first note was all it took for the hush to fall upon the crowd; on the second, understanding crashed on Roman. Ignoring the sensual pull of the song, he turned to face the stage. "Oh, fuck."

Beside him, Hai tutted and shook his head as he pulled two earplugs from a pouch he carried in his pocket. "It went well then – you telling her what to do with no explanation whatsoever." That was a direct gibe.

"There wasn't time to write it all down." The hairs on his arms rose. Her song seeped into him, twining with him, but he was immune. Everyone else was in peril.

"There's this old tradition called talking."

"I didn't fucking think she'd *sing*. The note was just a precaution. Does she seem like the singing type to you?" he snapped.

"She seems like the type who'll bristle at any order from a male."

"Fuck it, Hai – she sees me, she'll *run*. We can't lose her this close to the Blood Moon." He looked around the room. Every man in it was lost to Jennifer, eyes glazed, transfixed by her call; the women were clearly uncomfortable, though they couldn't fathom what was going on. Big shit was about to hit the fan. "Hai..."

The old man pulled one newly inserted plug out of his ear. "What?"

"Go to her. When the alarm goes off, get her out of here."

"Alarm?"

"Fire alarm – I'll set it off."

"And, pray, what do I do with her once outside?"

"Distract her."

"She's not two."

"Talk to her."

"Do your dirty work for you?"

He heard a man moan in bliss somewhere behind him to his right – it wouldn't be long before they all joined in. The ecstasy never lasted long. The subsequent pain would be severe.

Jennifer stood on the small platform, eyes half closed, completely unaware of the affect she was having.

"Lay into me later – we need to stop this now."

His mentor threw him the most scathing look before plugging his ears back up and nodding. He turned and strode towards the platform while Roman sped towards the kitchen. The fire alarm was likely to be near the kitchen. *Why the fuck didn't she just do as I said?* he seethed inside, though it was himself he was angry with. Hai was right, and it pissed him off. Something had changed last night when she'd let herself go in the garden – he'd sensed a wildness; a glimpse of recklessness. That it had turned him on was neither here nor there. He wasn't getting involved that way – not with her. What *was* relevant, was that her wolf had woken up after five years dormant. *Five years – of course it had to be five years.*

But that meant the shadow in her blood would also wake. And it had. Two minutes ago, he'd still doubted its existence. There was no doubt now.

And you went and put it there.

Where the fuck was the fire alarm?

A pained cry reached his ears. He pivoted on the ball of his foot. The same man who'd moaned in pleasure was now clutching his head in growing agony. *Shit!*

There! There it was!

Roman sprinted towards the small box on the wall and rammed the heel of his hand into the glass in a move he'd perfected from Hai at the age of eight. Its deafening ringing bounced off the walls, but it might be too late for the man doubled over in distress and clutching his ears, judging by the stream of blood that slipped through his fingers.

~*~

She hadn't sung this song since she was a child, and perhaps it was the wrong one to choose even though she still knew every word by heart. She'd never known her mother, the female having died just minutes after she was born. She forced herself never to think about her father.

The power of song, though, was something Jennifer had never given much credence to in the past – she'd had smell and sight and hearing; even touch was an exhilarating experience to a wolf. But song could conjure a memory – a feeling – just like a scent could.

She wasn't really aware of the song as she sang it. Rather, she slipped through song's tunnel, down its corridor of reality, until she landed in the seat of the music. It was strangely healing; addictively powerful. She hadn't expected to become so engulfed by the notes.

She hadn't lied earlier: she couldn't hold a note to save her life. So she was sure she must be ruining a few nights with her performance.

Half way through the first verse, she risked opening her eyes. She knew there was a reason she'd come on stage, but the reason was in fog – she couldn't remember it.

A man caught her eye, doubled over in his seat and grasping at his ears. He looked in pain. It crossed her mind her singing might be the cause (though she didn't think she was *that* bad), but she didn't care and didn't seem able to stop – didn't *want* to stop. *'They all deserve it,'* whispered an abstract voice that had seeped into her head, dancing over all the sharps and flats of the song. She couldn't deny she partly agreed with the voice. She'd had her fair share of pain, as had her gender. Men could suffer for a change.

'Yes, they should. They take – that's all they do. Take your body; take your freedom. They think they have the right to your existence.'

Red caught her eye. Blood was pouring down the man's hands from ... his ears? *That's odd.*

'No – it's as it should be. Don't stop singing.'

Don't stop sing... Don't stop... Don't... Don't sing. *DO NOT SING.*

Who had told her not to sing? She tried to reach the memory through her daze.

Other men in the pub – only men – clutched their ears now, grimaces on their faces. Before she could think further on that, a shrill howl filled the air.

What the... *Fire alarm.*

It stopped her mid-track. The song ended, the words dropped from her lips as she dropped the microphone. She covered her own ears, the wolf in her not appreciating the high-pitched wail of the alarm one bit.

Suddenly, a woman shrieked above the noise. When her gaze landed on her, she saw she was leaning over the man with the blood coming out of his ears. He was now on the floor, toppled over and unmoving. There was a *lot* of fucking blood. It pooled around his head.

Jesus Christ.

And then, everyone was crying out. There was mass movement, and bodies scrambled over each other to get out.

All at once, she remembered David. Her eyes went to where he'd been sitting. He was still there, staring at her in shock, his expression one of both devotion and terror.

His ears were red with blood.

No! "David!" She tried to get to him, but before she could move, one hand went over her mouth, another to her neck. Her scream never left her. Instead, a sense of nausea rose as whoever had grabbed her pressed into her neck.

The world went dark.

⁃ *Chapter Five*

The sound of waves, and the sea air filling her lungs, were the first things Jennifer noticed on rousing into consciousness. She didn't immediately remember what had happened, but when it came rushing back to her, she bolted upright, escape her priority. Only she wasn't upright; her struggles got her nowhere because her hands were tied behind her back, her ankles also bound.

Oh, god, not again ... not again ... not again...

She was lying on sand, a blanket thrown over her up to her shoulders. Some grains of sand had made it into her mouth.

...not again ... not again...

"Don't be scared. No one's going to hurt you." A male voice.

Terror gripped her tight, but she fought it. *Forced* herself to fight it. She wasn't ending up here again – she couldn't. She found her voice, her snark right there with it, and she grabbed onto the attitude she'd spent five years trying to eliminate because it dulled her fear. *Nothing left to lose now.* "In my experience, when men kidnap me and tie me up, I end up very much *hurt*." She managed to spit some of the sand from her mouth and wiped her chin on her shoulder.

"I deeply regret what I had to do. It was necessary."

"Bullshit."

"Yes, perhaps you're right. I've been pushing for him to tell you the truth for a long time now, but he's stubborn, and always has been."

"Him?" Fear clawed at her, but she focused on the pinch of the binds around her wrists – an old trick: pain, ever her saviour.

She finally got herself together and swivelled in the sand – as much as she could all tied up – towards the man who was speaking. The breeze flapped her hair across her eyes. When the strands finally moved, what she saw wasn't exactly what she'd expected, although she couldn't specifically say what she *had* expected.

A slight and old Chinese man sat cross-legged on a small rock just a couple of feet away from her. "Yes, him. The one who has watched over you for five years."

Her heart might as well have stopped. Except she could hear it beating louder than ever, thudding in her ears. *Him.* She'd been right – the note-sender was a 'he'.

That's what you're concentrating on? "Let me go."

"I would very much like to, but there are things you need to know. I'm not going to hurt you."

"You're already hurting me."

"The binds are necessary."

"Like silver chains and locked rooms?" she snapped back, assuming he'd know exactly what she was talking about if he was acquainted with the note-sender.

"I promise you, this is not the same as that."

"I don't believe you."

He stared at her for a few seconds, seeming to contemplate something, and then sighed. "He won't come to you himself for this very reason. So I'm afraid you'll have to hear it from me."

"You're *not* the note-sender?"

"No. I'm not the one who pulled you out of the sea five years ago."

God ... she'd been right about that, too. It *had* been him. The note-sender and her rescuer were one and the same.

"I'm not going to touch you. I won't lay a finger on you unless it's to untie those ropes, which I will do when I have finished saying what I need to. You will be free to go, I give you my word."

"Your word means nothing to me. Where am I?"

"Fraisethorpe Beach."

And where the fuck is that?

"You're just over an hour's drive from York."

And on the coast. Jesus, that meant she was well over two hours' drive from home. "David!" She suddenly remembered him, bleeding from his ears ... and that other guy. What the hell had taken place? "I need to go to him!" She threw herself around, trying to wriggle out of the ropes.

The old man said nothing, watching her.

That set her anger ablaze. "Is *he* here?" she yelled at him, furious. "My *rescuer* ... the one who also likes to take me *hostage*? Is he?"

The man sighed again after a pause. "Yes. He is here. He drove your car here behind me, so you can get home afterwards."

He knew where she'd parked. *Oh, god.* With a growl, she twisted in her binds, and with more than a little struggle, finally managed to sit up. "Coward!" she yelled at the tufts of grass and small rocks that peppered the sand along the bank. Windmills turned at the top of the beach. No one else was here – no one walking their dog at night, or anything. *He* was here, though, watching.

Humiliation ran through her. She'd given him a piece of

herself last night in her garden, although it hadn't exactly been planned. He'd watched her then, too. And now *this*. "You do this to a woman and hide behind an old man?" she cried out at her surroundings.

"I'm only sixty-nine," she heard the Chinese guy mumble.

She growled at him, willing her old werewolf strength to come to the fore, but her muscles remained pathetically human. "I'm *not* human," she said to him. "He lied to me."

"He did not lie. You were human ... at least for the most part. No one quite knew what would happen next. If you care to sit still, I'll tell you all about it."

"Untie me first."

"No."

"I won't run."

"You'll attack me, then try to run. While I know I could contain you, I really don't want to waste any more energy. Getting you out of the pub unnoticed was hard enough."

She paused. She remembered singing, then blacking out. "That was you?"

"It was."

She studied him. "Under *his* instruction."

"Yes."

"Can he hear me right now?"

"Yes."

"So if I called him a spineless dick with a sponge for a brain, he'd hear me?"

The man smiled. "Yes." Then, he raised his voice. "And in this instance, I'd be inclined to agree."

Okay, so he didn't *really* seem like he was going to have his wicked way with her. "What time is it?"

"Nearly eleven o'clock."

That made her stomach lurch. "I *have* to get to my boyfriend. He was bleeding."

"You'll be free to go in an hour if you *listen*."

Aaargh! She couldn't see a way out of this. Trying to calm herself, she closed her eyes, and took in a breath. As a wolf, she'd often do this, and the scents of the woods would always soothe her; now, she found the lull of the sea having the same effect. "You *don't* touch me; *he* doesn't touch me, and you untie me when you're done. Then, I get in my car and go."

"Yes. You have my word."

"I told you, your word doesn't—"

She started at the shrill sound that interrupted her.

The man pulled a phone from his coat pocket and answered it. After a moment, he raised his eyebrows and glanced at her. He put the phone on loudspeaker and held it out so she could hear.

"Spineless dick here. You have my word, too."

The phone went dead.

She couldn't for the life of her think of a reply. But there was something about his voice...

The man put the phone back in his pocket. "I think you pressed his button." He sounded amused by that. "My name is Hai, by the way. What would you like me to call you?"

She looked at him.

He stared back, his gaze steady.

He knows. He knows who you were; he knows what you did – what was done to you. She looked away. "Just call me Jennifer."

"All right, Jennifer. I'll begin with something that happened to a five-year-old boy that took place thirty years ago..."

~*~

It was weird listening to someone recount an episode of his life as if it were a story – a piece of fiction.

Roman tried not to hear Hai's retelling of his childhood, instead focusing on the database he'd just hacked. He couldn't stay on here long – two minutes tops. He'd done this many times when Selena – *Jennifer* – had been taken into intensive care five years ago.

He scanned the codes on the screen, knowing by heart where to find the one he wanted and noted it had changed since he'd last attempted this. He copied it and entered it into the decryption screen he had up, and ... bingo. He was inside York Hospital.

Now, all he had to do was find new arrivals in accident and emergency...

There. David Coates.

Fuck it, the information he was seeing would upset her. He'd spied the ambulance arriving just as they'd taken off and had hoped it wouldn't herald more bad news for her since she was about to receive the mother of all bad news.

He sighed.

As far as he could tell, David was stable, but unconscious. His profile listed him as having two contacts for emergencies: Jennifer Warren and Prisha Patel.

He pulled himself out of the database, cleared all trace of his having been there, and shut the computer down.

He had Jennifer's handbag next to him. Her phone was in it. He didn't need to check it to know the hospital had already called and left a message.

Hai's voice carried through the speakers fitted into his car. "They're nearer the surface when the moon is full, and being a Supermoon and Blood Moon, too, would ensure the siren's presence."

Christ, Hai ... think you can make my story sound just a little more interesting?

He glowered at his dashboard. He was annoyed at himself

for putting off the inevitable and confronting her face-to-face. And she *would* see it as a confrontation. That's not what he wanted, but he couldn't figure a way around it. As soon as she knew who he was, even if Hai explained it first, her instinct would be fight him, or flee. He didn't want either. He wanted her reason, but it was too much to ask after everything Bab had put her through, he knew that. Plus, she was not a reasonable person. He'd watched her intently while she was under Bab's imprisonment, and the female was emotion personified. Every feeling she carried was larger than life – engulfed her – and though detrimental in so many ways, it was also a beacon in a world where so many snuffed out that flame.

Perhaps that was why he hadn't been able to stop what happened after he'd pulled her out of the sea. She was already so much like the turbulent ocean.

Guilt hammered in his chest. He should be the one out there telling her all this, not Hai.

You are *a spineless dick.*

And that had pissed him off, too – that her flippant dig had got to him. He should have mastered that kind of reaction by now, but it cut too near to years of his father and Bab taunting him in similar ways.

He'd face her soon. But this way was better for her, he reasoned. Hai could introduce the idea in her mind gently – as gently as tonight's chaos would allow, anyway – then he'd show up and ... and what?

Shoot the final arrow through her heart, that's what. He cursed softly.

In reality, he hadn't fully expected her to embrace her human life, and she hadn't, but what he *had* noticed was a growth – a maturing – a resigned acceptance of her ills and vices and a willingness to change now her monster was hidden from sight. He understood it. His family were the monsters he'd spent a lifetime atoning for, and over the past five years separated from them after Bab's death, he finally could. *She* was his atonement.

He was about to rip all their efforts apart.

~*~

"So ... what are you saying? The boy became a siren? Because of the bite?"

"Not quite. After the incident was discovered by his parents, they finally confessed a dark secret: his grandfather, decades before, had spied a siren by the beach near his home. He hunted her and caught her. She put up a fight, but he was deaf – in the end that's how he escaped with his life. But not before impregnating her."

"Impregnating?" Her fury simmered. "You mean he *raped* her."

Hai held her gaze; his was sympathetic. "Nine months later, the siren returned to the same shores with babe in arms – why she returned is a mystery. There is a myth sirens are cold beings, but perhaps she was returning to bond father and child. Or perhaps she wanted nothing to do with a child created against her will. The baby was a girl – she would be the mother of the boy I've just told you about.

"But the siren's return had been foreseen, for the grandfather had the gift of vision. They were waiting for her. They murdered her and took the baby. She grew as a human – no signs of her mother befell her; no webbed fingers or toes, no gills, no black eyes... Their belief was that the human gene was dominant and had wiped out all traces of siren."

Jennifer snorted. Human superiority – where had she heard crap like that before.

"Turns out, the gene merely skipped a generation. It

would be the boy who carried it. It would be the reason he would hear the siren's call through his dreams, yet not be negatively affected by it. His talent for 'dreaming' came from them; they were calling him home. When the siren bit him, it was because she was at death's door. Upon dying, they become froth and waves, and merge with the sea once more, their wisdom shared with each other through every drop of the ocean. She chose to merge with him instead. We believe it was her last gift to him; the only way she could pass on the knowledge he had been denied through his human upbringing."

"Okay." Her head spun. Mermaids and stuff – she'd read a bit about them, but in the guise of fiction, much like how humans read about werewolves. All of this was ... a challenge to believe. "Why are you telling me this?" She was bloody uncomfortable. She shifted on her backside trying to find a better position.

"That boy grew into a man. Five years ago, that man pulled you out of the ocean where the white cliffs met the sea. Your lungs were full of water. His intent was to save your life, that was all. So, he breathed air into you. What he did not understand was that his breath held more than life, for this is also how sirens ... share knowledge." He looked away for a split second and Jennifer narrowed her eyes, her wolf's ears perking up at that little stumble over his words. "His breath held the blueprint of his siren gene. Your body absorbed it. The water never left your lungs – you never choked it up – it disappeared into your system, and then you breathed."

This might be the first time in her life she'd ever truly been lost for words. *So* lost.

So lost that she laughed – a small trickle of a giggle at first, but it quickly exploded into a guffaw at the *insanity* she'd just bothered to listen to.

Hai looked towards the heavens, not seeming too

impressed with her reaction.

Her laugh grew louder.

He laced his fingers together and waited for her to finish.

Thirty seconds passed ... fifty... Her laughing finally fizzled out. She looked up to find him staring back at her, patiently. "You're wrong," she said. "You think I'm a siren now?"

"That's not what I said."

"Then what?"

"The siren gene is a shadow in your blood, just as it is a shadow in his blood. Neither of you are *fully* siren, but you carry the heredity. If you were fully siren, you'd be living in the sea, swimming with the whales and eating the shrimp. But you have some traits. Singing men to death for starters."

Her skin prickled. *Holy shit.* She shook her head. "No. You've got it wrong. I was human. My blood was *human.* That's what he told me."

"Your blood *was* human. Because you were mated to a Trident."

She sat up and stared back at him, startled at how blunt that truth sounded. It was the first time she'd ever heard her past spoken of out loud.

"Tridents carried human blood; because of your mating, that blood was in you."

"But I never changed," she whispered. "I killed my mate the night before the full moon."

"You *did* change. You just never became a Trident. You became a human. Our mistake was in thinking that destroyed your wolf, but just as the Trident can only survive five years without a mate, the human in you – borne of the Trident, remember – only survived five years without a mate."

"Five years..."

"Three days ago, it was exactly five years since you killed your Trident mate." He paused, watching her as she let it sink in.

"So..." *Oh, my god.* "My human blood died."

"It did. But – and this is the part that had us stumped for a while – not before the siren latched onto it."

"What do you mean?"

"The siren's gene is compatible with only one other creature besides themselves: humans. The siren latched onto the human in you. It's been there ever since he breathed into your lungs five years ago, but both the siren and your wolf remained submissive to the human blood. Until now."

She was speechless. And scared. Her blood ran cold. *Or is that the siren's blood?* "How do you know all this?" she stuttered.

"For a long time we didn't. Five years of searching. But it's not only your blood we were trying to find answers for."

"His."

"Yes. But with him it's different: there are no male sirens – they're always female. That makes him an anomaly. The past few days, though, something is changing. It's affecting him as well as you, and we believe it's to do with the Super Blood Moon."

"I heard about this ... the eclipse on Sunday?"

He nodded. "The moon is almost in exactly the same location it was thirty years ago when he was bitten, and its phases are the same: a Supermoon and a total eclipse of the full moon, making it a Blood Moon, too."

"It's ... awakening the siren?"

"Awakening your blood shadow," he agreed, solemnly, "as the earth's shadow passes over the moon."

She said nothing for a while, trying to process it all. "But my wolf – she's been waking up, too."

"She has. We don't specifically know why, but we suspect because the human in you 'died', so to speak, it's made room for both the siren and wolf. The siren part took over your human blood as the human element faded, and the wolf ... well, we can't say for sure, but if neither creature is more dominant, perhaps they will share the space in harmony."

Her head spun. "So ... the human blood in me got taken over by the siren when its five years was up – which was three days ago – but my wolf, who never really left, also woke up when my human blood disappeared. This all happened, probably because of the Blood Moon since both creatures respond to the full moon, and now ... *both* the siren and wolf are in me? *Both* of them?"

"That's where we're at. That brings us to now."

What the fuck... Was she really accepting this all as *real*?

The image of bleeding ears branded her mind.

"*Can* the wolf and the siren coexist?"

"We have no idea. But I have no doubt we'll be finding out."

"What happens now?"

After a pause, he took a breath and stood. "Now I untie you, and you're free to leave."

"What?"

"That's what you wanted, yes?"

"Yes, but ... Jesus." She scowled. "You drop this atomic bomb on me and send me on my merry way? What's going to happen to *me*?"

His phone sounded again.

Her scowl deepened. He wasn't going to answer her fucking question, was he? "I know *nothing* about sirens!"

He ignored her and stared at his phone.

"What the hell am I supposed to do?" she pressed.

Hai finally glanced up. "First, I suggest driving to York Hospital. Your boyfriend is in intensive care."

The ground swayed under her, or seemed to. "Oh, no... Is he—"

"Alive. Stable, but unconscious. That's all I know. No doubt the doctors will tell you more."

"I did it, didn't I? I did that to him."

"Not intentionally."

"I shouldn't have sung." She'd tried. She tried really fucking hard to hurt no one the past few years. She'd failed.

Hai dropped her car keys on the sand in front of her. "I'm going to untie your hands first, then I'm going to stand back and let you untie your ankles. Then, you can take your keys and go. I'm told your bag and phone are in your car. It's parked in that direction." He pointed with his finger.

She twisted around to follow it.

"You'll see it just beyond the slope. If you come at me, I promise you, I can take you. But I really don't want to hurt you." He walked behind her, and she felt him tug at the ropes around her wrists.

"What the hell do I say to David?" But she wondered if that was the least of her worries. How did she go back to her life as it was? The one she'd battled to make just right.

It hasn't been right though, has it? Not really.

"The man who rescued you would like to meet with you now that you know his story."

"He should have told me himself," she ground out.

"He's programmed his number into your phone under the contact **Siren**."

"Imaginative."

She sensed the man smile, then her hands were free.

He stepped away just as he said he would while she pulled at the knots around her ankles. "He asks that you text him Sunday morning, no more notes – they're too slow. Then, you'll meet. You can't afford to wait any longer."

"I'm ready to meet him *now*."

"He insists you take tomorrow to process the

information."

She growled. "And why exactly does he get a say in what I do?" With ropes undone, she lurched forward for her keys.

Hai stood a few feet away with his hands clasped in front of him.

She brought herself up to her feet. "What if I decide *not* to meet him."

"Since none of us know what will happen when the Blood Moon takes place, I'd advise against that. You and he should be together on Sunday night. You're likely to need his help."

"I don't want his help."

"And he's likely to need yours," he said softly, "as much as he'd like not to admit it."

She fell silent.

"After five years aiding you, perhaps consider it."

She had more questions – *so* many questions – but freedom was calling, and so was David. And on the tail of everything was the worry this was all a trick; that her captor wouldn't let her go after all.

'You've got to get out.'

Without another word, she turned and sped towards her car.

~*~

Hai crossed his arms when he saw him approach. Roman wasn't surprised at the glare he got from his mentor. "I'm indebted to you, Hai."

"So what's new," he replied.

"I mean it. Thank you."

"I think you're being a fool. I understand your reasoning, but she's going to despise you more than if you'd met with her years ago. Especially after tonight."

"Maybe. I'll have to live with the consequences."

"She still doesn't know the crucial bit."

Roman pulled a face. "I know. She'll put two and two together soon enough."

"You're a coward."

"She won't listen if she hears it all at once. Better to let her come to the right conclusions bit by bit."

"I think you're underestimating her."

Roman shook his head, staring at the tracks made in the dirt by the wheels of her car. "I need her strong, Hai. Stronger than this."

"She seemed pretty strong to me."

"No. You should have seen her at the farm. She had a streak of rage for sure, perhaps even insanity, but it had been necessary for her escape … what she went through back then... It would have been enough to break most. She took herself to the brink and brought herself back. I need that from her again or I don't know if either of us will survive the coming moon."

Hai laughed.

Roman knitted his brows, then crossed his own arms. "And the funny thing is?"

"Do you really doubt her level of rage once she knows everything? I wouldn't want to be in your shoes."

"I don't need her rage, I need her *strength*."

"You may not get one without the other."

He sighed. "You might be right. What do I do?"

"Temper her rage – don't be afraid of it. Forge it into steel so she can hold it and wield it. She did that night five years ago when the storm beat down. *Jí fēng zhī jìn cǎo.*"

Roman smiled. Another day, another proverb – Hai was full of them. But as a child, Roman had swallowed up every one. In one of those proverbs, Hai had taught him more than his father had taught him in a lifetime. "And what does that mean?"

"The strength of a blade of grass is seen only in tempests."

Chapter Six

Only after pulling her handbrake and switching off the engine, did she realise she was shaking. A lot. Jennifer looked around at the hospital car park, half empty at this time of night. The clock on her dashboard read 12:57. She didn't even know if they'd let her in, but given he was in ICU, and probably hadn't had any visitors yet considering his parents lived down in London, she was hoping some kind of exception might be made. At the very least she could get more details about his condition.

But the shaking was distracting. She placed her hands on her thighs and tried to force herself still. She hadn't thought about anything that Hai guy had divulged during her drive back to York; she didn't even know where to start with it all and her brain felt pickled. It kind of felt like she'd dreamt the whole encounter.

The faint rope burns on her wrists and the sand still in her hair told her she hadn't.

Gathering herself, she picked up her handbag, put her phone in it – tried not to think about how the cowhearted note-sender had rummaged through her things – and got out of the car.

Think about all the crap tomorrow. Concentrate on David now.

And somehow, amazingly, she actually listened to herself.

She made her way to the hospital's entrance, looking out for the arrows to the department she wanted. She'd never set foot in here before, but it didn't take her too long to find, and after five minutes of elevators and long corridors, she found herself at the reception desk of intensive care.

She spied a notice for visiting hours on the wall. Yeah – she was *well* out of those hours.

A woman sat at the desk with her head down over something. Behind her, a man in a white coat – probably a doctor – was looking at papers on a clipboard.

She reached inside herself, calling for her wolf, wondering if that old animal magnetism still worked. She'd rarely used it on humans, but she'd known other wolves that had – they'd sworn by it. It was so subtle that humans never noticed, apparently.

Hesitantly, she made her way to the desk, eyeing the woman, but it was the man she kept her focus on. He was likely to be the one who responded, though you never exactly knew. "Excuse me?" In her mind, she kept her hold on her wolf. The animal seemed kind of nonchalant about her plan, though, which didn't bode well.

The woman, a middle-aged lady with dark hair and glasses, looked at the clock – made a point of it – then back at her. "Yes?"

Fuck it, this wasn't going to work. "Hi. I'm Jennifer Warren. I've only just received the messages on my phone about David Coates. I'm his emergency contact. I'm here to see him."

The doctor looked up from his clipboard, but didn't seem too taken by her presence. He turned around and went back to what he was doing.

Crap. What the fuck is that, wolfy? You used to be good at this kind of shit, didn't you?

Refusing to give in, she gave a wavering smile – she was

supposed to be visibly upset after all.

"Visiting hours are over, I'm afraid," said the woman. "I'm sorry about the news you've received, of course, but David did have a visitor earlier."

She frowned. "He did?" Who the hell would that have been?

The woman made some kind of sniffing sound as she picked up a file and opened it. "Erm ... here, yes. We have two emergency contacts listed for him. It was Prisha Patel that came by earlier."

Her heart dropped. Unexpectedly, a wave of jealousy washed over her. Yeah, she knew Prisha – she'd met her a couple of times and *really* didn't like the woman. She knew the feeling was mutual.

She might not love David, but he was *her* David. He'd been important to her for over two years – he wasn't *Prisha's*.

Yep – *there* was her wolf.

For a minute, she wasn't sure what to do. She was caught between past and present; the wolf world and the human one. A bitchy retort with a forceful ultimatum was on the tip of her tongue, but the part of her that had put all that behind her was too developed now to allow such an all-or-nothing reaction. "Well ... I'm glad he's had company, but I'm his girlfriend – he lives with me."

The woman eyed her. "Do you have ID on you?"

"Yes, of course." She popped her bag down and pulled out her wallet. Handing over the driver's licence, she glanced at the man. He was still absorbed by that clipboard. She might as well be invisible to him. "The address on there is David's address, too. If you find his wallet – he usually carries it in his jacket's inside pocket – you'll see that his licence has the same address."

The woman took her time studying her ID. Jennifer had

to stop herself from rolling her eyes at her mini display of power.

Peering over her glasses, she handed the card back. "David is in a stable condition; we're not expecting any immediate changes. It's only seven hours until visiting time. You can pop back in the morning."

The bitch. "With all due respect—"

"I'm sorry, we don't make any exceptions."

She felt the heat rise to her face. From frustration, yes, but also from the humiliation of being put in her place by someone who had no fucking clue what she was dealing with. She reached for her wolf again, but it was something else she found; a feeling at first – a lapping of coolness to calm her heat – and then a note.

That was all. Just a note.

It played out in her head – one note – until all she heard was the note. It weaved itself through her mind, lighting up synapses and neurons (or at least, that's what she imagined), until eventually, the note *became* her. Or perhaps she became the note.

For a minute, she feared she'd open her mouth and sing it because the sweet pitch felt like it needed an out – a way to escape before it detonated her mind. Instead, she sensed that 'magnetism' she'd tried to conjure earlier from the wolf.

But this wasn't the wolf. She understood with clarity, this was the siren.

An elusive coil of feminine power curled up her spine. It brought a flush to her cheeks, a glimmer to her eyes, and gently swelled the flesh of her lips. Not that she could see any of this, but she *knew* it. It couldn't be mistaken. Finally, that seductive coil stretched and seemed to seep through her pores. Not even as the wolf had she felt this *female*. As a wolf, she'd had to *fight* to get others to see her female power as equal to theirs – particularly the males.

This didn't feel like a fight. It felt like a natural destiny.

The doctor straightened his back, and finally turned her way. His gaze landed on her. She saw his pupils dilate; a slight gaze veiled his eyes. "I'm sorry. Please excuse me, I didn't catch your name."

"Jennifer. Jennifer Warren." She wondered if she'd accidentally sung her name.

No. She wasn't singing, she was talking normally, but it *felt* like she was singing. Words had become a thing of magic, music in every syllable.

This is insane.

It was also quite the rush.

"I'm Doctor Barrett. I treated David earlier; I'd be more than happy to take you to him."

The reception nurse's mouth fell open. "But, Doctor, I—"

"It's quite all right, Mrs Tate."

Her mouth closed, then opened and closed again.

"Miss Warren, would you like to follow me?"

"Thank you so much, Doctor. This means a lot to me." And she was going to hell, because she simply couldn't help turning back as they walked past the desk, and throwing the lady a small, victorious smirk.

Tears sprung to her eyes when she caught sight of David lying helplessly on the bed. He did look peaceful though; fairly content. No breathing apparatus were visible.

"He's stable and his heartbeat's strong. As you can see, he can breathe on his own... we're expecting him to wake up in the next few hours. We did put him under sedation to aid his recovery; there was swelling in the brain."

"Swelling?" She almost choked on that single word.

"Yes. A bit of a mystery – MRIs showed no anomalies at all. It's as if he's got severe concussion, but there's no bruising, or tumours – no sign of anything, actually."

"What about ... I mean, is there anything else wrong? Apart from the swelling in his brain?"

"His eardrums are perforated, and it seems that was caused by internal pressure in the skull. Again, we're not entirely sure why yet, but that's all. He'll be right as rain in a couple of days."

Her tears slipped. The relief she felt – the immensity of it – was a pleasant surprise. She often felt so disconnected from the human world and David himself, even though she tried not to.

"Oh..." The doctor saw her discomfort. "Here." He reached over the bed to the little bedside table and plucked a tissue out of a box. He handed it to her.

"Thank you," she said, taking it. "Does anyone know what happened? I mean, I heard about the, erm, chaos at the pub."

"I know quite little about that to be honest. The police spoke to our paramedics briefly – there was also another man affected."

Oh, god. She'd momentarily forgotten about the other man she'd seen on the floor, bleeding.

"My understanding is that there might have been a bout of food poisoning. I think the police were investigating a mass drugging of drinks."

"Drugging?"

"Spiking. Yes."

So, nothing about a woman fitting her description singing everyone to an embolism. It only made her feel marginally better. "What about the other man you mentioned? Is he in ICU, too?"

He looked at her uncomfortably.

She tugged on the siren in her a little harder, hoping her allure was still evident.

The doctor's expression changed to sympathetic. "Did you know him? The other man?"

"No. Um..." She probably shouldn't let on she'd been at the pub herself. "David was there with a few friends. One of those friends left a message on my phone, too. She's the one who mentioned the chaos. I think she might have mentioned the other man," she pressed. She wanted answers.

The doctor sighed. "I'm very sorry to tell you this, but I'm afraid he passed away half an hour after being brought in. He suffered similar symptoms, but the damage to his brain was irreparable and he'd ... well, he'd lost an alarming amount of blood." The doctor frowned, as if he couldn't quite understand that, and she should imagine he never would.

She felt like shit; felt herself grow small inside. *You killed him – well done.*

It didn't matter that it was by accident. That fact didn't stop her visualising a bullet burning its way through her brother's skull, nor the memory of exactly what it felt like to pull that trigger.

Bile rose in her throat. She swallowed it down, her breaths growing raspy. *You killed him.*

"Are you all right?" The doctor took her elbow.

She couldn't figure out why at first; then, she realised it was because she'd swayed. "Um ... sorry, yes, just feeling a little faint."

"Of course, you've been through a lot. Would you like to sit?" He caressed her arm.

She froze.

It was a tiny movement – hardly noticeable – and probably would have meant nothing if it weren't for the siren magic (or whatever the hell you called it) she was using.

A different kind of siren went off in her mind. She had no idea how to wield this creature she'd been told *just three hours ago* was inside her. What if she couldn't control the siren? What if she couldn't pull her back? Panic rose sharply. She had to get out of here.

She turned to make for the door, pulling herself out of the doctor's grasp, but stopped. She couldn't just leave David like this.

Hurriedly, she approached his side. Her hand went to his face and she gently cupped his cheek. He didn't deserve any of this; out of all the humans and wolves she'd ever known, he deserved this the least.

She had no idea if he could hear her, but she bent down and whispered into his ear. "I'm so sorry. Rest and sleep well. I'll come by in the morning to see you again." She stopped short of saying she loved him. At this moment, it tore her open that she'd never said those words to him because he'd earned them ten times over. Women killed for men like this – unconditional, supportive – and here she was, unable to love him no matter how hard she tried.

It's a blessing, David. Because I'm not worthy of your love – I'm really not.

She dropped a soft kiss on his lips, then walked towards the door.

"Miss Warren, would you like me to walk you to your car?"

A bit above and beyond the call of duty, isn't it? But she said nothing, knowing the siren had a hold on him. She also wasn't thinking straight enough to detach the creature from him. "No. Thank you, Doctor Barrett, I have kept you long enough and the receptionist was correct – I shouldn't be here at this hour. I'll come back in the morning."

He looked disappointed. "I'm not in until five o'clock tomorrow."

Jennifer smiled, politely, and left without looking back or glancing at the receptionist on her way out. *Please don't follow me*, she prayed as she reached the elevator.

He hadn't followed her, but he still stared, his stance clearly indicating he was attracted to her. She'd have to undo that little trick before she came back tomorrow ... if she could figure out how.

It was nearly half past two by the time she pulled into her driveway.

She was exhausted.

David's absence felt like a vacuum, but it was made bearable by the doctor's assertion that he would be just fine. A small part of her felt relieved he wasn't here. She needed time to understand everything she'd been through the past few hours – if this was a regular Friday night, she wouldn't have been good company. 'Silent and sullen', David called it, albeit usually in bemusement. He'd never minded her moods and there were times she'd taken advantage of that.

It was stopping now. She wouldn't use him again – she knew she couldn't. But she had to figure this siren crap out first. Was it permanent? Was there a way to undo it? What did it mean for her wolf?

She was so confused.

Shaking her head, and wishing it was enough to throw out all her thoughts, she got out of her car, only to see movement in the shadows down the side access to the garden.

Fear made itself known first, but anger chased it. *What the fuck is it now?*

"Who's there?" she called out, perhaps stupidly. Every now and then she still forgot she didn't have her old wolf strength. "I've had a really bad night, so don't fuck with me." She winced. Was that too harsh? Most of the time, she felt like she was far too blunt for the human world, but then, she'd been told she was far too blunt for the wolf world, too – ever since she'd been a child that crap had been spouted at her. Tonight, she found she didn't care. Sometimes, the two worlds did share similarities. A female who spoke her mind and called it like it was, was considered trouble. When a male did it, he was considered a leader and desirable.

At 2:30 a.m., after her shittiest night in five years, both worlds could fuck off.

The shadow moved, until a form emerged.

The fear faded completely, sheer annoyance filling the space it had taken. "Prisha."

The woman stood there, carrying the same expression Jennifer felt. "Hello," she said, curtly. Hardly a greeting. But then, Jennifer hadn't been expecting smiles and flowers.

"It's two thirty in the morning."

"So it is."

Oh, we're playing it like this, are we? Fine. "I've just got back from the hospital. Heard you'd stopped by there earlier."

"Someone had to."

The wolf in her growled, and she let it. She knew a bitch when she saw one, and just like that, all trace of siren disappeared. Only her she-wolf was present, and in the face of her breached territory, she wasn't about to tell the animal to sit.

For the first time in a long while, she felt utterly comfortable with her wolf. While the siren's emergence had been an alarming experience, her wolf was an old friend, and she knew her well. They'd been to hell and back together – more than once. She trusted her wolf implicitly. "I would have been there if I could have been. I didn't even know he'd been taken to the hospital."

"Really." It wasn't even a question. Her tone clearly told her she didn't believe her.

"David's important to me – why would I lie?"

"Hmmn..." The woman strode out of the shadows completely, but stopped about three feet in front of her.

She had to be careful here. Her wolf wanted to pounce, and she wanted to let it, truth be told, but Prisha was David's friend – probably his best friend from things he'd said – and he'd suffered enough. It was for David's sake alone this woman was still standing on her driveway.

Jennifer gave herself a silent pat on the back for working so hard on her patience over the years.

"I don't know, Jennifer, why *would* you lie." Prisha held something up between her fingers. It was a USB stick – that's what it looked like, anyway. "CCTV footage from the pub."

Jennifer narrowed her eyes. "Gosh. You stole footage?" *Probably hacked it.* That didn't surprise her. David said she was something of a genius with all that stuff. He often joked he was glad she was on the right side of the law, or she'd be emptying banks around the world. "And somehow, I'm the bad guy?"

"You were there at the pub. You're singing bloody karaoke the moment everything goes to hell, so I want to know where you disappeared to. Why weren't you at David's side when he got hurt?"

Singing ... shit. Could sirens affect their victims through *tape*? "You heard me singing?"

She frowned. "There's no sound, just footage. I saw enough. You were on that stage with the microphone, then people started freaking out and jumping over each other, and when I rewound, I could see you being pulled back by someone."

"Who?"

"You tell me."

"There's nothing to tell."

"Jesus Christ, I've never liked you. You must think I'm stupid."

"I don't think you're stupid, I think you're a hard-skinned bitch who wishes she'd got with my boyfriend instead of being palmed off to some balding banker for x-amount of pounds, and now you're sticking your nose in where it doesn't belong."

Prisha looked shocked, and then furious.

Jennifer almost felt bad, because if there was anyone who knew what it was like to be forced into a mating, it was her. But that also meant she didn't give a fuck that Prisha had successfully overcome her shitty lot in life – good for her – *so had she*. Only the shit kept on coming. "And I'm not lying – there isn't anything to tell. When everyone in the pub started panicking for some reason I couldn't fathom, I was grabbed from behind and pulled back by one of the security guards – that's what you saw in the footage. He was doing his job. I wasn't at David's side because I fainted, just like he did, and apparently, just like a few other people did. When I woke up, I realised he was gone and so were the friends I was with. It took quite a while to figure out what had happened, and where the hell David had ended up."

"You expect me to believe that?"

"I expect you to get the hell off my property."

Prisha fell silent as she glared at her. It was clear she knew something was off, but also clear she had no idea what that was.

Jennifer also had an inkling the woman would keep digging until she found the truth though, which was fucking irritating to say the least. Add an ounce of jealousy, and Jennifer knew how unstoppable such a female could be.

"All right, I'll leave. But you should have this." She

reached into her jeans pocket, and Jennifer tensed, not knowing what she'd pull out.

It was a small box, its velvety sheen emphasised by the security light shining from above her front door. "What is it?"

"I took it from David's rucksack when I was at the hospital. He showed it to me this morning." She opened the box.

A ring sat in its centre. A diamond ring. *Oh, no...*

"David's going to ask you to marry him."

She stared at the ring, speechless.

"I told him he was insane. I told him you were using him, and he's far too good for you – whatever the hell went down tonight, I *know* you know that's true."

Jennifer reached for the box, shakily.

Prisha all but slammed it into her open hand. "He doesn't deserve this." Her voice shook. "He might be your boyfriend, but I've known him since high school. People don't see it in him because he's quiet and kind – he's not the showy type at all – but he's always been the one to look after others. Maybe something in him seeks it out, I don't know, but he's always the crutch, and people always abuse it. His own sister was the same; his mother's not much better. And I see it in you.

"I want you to leave him. I want you to fuck off out of his life and give him the chance to have a good one with a woman who *loves* him; who would never treat him the way you are."

The words stung because they were accurate. Mostly. "That woman's never going to be you, Prisha."

Prisha took a step back and adjusted the bag on her shoulder. "You don't think I know that? It won't ever be me because I'd never in a million years land him in the shipwreck that is my life. Because I actually *care* about him."

The ring box in her hand weighed heavy; tugged her downwards; wanted to drag her into hell. "I do care," she whispered.

"Then leave him," said Prisha, making her way down the driveway towards the one road out of the village. Jennifer assumed she must have parked somewhere along that road. "And do it before I find out the truth about you, because I will – I know you're hiding something. And when I do find out, David will be the first to know about it. It'll be better for him if he's well shot of you by then."

With that, she strode off, leaving Jennifer reeling. That the woman was right was a bitter pill to swallow; that Jennifer had suddenly lived a flash of the past where she'd been the one dishing out similar words to another female with such venom, made the pill a taste of her own medicine.

She breathed out, exhaling history. *That was then, this is now.* She could wallow in her mistakes, but that didn't change the present, or anything that had happened tonight. It didn't change the fact she was ... god, she was *half-siren, half-wolf.*

That was it, wasn't it? That's what she was. Tonight's events suddenly brought that realisation crashing. She felt sick. She couldn't be with David. When she'd thought she was fully human, there'd been a chance – a glimpse of a future with him, even if it had always been uncertain; even if she'd always kept a part of her from him. But now...

A movement from above her caught her eye – a twitch of a curtain from the house next door. *Jack.* Oh, wonderful. Had he heard all that?

Is it really worse than him watching you masturbate in your garden?

She fumbled for her house keys, the ring box burning David's heart into her palm, and let herself into her house, pushing her nosy neighbour to the back of her mind. She had more pressing matters. Having her wolf back was cautiously comforting, but being a siren was something she knew nothing about. What happened next, she had no idea. But it was becoming more and more obvious David – her only safety net – couldn't be a part of it.

Chapter Seven

Your kind will all be gone by the time the moon begins to wane again. You're not facing extinction in years to come – you're facing it now. Right now. You can't stop it. Neither can I."

Jennifer turned in her sleep, aware she was dreaming; unable to wake.

"But you, my darling, do not have to die with them. You are a part of the next stage of evolution." Bab put down his drink, shuffled off the sofa and approached her, staying low, prowling around the coffee table.

She felt sick. Sick with fear, but the fear was a physical thing as was the vomit she swallowed back down. She tensed, ready to bolt.

He knelt in front of her, very still. If she didn't know him, she'd mistake it for an act of reverence. "Don't fight it," he whispered. "Become it."

She felt drunk – stupored – even though she'd only had the tiniest sip of that bourbon he'd forced down her throat.

"Come close, Selena. Sniff my neck."

She frowned, fearful, not understanding his meaning.

"It's all right, I promise. Just smell me. Here." He turned his *head away from her and exposed his neck. "I won't hurt you."*

A moot promise coming from the man who had already hurt her so much. Nevertheless, she saw no options with Gabriel to her right, Bab's ever-silent brother standing guard a few feet behind him, and the door too far away for her to reach in one piece. She leaned forward as much as she dared, and sniffed the vein protruding from his neck.

No! Her thighs clenched, and she scooted back, alarmed – alarmed at the too-pleasant heat that spread from her bare crotch.

"See? I smell like him, don't I?"

Gabriel. He smelled like Gabriel.

"I smell like your mate."

She whimpered, disgusted, despite her body's arousal. It was a repulsive abnormality.

"It was Gabriel's blood I injected into my veins this morning."

Good god! *She stared at Gabriel, but he had his head turned away from her. In shame? His posture indicated he wasn't best pleased.*

Bab had told her about how the humans at Head Office – him, his brother, and a handful of others – injected Trident blood into their veins so they could overpower them, and control them better.

She jolted in her seat as Bab's fingers stroked her skin, just under her bellybutton.

She hissed. Don't touch me! *The words never left her mouth.*

"There's no pain, is there?"

Tears of hot humiliation filled her eyes. No, the common jabs of betrayal pain weren't there.

Still, Gabriel growled.

Instinct.

A very low growl at the impostor wearing his scent. His eyes flashed as he turned towards Bab.

Bab's own eyes momentarily glowed in response, and Selena gritted her teeth as his thumb brushed against the top of her pubic mound.

But he halted all movement, then slowly retreated, stood, gave his shoulders and neck a stretch, and then looked at his watch.

Gabriel bristled; his every muscle poised for attack.

Bab's brother took a step forward, his stance one of wariness, ready to defend Bab.

Something fluttered against her feet. It almost jostled her out of the sick nightmare of a memory because she didn't remember this part – this bit hadn't happened five years ago.

She looked down to see a slip of paper curling around her ankles in a breeze that wasn't there.

The note-sender!

In relief, she bent to grab the paper, afraid dream-Bab would reprimand her for such an action.

He didn't notice. He couldn't see the note. He swiftly turned, picked up his glass from the coffee table, swallowed the last of the whiskey, then put the empty vessel back down with a clank.

Hurriedly, she looked down at the written message: **It's you I tried to protect.**

She blinked, confused. What did that mean?

Bab was talking again. She hadn't caught what he'd just said.

"...we'll catch up tomorrow night, Selena, when the moon is fully round and you're the last of your kind left on the planet...." His voice faded again. She couldn't concentrate. She sensed Gabriel bridling, Bab goading him ... and then Bab's brother cleared his throat, and said something in a language she didn't understand...

Ice enveloped her before she could comprehend the scene had changed; had torn her from the disastrous heat of the living room and plunged her into raging waters that pillaged her mouth, throat, and lungs.

She couldn't breathe, and though she fought to swim upwards, it was downwards she raced. Everything hurt, and she'd changed her bloody mind: death wasn't what she wanted, despite everything she'd been through; despite the burn of her mate's exit from the world.

This was worse.

She struggled harder against the current – a new captor she'd willingly thrown herself to.

I don't want to die!

Instinct could never be bargained with. Every last inch of her screamed for air, and though she knew it would be her end, she could not help but open her mouth, seeking oxygen where there was none.

The cold of the vast ocean rushed into her lungs. NO!

But she was no match for the hugest body on Earth. The sea possessed her every cell, pushing pain to new heights, and then ... there was no pain.

None.

Sensations floated away, just as the light from the surface continued to do ... it was so far away. When the light was nothing but a pin prick in the furthest ether of her consciousness, it occurred to her, hazily, that her eyes might be closed. Why else would it be so dark?

As the pin prick became consumed by wet blackness, she thought she felt a pull on her arm. And that was all she thought before she died.

The blackness of her bedroom might as well have been the blackness of the ocean, fathoms deep, as Jennifer awoke, gasping and retching for air.

At first there was no breath, and she imagined for a crazy second that, this time, she really had died, and the past five years had been nothing but an interlude. But then, finally, the scream came – more of a caterwaul, really – a bay into the room as she leapt towards the other side of the bed. "David! David!"

She shouldn't wake him, but she needed him – she really needed him after that untimely sojourn down memory lane.

"David ... Dav—" Oh.

She'd forgotten.

Last night's events came rushing back, as unforgiving as the sea, and Jennifer did for the first time what she hadn't done since seeing her brother mutilated and helpless, begging for her safety: she sobbed.

Overwhelmed – already drowned – she crumpled onto David's pillow, his side of the bed far, far too cold, and sobbed.

She didn't know what had pulled her out of sleep. Not the nightmare from last time.

The room was still dark, so she knew it must still be before dawn.

Beep.

Aah ... that was the sound that had woken her.

Groggily, she shifted her haphazard position on the bed, realising she'd fallen asleep lying sideways, hugging David's pillow, his scent on it her only comfort. She could feel where her tears had dried on her face.

Beep.

Her bag was on the floor by the chest of drawers, and the *beep* reminded her she'd left her phone switched on in case the hospital called.

Aching in ways only humans could *(though, you're not human at all, are you?)* she climbed off the bed with a small moan of discomfort. Her wrists and ankles stung a little from the ropes. They hadn't been overly tight, but she'd struggled against them.

Reaching into her bag, she brought out the phone, her hand brushing against something that made her go back into her bag.

The sheets about sirens. She'd left them in her car's glove box, hadn't she?

Guess who put them back in your bag.

With a sigh, she made her way to the warmth of the bed once more, phone and paper in hand. Her life had been hijacked whether she liked it or not, but the truth was, it had been hijacked five years ago when she'd been given it anew. *She* hadn't chosen her new name, her new location, her new car ... it had all been decided for her, not that she could really have refused it at the time – she'd have had nowhere to go except prison.

She was the idiot to think she'd actually escaped; had actually gotten a *real* chance at redemption.

You don't get redemption by escaping.

Finally curled up under the duvet, she glanced at her phone. It was nearly four o'clock in the morning, and the three text messages she'd received were from Amanda checking on her and asking what the hell had happened at the pub because she'd drunk too much and couldn't piece the bits she remembered together. She and Shauna had apparently staggered back to Amanda's flat just ten minutes from the pub. Shauna had just thrown up.

She wasn't going to reply – not now. She'd send an 'I'm okay' text after breakfast, but she didn't want to get into the whole 'David's in hospital' conversation right now. Her attention wandered to the information sheets.

You're a siren.

Hell, it wasn't like she'd never thought they existed, it was more that she'd never thought about them at all. Sirens? She kind of knew the mythology – roughly. It's not like she ever went looking them up to find out more.

She turned on the torch on her phone to read the text better.

Since the seventeenth century, Sirens and mermaids have been synonymous with each other, and most differences between the two creatures faded into oblivion. However, there is one major difference to be found if one is to research thoroughly: Sirens are always and only female, unlike the mermaid, which finds her counterpart in the merman. Sirens cannot mate with their own kind, but must come to land and find a human male willing – or sometimes not – to copulate with. In addition, some of the research has concluded that mating cannot take place in the traditional sense, as Sirens have no vaginal cavity leading to the womb. It is suspected that mating takes place through the passing of breath from human to Siren, on which the male's blueprint is carried and can be transformed by the Siren to create new life within her.

Jennifer blinked. Then, blinked again. She'd started to drift off while reading in the low light of the torch, and she didn't at first understand what had her wits on alert. Something in the text ... something that had her feeling alarmed, though the feeling had no footing until she read that last sentence again: **mating takes place through the passing of...**

Shit, shit shit! She bolted upright, grabbing the sheet and straightening it out in front of her. Angling the light, she read it again: **mating takes place through the passing of breath from human to Siren...**

She shook with shock, which quickly turned to white hot fury. She was going to fucking kill him.

~*~

He'd been slapped awake.

Okay – no. But that's what it felt like, because he could feel *her*. Fuck.

It was only a matter of time, dimwit.

Roman sucked in a breath, tiredness falling off him rapidly as he took in the full weight of her emotions. It was quite a thing to get used to – someone else's feelings embedded with yours. Just as one drop of ocean connected that drop to the entire sea, it turned out sirens could connect with each other through the vast body in a similar principle, from one end of the earth to the other. Like humans, they were made up of 60 percent water – *more* than 60 percent if they were a full-blooded siren. The ocean lived within them, and some vibration of the water threaded each siren together.

The ability had been passive within him until he'd saved her life. Sure, he'd had the dreams, and he'd had empathy. Always empathy – an innate ability to simply *know* what others were feeling, and to some extent, thinking. God, his father had hated that skill. Perhaps because it had opened the bastard wide to his son. Bab had cared much less that Roman could get under his skin, but Bab had had far less of a conscience. 'Care' wasn't anything he'd been capable of.

With trepidation, he reached for his phone, and just as he predicted, the first message came in.

You bastard. I trusted you.

He exhaled and tried to stay calm. Hai was right: he was a coward. His entire life he'd revolted against his family and their actions yet had never been able to fully extricate himself from them – not after the siren had sunk her teeth into him –

and then, five years ago, he'd gone and done *that*. To the one person he'd tried to help of all people. He'd never forgive himself, not that it mattered, because it didn't look like she'd ever be able to forgive him either. And why should she after everything she'd endured? He'd only added to it. *Like your brother, like your father, like your grandfather...*

His fingers flew over the buttons.

You read the sheet, then.

A lame reply, but even though he'd rehearsed this moment in his head, it had always been face-to-face – with his getting something of a pummelling. The time taken to send each text made this his least preferred method of communication, but he couldn't risk losing her yet by showing himself.

You did that to me.

I didn't know. I was trying to save your life.

And if she bothered to *try* and reach out, she'd be able to feel him, too, and understand everything he was saying was true. She didn't know she could do that, though, and he very much doubted she'd now want to.

You raped me.

I didn't. I didn't know, I swear. And there was no pleasure in it.

He winced. That wasn't strictly true, but it was definitely true that any pleasure had been mixed with a hefty amount of horror and subsequent disgust at what had taken place, all his worst fears about himself realised through a fucking *accident* of all things.

I was thinking as a human. I AM human. Mostly. All I was thinking about was getting you to breathe again. I did not know.

You GAVE me the information right here in front of me. You didn't know putting your breath in my lungs was the fish version of fucking me? Clever dick, aren't you?

He raised his eyebrows as he read her retort. He would have smiled at her gibe could he not feel her pain.

The sheets I gave you, I only learned most of that after it happened. It was the incident that spurred the research. My father's text books said very little. Most of what I know about sirens I learned over the past five years. Everything I know is on those sheets now.

Everything? There's fuck all on here. Wolves have shelves of textbooks dedicated to them. This is all you know about sirens?

Sirens are a mystery. Almost nothing's written about them. There's a way to research more, but it will take time and might be dangerous. Have you read all the sheets?

I've read enough.

Read all the sheets.

Fuck you.

He held back his own retort; she didn't need that. She was backed into a corner – that wasn't her fault.

> Read all the sheets. You need to
> know everything you can.

And I should listen to you, WHY?

> I'm not your enemy.

I don't trust you.

> I've given you plenty of reason to trust me.

You RAPED me. While I was DEAD.

He growled into the emptiness of his room.

> I'll apologise for all eternity if I have to, but I'll also re-
> peat: I DID NOT KNOW.

Did you stop once you'd figured it out?

Christ... It sounded so bad he almost disbelieved himself.

> I couldn't stop. I tried. I can show you if you like. There's
> a way. I can show you what happened that night. You
> can feel everything I felt and see everything that took
> place through my eyes. You can know my mind.

You've got to be fucking kidding. I don't EVER want to be that

close to you again.

He sighed. She was closer than she thought – it really wasn't an option, and yes, he felt fucking guilty about it.

> **Hai told you about my family – my brother, my grand-father. I NEVER wanted to be like them and by god I TRIED to stop. I was pulled in, it was too strong. It was like a current. I couldn't stop.**

Fuck you. FUCK YOU. I'm done. No more texts, no notes.

Shit!

> **NO. PLEASE.**

He pressed 'send' and sat up, ready to leap at the door, as if he could stop her miles away with his movements.

> **What happened – it's not the same as for wolves. It's NOT like what happened to you before. We're not MATED or anything – not like that.**

He pressed 'send' then carried on.

> **But there IS a connection I can't do anything about. It's not a result of what I did, but it's accentuated by it. Read the sheets. It's not all on there, but I can explain the rest in person.**

His phone was silent for a good five minutes after that. If he hadn't been able to sense her presence he'd have thought she'd kept her word and fucked off.

Finally, the beep sounded.

When?

This is it, then. He wondered for a second whether he should tell her first who he really was.

No. She wouldn't meet him if he did – he knew that. And he *needed* her to meet with him. How he'd get her not to run, though, was something he hadn't figured out. He didn't want to tie her up again – that didn't exactly set a good precedence.

Tomorrow night. At the same beach we took you to tonight.

No. That's a two and a half hour drive for me. And I'm not meeting you anywhere secluded.

Fucking wonderful. He frowned. Meeting anywhere crowded would make it easy for her to slip away; easy for a crowd to turn on him if she happened to cry wolf. But he had to give her this. He couldn't expect her to willingly put herself in danger, even if only perceived, given what she'd just discovered. *Given what she's going to discover once she sees you. You're an idiot, Roman.*

Yeah, an idiot with no choice.

Okay, meet me outside York Cathedral. 8pm. Front entrance.

How will I know it's you?

Oh ... there was the billion-dollar question. He grimaced.

You'll know.

⬝Chapter Eight

T he next time she woke up, it was to the sun streaming in through the living room window. Jennifer hadn't gone to bed after that texting spree last night – she'd been too angry. Instead, she turned on the TV and flicked through channels, hoping anything would catch her attention and take her mind off everything that had happened, which it didn't. She'd finally turned it off and had fallen asleep on the sofa in her fluffy robe. She loved the softness, even if it was synthetic. It was the closest thing she had to fur. She'd often played with Stephen's fur when they'd been pups; he'd found it funny to shift, knowing she couldn't, but she'd squeal in delight while bringing him in for a cuddle. They'd been three and five – just before all the horror had taken place on the Surrey pack's land. The *first* time. So many wolves had been slaughtered. She'd cried when she'd learned Elana – one of the females she'd loved most – had been killed. She'd been a bit like an older sister she'd admired, but mostly, like the mother she'd never had, even if Elana had only been fifteen herself. At the age of three, she'd been her hero.

Those memories weren't welcome. She pushed them aside, and sat up, feeling slightly disorientated. The clock above the fireplace told her it was just gone nine o'clock. She reached for her phone on the coffee table.

No more texts.

She could do with feeling less confused. It should be straight-forward: he'd taken advantage; he'd violated her.

The confusion came because she didn't actually feel violated, and she bloody well knew how it felt to be so, what with Gabriel and Bab, and that other male wolf when she'd been fifteen.

Yeah ... it should be straight-forward.

It wasn't.

Whatever-his-name – her note-sender – didn't feel like any of those other males, despite his confession. She was angry it had gone down that way, but she was also alive. She hadn't wanted to die, and his actions were the reason she was here.

She had eleven hours until she'd finally see him in the flesh. Maybe then everything would fall into place.

Jennifer rose from the couch, re-tied her falling robe, and made her way into the kitchen, missing David's cheerful morning greeting. He'd no doubt have had a coffee on the go for her if he'd been here. She'd head to the hospital straight away, or... Maybe not.

An idea took root.

She'd call in first to check on him. Providing he was doing okay, she'd take a walk in the Dales first. She hadn't been for a proper trek in a while.

Smiling, she filled up her cafetière. The smell of leaves and wood and bark ... that would hit her sore spot. That would go some way to making last night bearable, and maybe it would ease the confusion.

There didn't seem to be any sign of the siren right now – it was all wolf inside her, and she *had* missed the animal. She couldn't say she really missed feeling completely human.

Studying the blades of grass poking up through the gaps between her toes, Jennifer took a deep breath and filtered through all the scents she could pick up on: all of them. Her wolf was truly back. The only part of her wolf that hadn't returned was her strength.

Why it hadn't returned, she could only guess at. Maybe it was because the siren overruled it. Were sirens strong? The information sheets hadn't said anything about that. She'd read them all. There'd been a lot to take in – things to do with conjuring lust and controlling the emotions of others. She didn't know how much of it to take with a pinch of salt. How much was real, and how much were the ramblings of drunk or delirious sailors centuries ago?

Feeling calmer than she had in the past twenty-four hours, she pulled the ring box that she'd brought with her out of her small rucksack. She could finally think about this properly, standing here with nature surrounding her and her wolf by her side.

Jennifer opened the box. Her heart did that guilt thing again, where it felt like it folded in on itself. The diamond was a beautiful one. "What am I going to do with you, David?"

Her answer was a drilling from a woodpecker some two hundred feet away.

"I can't say yes – not to this. And you deserve the truth, but I don't know how to tell it." And no, it hadn't escaped her notice that withholding the truth from David was much like her note-sender withholding the truth from her. Perhaps his silence all these years wasn't too far off what she was doing to David. She was a coward, too.

She stroked the band of the ring. He must think she loved him even though she'd never said it. "What a mess," she whispered. "I'm so sorry." She missed him, she adored him, she needed him in so many ways, but... "I'm just not sure I'm capable of love. Maybe I can't love because I was always supposed to be mated; maybe I'll never love now that wolves don't need to mate anymore. I just don't know." At least the air was very forgiving; the trees understood. "I'm damaged. And I used you to fix me, but I don't think it completely worked. I'm truly sorry about that."

That's what she needed the guts to say – just like that, to his face.

But maybe leave out the wolf and mating bits.

Her monologue was interrupted by a rustle.

Ears pricked, she shut the ring box and slid it back into her bag while searching all the gaps between the foliage for anything that looked out of place. She'd seen no one on the Dales as she'd made her way to this small copse, but it was now about eleven thirty, and on Saturdays, dog-walkers were common. Though the rustle hadn't sounded like a dog had made it.

She picked up her rucksack, closed it, and slipped it onto her back. Time to head home anyway; she needed to get to the hospital. She needed to say to David everything she'd just said to the ring.

Preferring to walk barefoot, she picked up her trainers, her socks tucked into them, and made her way out of the copse.

Someone entered the cluster of trees, right through the gap she wanted to exit by.

She stopped, her muscles tightening, ready to leap if she had to – a purely instinctive reaction. But she relaxed when she saw who it was. "Mr Stewart."

"Aah!" Her neighbour looked up and smiled. "Deary ... hello. I thought it was you I saw from a distance."

"What are you..." She paused, wondering if she should be wary of the hunting rifle he held in his left hand. "What are you doing here?"

"Morning walk. Loosen up the hips."

"Oh, I see." She gestured at the weapon. "I didn't know you hunted." Hunting season for some of the birds opened beginning of September if she remembered correctly, though she hadn't heard any shots around here.

"Ooo, yes, isn't she a beauty. She was my father's before me," he grinned.

"I was going to place it at around fifty years old."

He studied her, and his eyes seemed sharper than usual. She suddenly felt like a deer caught in headlights. "Know a bit about guns, do you?"

Damn. She scolded herself for her carelessness – highlighting anything unusual about herself just wasn't a good idea. She wasn't thinking straight. "My father knew quite a bit – he taught me some. Not a lot," she lied. "So ... you're out hunting now? Despite your hips?" she couldn't help but add.

Having relaxed on seeing it was her neighbour causing the disruption to her moment of solitude, she was now feeling a bit uneasy. One plus one was not equating to two, but she couldn't figure out why.

"Needs must." He lowered his voice. "Lots of strange happenings over the centuries in these Dales?"

"Really?"

"I grew up in Hull. Legend tells of a beast down that way that killed dogs and other animals. The Beast of Barmston Drain they call it."

Her mouth went dry.

"It's just a story made up, they say, because so many have drowned on the banks of Barmston Drain, but *I* saw it. I swear I did. Half man-half dog – chased me and my friend when we were boys. Just ten, we were. I was the lucky one. I got away, but poor William didn't. They found him later, washed up on the bank. They said he fell. He didn't bloody fall – there were chunks taken out of him. Damned beast tried to devour him."

Trident.

He took a step closer to her.

She took a step back.

"As I got older, those legends spread. The beast turned up in various places across Yorkshire, and right here in these Dales. I've suspected more than one for it to make such a ruckus. A beast is an animal – animals breed. And sure enough," he raised his rifle a few inches and shook it in a show of defiance, "I've killed one before."

What? "You've … killed one?"

"Aye. The thing ran on two legs disguised as a man, but I knew it wasn't a man, and sure enough, after I shot it, it turned into the biggest damned dog I'd ever seen, right in front of my eyes."

A wolf. God damn it, he'd killed a *wolf*, not a Trident. A Trident turned back into its human form when shot.

A natural protectiveness in her rose for her species, always on the brink of fucking extinction in one way or another. "Sounds like it was just a wolf, Mr Stewart. I hear they lived in these woods not too long ago." *Yeah – in peace. Until men with guns demanded more land.*

"Wolves walk on two legs, do they?" he huffed.

"I doubt the beast you speak of was a wolf. Perhaps what you saw was—"

"I saw a *werewolf.*"

So … he knew about werewolves. Shame he had the wrong end of the stick. Human urban legends had Tridents and werewolves as one and the same. They couldn't be more different – wolves were gentle by nature, and reclusive. Only the rare rogue wolf might be considered dangerous, and while this 'beast' might have been a rogue, she doubted it very much since it had tried to devour the boy he'd spoken of.

Werewolves didn't eat people; Tridents did.

She swallowed, trying to battle her swell of anger at his killing her kind. "Mr Stewart—"

"Jack."

"Jack – yes – I'm sorry. I'm afraid I must go. David was taken into hospital last night, and I'm off to see him."

"Oh, no. Nothing serious, I hope?"

"Erm—"

"Mind you, if you're careless about who you involve yourself with, you're bound to end up hurt."

What did he just say? "I beg your pardo—" Her sentence was swallowed by her intake of breath as four more men emerged from the edges of the copse.

Blood drained from her face. She recognised them all from the village. They were Jack's friends; they often met together in the only pub there. They'd been friendly enough to her – smiled, waved. Clearly that had been for show. They didn't look that friendly now.

All of them carried guns.

The reality of her situation crashed down on her: they knew about werewolves. *They know what you are.* And these weren't the kinds of humans who liked wolves.

"There's lots written about werewolves," said Jack, taking another step forward. Only this time, when she tried to step back, she was met with a solid body, and hands which clasped her arms from behind.

"Ouch!" Fingers dug into the flesh of her upper arms so hard she knew she'd bruise in seconds. She fought the urge to attack; forced herself not to struggle. Five guns vs. her lack of werewolf strength – she was quite aware of the likely outcome.

"I devoted my life to researching the beasts after I'd killed that one, and realised what I was up against."

"Books don't tell you everything," she replied through

gritted teeth.

The hands on her arms dug deeper. She cried out in pain. A quick glance behind her told her it was the goddamned *vicar* who had her pinned.

"Aye, but they tell you how to spot the bastards, and I became quite proficient in it over the years. They're hermits – they like solitude. Even if a wolf is part of a pack, the pack is isolated. They live near woodland, or open grass if secluded enough. They're always meat eaters. They're strong – they'll manage well enough by themselves and never ask for help. There's a certain look; a rugged intensity from the males; a raw allure from the females, and of course the *lust* every full moon." He met her eyes with both interest and disgust.

She recoiled inside.

"That's the devil's doing, Miss Warren," whispered the vicar into her ear. "That's why the beast must die."

She couldn't quite believe what she was hearing. "I've never done anything to hurt you – any of you." She took in the other three men standing off to the sides: the butcher, the baker ... it was just the bloody candlestick maker that was missing. Instead of the candlestick maker, it was the guy who managed the bank in the village.

Jack sniffed as he unlocked the barrel of his rifle, and inserted two bullets, undoubtedly silver because she could sense the metal from where she was. "It's only a matter of time before you wreak havoc. I saw you in your garden." He looked at her, his gaze heated. "That was the nearly full moon that was. Dead giveaway, and when you add up all the other factors, I was left with no doubt. Pretty thing like you locking yourself up, alone, in a village like this. It's not a normal moon coming this month. It's already got you by the pussy – I *saw* you – and it'll have you killin' on Sunday night. We can't have that."

And I'll bet he liked what he saw, the sleazy git. "What you saw was nothing to do with the moon for fuck's sake."

She yelped as the grip on her arms tightened once more. "Language, Miss Warren," growled the vicar, and she just couldn't help it – it was instinct. She growled back.

Her teeth bared, and after years of dormancy, she felt her fangs emerge; her canines elongate. Though she knew this was as much of her wolf that could emerge having never fully turned, she was certain her eyes were also glowing. If she'd had any hope of trying to convince them she wasn't a werewolf, that hope just fell dead in the water.

She wished for her werewolf strength to no avail. What was the point of fangs if she didn't have the power to use them?

"There it is," spat out Jack, his face twisted in contempt. Gun cocked, he took two strides until he was directly in front of her, then gripped her cheeks with his hands, forcing her head up to meet his. "*There's* the beast. Don't you worry, lassie, we're going to put you right out of your misery."

"Strip her first, Jack," said the vicar. "I'll cleanse her before you kill her. If there's a soul to be saved, we might as well save it."

Her growl grew louder. "Don't you *dare* lay a finger on me, you cunt. You want to shoot me, do it now. You think this is the worst that's ever happened to me? It won't be *me* going to hell, but five old perverts who can't get any on their day off!"

Jack laughed and let go of her face, though not without a shove which flung her head to the left. Her cheeks throbbed. "You're right, Vicar. A mouth like that needs cleansing."

She was yanked backwards, and then the vicar's arm went around her neck in a choke hold while his other hand roughly pulled her rucksack down, taking her jacket with it. She dropped her shoes, which she hadn't even realised she was still holding.

Her hands went up to the arm around her neck, pulling, trying to release his grip a bit so she could breathe with more ease, but with four rifles aiming at her, she wasn't sure what would happen if she succeeded in pulling him off her.

Her neighbour stared at her while he fumbled with the button and zip of her jeans. "Any last words you want to say, you can say during your cleansing." Down went her trousers, and from what she could feel, her underwear went with them.

If she hadn't been through all this crap before, she might have cracked at this point, but she got a hold on herself, closed her eyes, shut everything out, and tried to think. Five against one, and she had no strength. There had to be a way out, though. Being molested by five old men wasn't on her bucket list any day of any goddamned year.

Her top was cut off with what felt like a knife; then, her bra was unhooked and roughly tugged down her arms as two further hands held each limb out.

She kept her eyes closed, but they snapped open when something cold and wet streaked across her face and breasts, making her gasp. Jack held a bottle in his hand.

"Holy water," explained the vicar, still anchoring her by the neck. Using his other hand, he brought a cross up, and held it in front of her face.

God ... it was silver, too.

She hissed, trying to pull away from its unnatural heat, but many hands had her pinned now, most of the men having dropped their rifles on seeing she couldn't break free. Jack still pointed his at her.

If her muscles weren't weak before, they were verging on useless now in such close proximity to the silver.

The vicar started to chant – in fucking Latin, too. This was so cliché a wry laugh slipped from her lips.

He brought the cross closer to her face.

She closed her eyes; didn't want to see their gazes on her naked body anyway; didn't want to think about the horrific fact that despite her revulsion, her chest and crotch grew warm with some contorted version of desire – it was the devastating, twisted legacy of what she'd had to endure at the hands of Gabriel and Bab, and now through nightmares. Part of her wondered if what they'd injected her with had damaged her permanently in this respect. Perhaps a craving for her unwanted 'mate' would forever be enmeshed in her system.

She forced that thought out of her mind and ignored her body's learned reaction. *You've had worse done to you. Even if they fuck you it won't be as bad as anything you've already been through. Just don't let them put a bullet in you, 'cause there's no coming back from that.*

"Sing," she said suddenly, the plan coming out of nowhere, and with it the understanding it was her only way out – assuming it worked.

The vicar kept on muttering his pathetic prayers, his cross staring her in the face.

Jack frowned. "What are you talking about?"

"I have a last thing I want to say. But it's a song. It's a lullaby my mum used to sing to me."

Jack smirked. "How sweet, lassie." He looked at the vicar.

Jennifer saw him nod, but he didn't stop chanting, and didn't relax his hold on her.

Jack put down his rifle, stood and crossed his arms, still smirking. His stare slid down her frame, hovering on her breasts, then lower.

She might just enjoy melting their brains.

"Go ahead. Been a while since I've been this entertained."

She battled to remember exactly how this would play out. Truth was, she couldn't really remember too much about what had happened at the pub while she'd sung. But she *had* read the information sheets about sirens this morning. If she'd interpreted it right, after she started singing, their first reaction would be intense arousal – which she really wasn't looking forward to – but it would be followed by crippling pain owing to a pulverised brain. The result would be death, and hopefully not hers.

For one scary second, she had no idea if she could pull it off, because she didn't feel like singing at all. Fighting, screaming, kicking, yes. Singing? Not even a little bit.

However, she followed the motions, opened her mouth, the first syllable of the song escaped on a note, and that was all she had to do. The siren heard the call, surged past the wolf and took care of the rest.

It was like being in a trance of which she was both the captor and the captive.

Notes became a melody, and she travelled into it somehow, her mind falling back as a form of magic she wasn't sure she'd ever have a hope of understanding, took over.

She wasn't quite in her body anymore – it had been the same at the pub. She was still aware of movement; of what was happening around her; of the faint moan in her ear now the vicar had ceased his prayers; of the men coming closer; of a hand grazing her right hip, then sliding behind and squeezing her bottom; another moan and a curse, and then a wet mouth on her left breast.

But it all took place in a haze – distant. She was the song, and she was the siren.

Relaxing against whoever now held her upright, she allowed herself to drift headlong into her deadly secret; let them do whatever they wanted to her – she knew how this would end.

The end began much sooner than she'd dared hope.

Still in the midst of her mind-fog, she heard a louder, more agonizing moan, which escalated into a scream. Through glazed, half-open eyes, she saw Jack clutch his head.

Other hands fell from her body; more screams sounded.

Five men squeezed hands over their ears in desperation and outright terror... And she sang. Perhaps she'd never stop, for it was rather freeing, this blissful, empowered place where she was nothing but rhythm and resonance.

Indeed, she had no idea she'd stopped until after the song had reached its natural conclusion. A tingling of her physical form, like pins and needles after numbness, was what gradually brought her back into herself. The homecoming was bitter-sweet.

And confusing as hell.

As the pins and needles subsided, all the aches and pains of her capture and abuse returned. She could feel where they'd been, the cool air on her skin drawing her attention to where their saliva coated it.

Vomit surged up her throat, but was repressed by the shaking that took over.

Muscles trembling, she sank to the ground, not knowing whether to laugh or cry as she took in the destruction she'd caused. She was alive, but ... *Holy fucking Christ.*

As if she sat in the centre of some macabre fairy ring, five men lay dead in vast pools of blood that seeped into the soil and encircled her in a rusty red band. Their faces were twisted in torment.

The sound of her phone made her jump. Another beep. Another text. *Him.*

Still shaking, she found her rucksack behind her and pounced on it, fumbling to open the pocket that held her phone. She yanked it out with a whimper, desperate for some normalcy – if anything could be called normal – even if that came from an obscure man who she wasn't sure she trusted.

It *was* him.

She pressed the notification, and tears filled her eyes as they widened at what she read, capital letters yelling at her from her screen:

**RUN HOME NOW. PACK A BAG. BE QUICK.
STAY HIDDEN. THEY ALL KNOW YOU'RE WOLF.
THE WHOLE VILLAGE ARE WOLF HUNTERS.**

⁃ *Chapter Nine*

I t ached to see because the light was so bright. A bright white. David closed his eyes again with a groan, then attempted to face the light once more.

He heard a gasp from somewhere to his right, then a scuff on the floor – a chair moving. "David?"

"Jen?"

A pause.

"It's Prish."

Aah. "Prish..." It hurt his head to talk. He'd been in a bicycle accident as a kid, and he'd gotten concussion as a result. This felt just like that. "Where am I?"

"York Hospital."

She came into view, her dark hair offering his eyes some relief against the brightness, as if the blackness of her hair sucked it all up. He didn't mind – this hurt far less. "The pub..."

She took a step towards him, and he felt her hand on his arm. "You remember?"

"Jen ... where is she? Is she okay?" Panic snared him. He couldn't recall the last thing he remembered, but he did know she'd been there with him.

"Calm down. She's fine, I promise. She came in to see you last night, but it was late, past visiting hours. I don't think she's been in this morning, though."

He let out the breath he'd been holding. "Good. Good she's fine."

"Do you remember what happened?"

He tried to shake his head, then thought better of it when the movement sent bolts of agony through him. "No."

"Nothing at all?" Was that disappointment in her voice? "The police seem a little confused as to what took place, so anything you can remember ... anything at all..."

"Prish, there's nothing. We went to the pub, we had dinner... Jen got up to sing – it was a karaoke night – but I don't even remember if she did her song or not. I don't remember hearing her sing. Maybe she backed out."

Prisha frowned. He could see her much better now his eyes were getting used to the light. "Okay," she smiled, "please don't strain. Rest. I'm going to let the doctor know you woke up."

"Do you know when Jen's coming?"

Looking away, she shook her head. "No, sorry. I'm pissed off she's not already here; that she wasn't on standby counting down the hours until visitors were allowed back in."

"Prish," he whispered, feeling distressed. He couldn't handle the antagonism between them right now.

"Shit, I'm sorry. Hey, forget I said that, okay? I'm being a bitch, and that's the last thing you need. I'm going to go get the doctor. Be right back." She left his field of vision.

He hoped to god he was allowed more painkillers – his head felt bloody horrendous. But nothing would feel better until he saw Jennifer standing in front of him. He hoped she really was all right. In his mind, he had a hazy image of her being grabbed from behind by some man, but he wasn't sure he hadn't dreamt it, and Prish had said she'd been here last night so...

Nevertheless, he needed her here. He hoped she'd come soon.

~*~

Prisha tried to push away the knot of anger burning in her gut as she sought out the doctor for David. She'd barely slept last night after getting home. Instead, she'd played the CCTV recording that she'd illegally acquired, over and over again until it pretty much became branded in her mind. She wished it had sound, but it didn't. Something about it was off though, and the 'disjointedness' took place the moment Jennifer picked up the microphone. It was something about the way the audience moved – or didn't move to be exact. They'd all stopped what they were doing and sat stock still – it was eerie. It made Prisha wonder what the hell Jennifer had sung. Or had something else taken place? Had she said something, or...

One of the nurses she recognised from last night came into view. "Excuse me." She stopped her as politely as possible. "David Coates in ward number 2 has just woken up."

"Oh, good," chirped the nurse. "I'll ping the doctor and come straight over."

"Thank you."

The nurse hurried off to the reception desk, and Prisha headed back to the ward, though she didn't go in. She took a seat in one of the chairs outside it.

She had to think.

There was a huge chunk of something she was missing, and it seemed the only way she was going to find it was through dark and dodgy methods. David would not be pleased, and guilt tugged at her for betraying him, because it *was* a betrayal of sorts. Greater in her, though, was the need to see him safe and sound, one hundred percent healed and never,

ever put in this situation again.

Since this situation seemed very much to do with Miss Jennifer Warren – from whom David was blind to all faults – Prisha would have to take matters into her own hands.

~*~

Dried mud caked her feet inside her socks and shoes, and she'd had to hide a couple of splats of blood under her left sleeve. None of that compared to the smell of the men that still lingered on her skin. Totally gross. But there was no time for a shower.

Her jacket had a hood, and she made full use of it, tucking her long, strawberry-blonde hair as far into it as she could. A few strands found their way out as she picked up pace – nothing to be done about it. She had no time. 'Be quick' the message had said. In and out. *They all know you're wolf.*

And worse. They were wolf hunters. The whole goddamned village.

One of the five men had carried a shotgun. She'd taken it, checked the full chamber and the safety, and tucked it into the inside pocket of her jacket. It was a last resort. She didn't want to go brandishing a gun about, but having learnt to shoot since the age of five, having one on her person made her feel safer.

The church of her village came into view. How fucking sad. And how really fucking stupid of her thinking she'd found somewhere she might be able to finally call home – if not now, then in the future – only to discover she'd walked into some wolf hunter's paradise. *Jesus, you know how to royally screw up, don't you?*

The *whole village.*

She wondered how long they'd known for. She'd been living here the best part of a year, and they'd been friendly – all smiles.

Angry tears surfaced. She couldn't believe she'd fallen for it. *That's what you get for hoping. Haven't you learnt yet? You don't get the good things – that's not who you are. Killed your bastard of a mate, ended up drowning; got pulled out the water, ended up a siren; got given a new identity, ended up living among bloody wolf hunters!*

The only good thing she'd ever managed to do was find the miracle that was David, the first person, human or otherwise, to have ever loved her unconditionally. And now, he was in hospital because of her.

You're not one of the lucky ones who gets the easy way out.

She could see her cottage now. She could also see Martha who owned the flower shop. *Does she know you're a wolf, too?*

The answer must surely be yes.

Do they all know Jack and the gang went hunting for you earlier?

Again, she had to assume yes. Which meant her time was up the moment Martha laid eyes on her, which would be ... now.

"Miss Warren," Jennifer heard her gasp, though the older woman tried to dial back her surprise at seeing her.

Because she expected you to be dead by now. Her best bet was to act like she'd never run into the men. "Good morning, Martha," she greeted in the best cheery voice she could muster. "Beautiful day isn't it? Bit of a chill in the air though – glad I've got my jacket."

Pack a bag. Be quick. Stay hidden.

She had to force herself not to run, though. She hoped her stride looked relaxed, like she hadn't a care in the world.

"Ah, Miss Warren ... er ... don't suppose you've seen Jack this mornin'? He said he'd pop into the shop, but he hasn't been yet."

Fishing for information. "I'm afraid not, sorry. I've been up in the Dales and haven't seen a soul – not even dog walkers today. I'll catch you later, Martha."

She didn't hang around for any reply to that, but pulled her house keys out of her pocket as she approached the pathway to her front door. *Pack a bag. Be quick. Stay hidden.*

Once inside, she shut the door, and *now* she ran.

She sprinted up the stairs, not taking her rucksack off her back – it had her wallet, phone, and keys in. Grabbing an overnight bag from the top of her wardrobe, she shoved in underwear, socks, a handful of tops, another pair of jeans, and her boots. The toothbrush and toothpaste went in next.

There was a scream from outside.

She stopped all movement and turned her head in that direction, pricking her ears...

"They're dead! They're DEAD!"

Oh, fuck. Time's up. She zipped up her bag, then heard glass smashing out the front. Racing to her bedroom window, she looked out to find a brick had been thrown through the windshield of her car. The biggest problem, though, was fourteen-year-old Thomas jamming a knife into her tyres. "No, no, no..." *Now fucking what?*

Heart hammering, she pulled away from the window. She could grab one of their cars – no one ever locked them around here. *And how many miles will you make it before you're caught by the police?*

Shit.

Her phone beeped.

She struggled out of her rucksack and pulled the phone from the front pocket.

"WOLF!" came a cry from outside. "Wolf! Wolf! Wolf!" Not just one voice, but many. It was a chant, and it was chilling.

Gearing up the crowd. They're going to drag you outside and kill you slowly and publicly. She checked the text message she'd received:

BACK GARDEN, JUMP THE FENCE INTO DEEP POOL LANE

That would be the neighbour's fence facing south, right at the bottom of her garden – Deep Pool Lane was at the end of that neighbour's garden.

Glass shattered, shards flying at her as a brick landed on her carpet with a thud.

She screamed.

Everyone had joined in on the 'wolf' cry – it sounded like the whole fucking village was below.

She didn't need to be told twice. Ramming the phone into her back pocket, she slipped the rucksack on her back, grabbed her overnight bag, and sprinted down the stairs towards the back doors of the living room that led into her garden. The coast was clear. Relieved they hadn't jumped fences themselves – not yet, anyway – she ran down her garden, and gave her she-wolf a motivational nudge as she leapt at the fence that bordered the end of it. Having human strength sucked big time, but she made it over with a grunt – what was another bruise to add to the list – only someone had caught on to her escape plan.

"She's running that way!" they shouted – it sounded like a young girl.

Tattle tale, she silently retorted. Just one more fence to go at the bottom of this garden.

She saw heads bob along the top of both fences running parallel to her, and she groaned. They could tell where she was heading. She just needed to get there first.

And then what?

She didn't know. She suddenly realised she'd followed that text blindly having no clue as to what would happen once she'd reached Deep Pool Lane. *Too late now.*

She took a leap at the second fence, and cursed because this one was higher, and her bags were starting to feel heavy.

The screaming crowd closing in on her was motivation enough, though, and she found herself over it, if somewhat clumsily, landing heavily on her side – more mud; not very soft.

The yelling of the villagers was so loud now she feared she had seconds left 'til she was lynched.

Car tyres screeched.

She looked up.

A dark blue Volvo pulled up sharply in front of her, passenger door flinging open. "Get in!"

Hai.

She didn't think twice. Scrambling to her feet with her bags, she all but dove into the car head first, tucked her feet in, and then they were speeding down the bumpy lane. Her head bashed into the dashboard. "Ow."

"Shut the door!" yelled Hai.

She fought for balance with both her bags as she sat herself upright in her seat. Reaching over, trying not to fall out of the car, she pulled the door shut with a small roar at the effort. Her eyes widened as she caught sight of people piling into the end of the lane, blocking their exit. "What do we do?"

He accelerated. "Go faster."

He had to be joking. "You're going to hit them."

Hai looked at her and smiled. "They'll move."

He floored it.

She held her breath, her heart in her throat, but he was right – they moved. There was angry screaming, yelling ... but when they realised the car wasn't about to slow down they either ran, or sidled up against the edges of the lane on either side. Some fell into the brook that ran down one side of it. "It worked ... you did it." She turned and glanced out the back window, the regrouping villagers becoming smaller until they were specks in the distance.

"Do not be ruled by panic. If you are patient in one moment of anger, you will escape a hundred days of sorrow."

"I think I missed that boat, Hai. I killed them. I killed five men."

"Ah, Miss Warren, even a rabbit will bite if cornered, and *gŏu jí tiaò qiáng*. You showed great courage. As they say, *fù tāng dǎo huŏ* – you waded through scolding water and burning flame."

Say what? "No – I sang."

Hai looked at her, sympathy in his eyes, and softened his tone. "Sometimes the end justifies the means."

She shook her head, tears stinging her eyes at everything she'd just lost. "My human life is over – if I ever even had one."

"In the face of evil, I would rather be a broken jade than a brick intact, wouldn't you?"

"What? What does that even mean?" What the hell was with all the Chinese proverbs?

He raised his eyebrows and let out a sigh, indicating to turn right onto the main road, finally slowing the car down. He shook his head. "You're just like him – difficult to teach. Open your mind, Miss Warren. Change your way of thinking. *Huò xī fú zhī suŏ yĭ, fú xī huò zhī suŏ fú* – calamity has its roots in prosperity, prosperity has its roots in calamity. Perhaps your life is just about to begin."

Chapter Ten

Leaving David had been hard. They'd injected him with more painkillers, and he'd eventually drifted off, though not without asking for Jennifer once more.

Prisha gazed at her open laptop, her anger thrumming just under the surface. She needed to keep a cool head.

A hundred Jennifer Warrens glared back at her from her screen. She only needed to see the ones in the United Kingdom – at least to start with.

Turning to the second laptop on her desk, she moved up the screen a little until she had all of Jennifer's current information in front of her: personal details, address, medical history ... the medical history was interesting, but it all pointed to a background David had already alluded to: abduction, and repeated physical and sexual assault. It was harsh. A faint unease grew over her actions – she shouldn't be prying – but she was tired of half-truths from the woman, so she had to do this.

As far as she knew, Jennifer *still* hadn't been in to see David at the hospital, and that got her back up more than anything else. Even more than the subtle blip in Jennifer's medical history: all the shitty stuff had happened to her five years ago, but before that? Nothing. Zilch. Not even a cervical screening on record. Not a blood test; not a check-up for a cold ... which all led to one very disturbing conclusion: identity theft.

While there was still a chance there might be a simple explanation, it was looking more and more unlikely. So, here she was, searching through every Jennifer Warren she could find in this country who was roughly the same age by five years either way – anyone from twenty-five to thirty-five could fit the bill with some expert meddling. She was good at spotting expert meddling.

Two hours and two cups of coffee later, the United Kingdom, the United States, and Canada had turned up nothing. Australia, however, had a very interesting 'Jennifer Warren' – or they used to have. She'd died seven years ago at the age of twenty-eight. Her father had been her only living relative, but he'd been of ill health and had passed away one year after his daughter – one year before his dead daughter mysteriously showed up in Britain with no other family. No one to say, 'Hey, why is Jennifer's ghost living in England now?'

Bingo.

Prisha saved the information, and also sent a copy to her printer. Scrolling back down the screen, she took note of Australian Jennifer's last known address. Moving over to current Jennifer, she brought her address history that she'd hacked up on laptop two's screen. The medical history might be missing, but no way could her address history be – not if she didn't want the new ID to get flagged up.

There: Queensland, Australia – the exact same fucking address as the dead girl.

Prish sucked in a breath, half in shock. That proved it. Even though she'd suspected a lie from Jennifer for a long time, all-out identity fraud was ... well, it was criminal. There was enough here to put her in jail.

Current Jennifer had conveniently immigrated to Britain thirteen months after Australian Jennifer's father had died, and lo and behold, here were her approved and signed immigration documents filling up the screen in front of her. According to those documents, Jennifer's British address at the time had been the flat she used to own in York, yet...

Prisha frowned in concentration. On the day the immigration document was signed Jennifer had been in hospital in Dover. That hospital stay was in direct relation to the whole abduction thing that had taken place five years ago. "That's one hell of a coincidence."

She opened a new tab on laptop number two. Within five minutes, she was inside the database for the hospital in Dover. Another minute of searching for Jennifer Warren, and she'd found her. The information in the database tallied with what else she'd found on her medical records, but there was an exception.

The detective in her fully awakened, she brought the cursor to the section on the screen causing her pulse to quicken, and highlighted it. When Jennifer had been brought into the hospital, she'd had no name. She'd been listed as 'Patient 142'. Only two days after her admission did her record show her as Jennifer Warren.

The same Jennifer Warren that had died halfway across the world two years previously.

Her immigration documents had clearly been forged *while she was in hospital*. Someone knew what they were doing and how to fucking do it – quickly, too – and it hadn't been Jennifer because she'd been unconscious in that hospital at the time. Clearly, she'd embraced her new identity on waking.

"So who helped you, Jen?"

And more to the point, who the bloody hell *was* Jennifer?

But there was one thing Prisha had absolutely no doubt about. While David was with Jennifer, he was in big trouble. And she couldn't have that.

~*~

Hai unlocked the door and beckoned her in. This wasn't Hai's one-bedroom flat, but *his* – the note-sender's. She knew this because of the scent. Now her wolf had re-emerged, she could place his aroma as the same that drifted from all his notes she kept in her wooden box. It enveloped her like the warmth of a fire on a cold day and seeped under her skin. Worryingly, the heat centred low on her abdomen and sparked another sensation she was far too familiar with. That wasn't okay at all. She was going to have to do something about that because there were other layers to his scent that made her uneasy – his siren for one.

She could smell the siren in him and she had no idea what to make of that. Did sirens have a smell? Or was it only because of her wolf's keen senses that she could make that connection. She had no answers, nor did she have an answer for the vague familiarity that crept into her mind with his aroma. She couldn't decipher it with all the layers to sort through, but the familiarity was … unnerving. Her immediate feeling about it was one of danger, which conflicted with the protective warmth his scent also exuded. And it *all* conflicted with her arousal, but since she apparently got horny over nightmares of rape and old perverts assaulting her, she decided her irrational bodily reactions were due to her incredible fucked-upness. She was the definition of 'damaged goods'.

"This is his place," she said for no reason other than to hear her voice aloud. Maybe it would disperse the headiness she felt from his musk.

Hai nodded as he led her past the living room and into the bedroom. "It is. He insisted I bring you here – you'll be safe here."

"I can't stay here."

"There's nowhere else to go. The police will be looking for you now; they'll have your work premises covered, and they'll be questioning your boyfriend about you the moment he wakes. They'll arrest you on suspicion of murder, not least because of the way the five men died. Their injuries match those of your boyfriend, and those of the other man from the pub who died last night."

God, he was right. "But ... they can't prove anything."

"Maybe not, but it'll certainly bring up questions about your past. It's publicity we could do without."

"I need to see David."

"I don't advise it."

"He'll be out of his mind with worry. He—"

"Jennifer, please." Hai looked at her kindly, but firmly. "I know you might not want to hear this, but the kindest thing you can do for him now is let him go."

"I can't just—"

"News of the wreckage to your home – it's his home, too – will reach him soon, along with the news that you've disappeared and can't be found. Coupled with what happened last night—"

"He'll think I've been abducted, especially given my past."

"Most likely, yes. Jennifer..."

She looked at him through blurry vision.

"Let him think it."

"No."

"Consider it."

"He'll be devastated."

"He'll be *safe*. Safe as long as you're out of the picture."

Her heart broke a little. "I could just tell him the truth."

"And make him a target for anyone who wants you dead. Wolf hunters in the region know you – you need to leave."

Her tears heated with her anger. "Did *he* know about the

wolf hunters? My 'rescuer' – who *still* won't show his face – did he know?"

"Of course not, and I should imagine he's kicking himself right now for not checking more thoroughly. We believed wolf hunters to be as extinct as wolves nearly are; hunters weren't on our radar."

"How did you know to come for me this morning?"

"He felt your panic. Your emotions and his are tied. You could feel his if you tried."

"I *don't* want to be that close to him."

"I'm afraid you are whether you like it or not."

"He said it wasn't like wolf mating."

"It isn't. There are no physical ties; no physical bond. You could live on the opposite ends of the world for the rest of your lives and neither of you would suffer for it. The bond is an *emotional* one, but it is total in what it is. You cannot extricate yourself from him, and he cannot from you. Even from the opposite end of the world, he would feel your feelings, and you would feel his."

Dear god, that sounded worse than a mating bond in so many ways, though she'd never have imagined that was possible – not after Gabriel.

"The full moon tomorrow night – it's a special one."

"So you've said."

"We don't know how it will affect either of you. He's the first male to have siren in his blood that we know of; *your* siren should never have been able to be birthed through him. Throw your wolf into the mix and we must be vigilant."

It sounded just as messy as a wolf-Trident pairing, though she supposed if the male wasn't actually a psychotic killer this time around, she was one up on her luck. Whoopy. "Is he coming? Back here, I mean?"

"He plans to keep his promise to meet you at the

cathedral tonight, though you'll have to be extra careful with the police looking for you."

"Why not here?"

Hai sighed. "Honour."

"Honour?"

"He wants to give you the chance to run, but he sincerely hopes you won't."

"Run?"

"When you see him. He doesn't want you to think you're trapped."

She dropped her bags with a huff and threw her hands up in irritation. "Kind of late for that with the siren version of I-can't-believe-it's-not-mating, wouldn't you say? And the fact the last five years of my life have been a lie."

"Not a lie – an interim. We did not know for sure you wouldn't remain human in every way. If you had, there'd have been no need to say a word."

It was her turn to sigh. This was chaos. "So, what's the big secret? Is he half fish, or something? Am I meeting a man with goggle eyes and gills?"

There was a pause, then Hai laughed. Harder than she'd expected – she didn't think she'd been that funny.

He was still laughing after she'd repositioned her bags more neatly down on the floor by the bed. She rolled her eyes, but felt a little lighter. It had been a long time since she'd heard unbridled laughter. She couldn't stay annoyed.

"Oh, d-dear..." Hai wiped his eyes. "My dear, you are a joy."

She snorted. A joy was something she'd never been called by anyone – ever.

"Right." He breathed in and steadied himself. "The bathroom's the next door down the hall – I'm sure you'd like to shower. There are clean bed sheets in the wardrobe. We didn't exactly have time to change them or tidy in our rush to get to you, but you're welcome to make the place your own."

She looked around. There wasn't too much 'stuff' lying about.

"You won't find anything personal of his here."

"You're a mind reader?"

"Ha-ha!" For a minute, she thought he was going to crack up again, but he didn't. "No. I see the curiosity in your eyes. He's never had anywhere he calls home – it's always been where he lays his hat. All personal items that identify him, he carries with him. You're welcome to go through all the cupboards and drawers to satisfy yourself."

"Why are *you* here, Hai? Do you just do what he says? What is he to you?"

Hai's smile faded a fraction; his look became thoughtful. "He's like a son to me, and I'm more than a father to him. I'm his whole family in a way – you remember the story? How brutish they were?"

"You hinted at it. You didn't go into specifics."

"No." Now he looked solemn. "If you ... decide to stay and brave it out after meeting him, perhaps he'll tell you of it one day."

"One day? Hai ... I don't plan to stay. I might not know exactly what happens next, but I'll figure it out. Emotional 'bonding' or not – or whatever it is – that's not part of the deal. It never was."

He lowered his eyes, disappointment evident, and shit, she didn't need to feel bad about that. This guy was sweet though. She liked Hai.

"I understand," he said. "I need to be off now. There's a city map on the coffee table in the living room if you need to find your way to the cathedral. It's a twenty-minute walk from here. Please be careful journeying out."

"I will be careful."

"Good. I have keys, so there's no need to open the door to anyone, and I suggest you don't. Stay hidden. There's food in the fridge – make yourself lunch."

"Thanks."

He smiled and nodded, and then turned and left.

After she heard the front door close, she relaxed a little and took off her jacket. A shower was *way* overdue, and while a part of her wanted to explore her new surroundings, she wanted to wash the blood and mud off her more.

The bathroom was equipped with everything she needed from shower gel to towels. There was even moisturiser, though it was basic and unscented. She didn't mind – so many scents were too strong for her.

She reached into the shower cubicle situated in the far corner of the bathroom and turned the water on. After the stream turned hot, and she was satisfied with the temperature, she made quick work of stripping, wondering if she should burn her clothes. Not that that would get rid of the dark bruises on her upper arms from where the vicar had gripped her so tightly she thought he'd dislocate her shoulder.

The spray felt gorgeous. Getting all the way under it, she closed her eyes and sighed, doing nothing for a while but heating herself up under the water.

It was sublime.

Unbidden, tears surfaced. The morning's events played over: bound and stripped. Gabriel's face flashed behind her closed lids, a silver necklace, chains binding her to a bed, Bab's hand against her—

Damn it. Why was it never David she saw? They'd made love many times, she'd come, so had he... Was hate stronger than love?

You don't love him.

But he loved her. And he showed it to her in every way – why wasn't that enough?

She couldn't just leave him stranded, never knowing what had happened to her. That's how she'd left her dad. Her only comfort was that she was pretty sure her dad must think she was dead by now given what had happened to Gabriel and Bab. He'd never guess she might have survived – female wolves didn't without their mates. At least, they hadn't back then. Now the rules had changed, she wasn't sure.

But her presumed death would at least offer a small amount of closure should her father choose to believe it.

David, on the other hand, would be told that she'd visited last night – he wouldn't think she'd died, no matter the state of the house. He'd worry she'd been hurt in the most awful way and was still suffering. She couldn't do that to him.

She let the spray wash away the tears that had fallen and got to work with the shower gel. She wasn't stepping out of this shower until every trace of this morning had been scrubbed away.

~*~

"The Volvo's parked at the very back of the parking lot," said Hai. "It's not out of view, but there's no reason anyone should take a closer look at it – not immediately, anyway."

Roman had waited for Hai in a Travelodge on the outskirts of York. "I'll get rid of it now; get us a new car. Her face is already on the regional news; I'm hoping it doesn't go national. The Volvo's been mentioned, but no one got a clear enough look at you, so I think you'll be fine. You told her to stay out of sight, right?"

"Of course. Whether she listens is an entirely different matter."

"How was she?" He mumbled the question, trying not to sound as angry as he felt. He was warring with himself – letting her buy a fucking house in a village full of goddamned hunters. Jesus Christ, he'd not seen that coming, and he couldn't believe he'd been foolish enough – caught up in everything else too much – to not even consider checking. It hadn't crossed his mind at all.

"She's survived far worse. You know that."

"That's not what I asked."

Hai clenched his jaw, and Roman immediately regretted being so curt with him. "She's a bit dazed," Hai replied. "The shock of it I should imagine; doubt it's all sunk in yet. But she's fine. I think you should meet her at your flat though."

"No."

His mentor pushed air out between his teeth. "The two of you are going to drive me to insanity. You're both as hard-headed and guarded as each other."

"Showing her who I am in *my* flat? With *my* scent permeating the walls? First thing she's going to associate me with once she sees me is my brother – I can't help that – but add my scent to that pivotal moment and she'll *never* get him out of her system while I'm around. She doesn't need that, and neither do I. She'll feel trapped. As much as I hate the idea, she should have the option of escape. She'll feel cornered if I reveal my identity inside the four walls of my home."

"Escape? There's no escaping the full moon if it affects her like it affects you."

"I won't leave her stranded; I'll be there if that happens."

He paused, studying him carefully. "She listened well enough tied up on the beach. Have you considered a little bit of force is actually what she needs?"

Roman glared at him. "I can't believe you just said that."

"She's a she-wolf. Her nature demands she's dominated,

even if she tries to fight it. She'll listen to an amount of force – positive force, not negative force. But leave the run wide open with no boundaries and she won't listen to you at all. All she'll listen to is the call of freedom, even if it leads her straight into a trap. Stop thinking like a human. She's a *wolf*."

"Part siren now."

"A wolf first."

"Damn it, Hai, I'm *not* my brother," he said, louder than he meant to as he shoved his coat on. He grabbed the car keys from Hai's hand.

"You don't think I know that? Since you were six years old I've all but raised you. You'll never be your brother, or your father, but you *do* run from your own authority time and time again because you're too afraid of your family's heritage."

"Every woman in my family for the past two centuries has been treated like dirt; hurt; bruised and worse because the men threw their weight around – *that's* my heritage, and I won't be a part of it."

"You're not a part of it. But for five *years* you've aided Jennifer from a distance because you fear your own reaction around her. That's not going to help her either, not anymore."

"I don't have time for this, Hai."

"Don't you know yourself? Don't you trust yourself?"

He let the door slam shut behind him, fury rising over Hai's words, the wound they kindled as raw as it ever was. Hai should know better.

After saving Jennifer's life five years ago – after realising what saving her life had actually meant he'd *done* to her – he'd made himself a vow he'd never lay a hand on her again. He'd protect her the best he could – he wasn't about to shirk his responsibilities – but from a distance.

Yes, he feared his actions around her. No, he didn't trust himself. How could he when he'd gone and put the siren inside her? Another beast for her to conquer.

Everything he'd tried to prevent Bab from doing to her, he'd done instead. He hadn't escaped his family's heritage; it was right there, laughing in his face.

Chapter Eleven

S he hadn't packed her fluffy robe, and it was stupid how much that upset her when she realised it after coming out of the bathroom and drying herself down.

Instead, she'd put on a clean pair of black jeans she'd thrown into her bag, along with a long-sleeved top – pink with white flowers. She'd wanted to throw her bra away after the events of the morning, but she hadn't thought to pack another – knickers, yes; bra, no.

She'd considered not wearing one at all – she'd have preferred it in all honesty – but she couldn't shake the sense of vulnerability she felt when unclothed in any way now. It saddened her and frustrated her. *Another mountain to overcome.*

Just as well she couldn't shift; wolves didn't wear clothes when they shifted.

Dressed and at a loss as to what to do for the next few hours, Jennifer wandered around the flat, her arms hugging her chest. Just as Hai had explained, this didn't look like a home, but some in-between abode. It didn't feel cold, but it didn't hold the warmth of a hearth either, except for...

A frown creased her brow. *Except for his scent.* It was a mix of sand and salty sea, with a hint of cypress, and she could do without the inconvenient awareness that ignited in her navel. It was likely due to their siren connection and she was so done with that kind of tie, especially to a man she'd never even met. Even if he insisted it was not like physical mating, she refused to ever be that dependent on a male again. Plus, there was that odd uneasiness that came from that strange sense of familiarity she couldn't place.

So, she blocked his scent out; pushed it to the far recesses of her mind as she ran a hand over the kitchen counter on her way to the fridge. She should eat – it was gone half past one – but she didn't feel hungry.

Heading away from the fridge, she spotted a remote control on the small breakfast table. The TV was fixed to the wall in the corner of the kitchen-diner. She hadn't grown up with a TV – most wolves didn't. It was a strange creation that took you away from nature and tumbling down a rabbit hole of twisted facts and alluring fiction. But she turned it on now since she felt restless, and almost dropped the remote when the first thing she saw was her face. It filled the entire screen.

"Oh, shit."

"...is wanted for questioning in connection with the five deaths that took place this morning in the Dales just north of the village of Summerbridge. Eye witnesses say they saw Jennifer Warren race away from the scene, covered in blood, and with an accomplice in a dark blue Volvo."

Racing away from the scene? Covered in blood?

The reporter drabbled on, but she zoned out, gaping in shock. They'd lied. She hadn't been covered in blood – just two patches on her arm they wouldn't have seen – but they'd say anything to get her locked up, wouldn't they? They'd conveniently left out the part where her house had been vandalised by the villagers themselves. She was suddenly very sure that the police had a whole load of fabricated information they hadn't released.

God damn it, this ruled out going to the hospital. Numb,

she turned the TV off. Maybe she could still risk it after dark – perhaps after the meeting at the cathedral. The hardest bit was not getting spotted on entry, but once inside, she could use the siren's magic on the doctor once more.

What if he's not there. Oh, god! What if David sees the news.

He would. He probably already had. Even if he hadn't, he'd be first up for questioning by the police. *They'll be waiting for you at the hospital.*

Tears burned her eyes. She couldn't risk seeing him – there was no way around it.

Something clattered, making her jump, and she realised she'd just dropped the remote on the tiled kitchen floor. She picked it up and winced, but it looked undamaged. And all at once, she felt tired. Exhausted.

As if a cloud veiled her vision, everything went kind of dark, and she felt faint – light-headed.

Placing the remote on the counter, she headed for the bedroom. She needed sleep – had hardly got any last night. She couldn't face anything right now, and not in this state. Just wondering how the hell she was going to get to the cathedral without being spotted was enough to press her panic button. She'd thought Hai was being overly cautious, but seeing her face on the screen like that...

In the bedroom, she grabbed her phone from her bag, and set an alarm for six o'clock. She'd eat something before leaving.

She pushed aside the disappointment she felt at seeing no text messages.

Sitting on the bed, all she wanted to do was collapse on it, but...

Hell, the bed smelled good. It smelled *really* good. It smelled like safety and protection and the assurance of every note he'd ever sent her. *This is the dependence you don't want, re-member?*

But her wolf lavished in it. She damn well knew what the wolf was doing: seeking out the dominance behind the scent.

She bad-mouthed her annoying canine, calling it all manner of names, but the animal ignored her, instead whining for her to get under the sheets and roll in his scent.

"Not on your life," she mumbled. But she yawned, too bloody tired to fight her wolf all the way. Her eyes were dry with her fatigue, and she was scared. More scared than she'd like to admit.

She slipped under the top sheet, and sighed as her head hit the pillow, billowing his aroma further around her, into her...

A small part of her cried for David; for this accidental betrayal towards him, but the allure of the scent was far too strong. Her wolf relished the power of it; the siren ... she had no idea what the siren thought. It was currently the wolf at the fore of her consciousness, and the damned animal really needed to understand she was *not* going to submit to any male ever again, no matter what he fucking smelled like. The need for male dominance was the vice of her species; of her gender. Male dominance had hurt her over and over again in unthinkable ways. *Don't think about that ... don't ... don't think...*

Consciousness slipped away as another yawn led her into sleep.

~*~

"But you, my darling, do not have to die with them. You are a part of the next stage of evolution." Bab put down his drink, shuffled off the sofa and approached her, staying low, prowling around the coffee table.

Behind his back, Roman curled his hands into fists, old rage surfacing. He thought he'd talked some fucking sense into Bab *yesterday, but here he was, Trident blood in his veins, accentuating the beast that had always been inside.*

Roman was trancing. After ditching the car and acquiring another, all on very short notice, Roman had needed to feel calmer, especially with tonight's meeting ahead of him, and not least because the moon's coming presence was something he could already feel on the scales coating his neck.

Sometimes trancing calmed him – took the edge off everything – much like a meditation, so he'd found a space on the floor of his room at the Travelodge, concentrated on his breathing and had drifted off. But he really wished it hadn't brought him here of all places, to this god-awful memory.

The she-wolf was at the end of the line. He could see it in the trembling of her nerves and the shadows under her sunken eyes. But still, she squared her jaw; lifted her head that little bit higher in defiance. He'd never seen anything like it. His mother's light had gone out a long time ago from the way his father had treated her; Bab's women never lasted more than weeks, though sometimes, if he liked them enough, he'd tease them for longer, gaslight them, confuse them into doubt until they were too weak to see clearly, and by then, it was too late. By the time the fists and force came out, they were so buried in the insecurities he'd manipulated them into taking on as their own, they could see no way out.

But those were all human women. Wolves and Tridents could smell Bab's lies, so his fists came out from the start.

Roman's consolation was that the she-wolf would heal fast; his consolation was that stubborn bitch inside her that refused to submit. His everlasting regret was his life-debt to his family.

His father, and now his brother, saved his life every full moon since the siren's bite had rendered him a slave to the ocean once a month. Each month when the tides swelled, the small spattering of scales on his neck spread. Every year, the spread had increased until now, at thirty-five, it covered half his body. He couldn't care less about appearances – that wasn't the problem. The problem was the mutation itself. With the spread of the scales came suffocation. The air no longer sustained him, and his skin became crisp without the salted sea on it. The first time it had become a problem had been on a full moon, ten years after the bite. He'd been fifteen. He'd fallen on the floor of their kitchen after dinner, muscles seizing, throat constricting, and gasping for air. His father, already suspicious something like this might happen in due course, had hauled him to the beach and bound him to a rock under the waves.

He'd been fucking terrified. His father hadn't explained a thing about what he was doing or why. Roman had thought he'd finally lost it and was murdering him in rage.

Only after his muscles relaxed and the fits had stopped, did he realise he was breathing – under the water.

There he'd stayed all night until the moon had set. His scales had receded back to that small spattering across his neck, and he'd begun to choke once more as his gills receded with them and water found their way into his lungs. At that point, he'd been untied, and pulled out of the sea. Bab had been standing by his father's side, both of them having kept watch on him all night.

"You careless fool," his father had said in disgust. "You had to follow the call of a siren, didn't you. This is your penance for being so weak. We'll have to anchor you to the ocean bed every full moon."

He'd been cold, wet, and exhausted, and it wasn't a prospect he looked forward to. "You don't need to anchor me – I'll lie here willingly."

"Idiot child, you don't understand. You weren't even of sound mind. The call of the ocean, to a siren, is as tempting as a call of the siren is to a human. You would have swum off if we hadn't tied you to the rock, and you will if we don't do the same next month."

And so it was that every month, when the moon was round, he

was bound to the bottom of the sea, freezing and terrified, and left there until his humanity returned and the water no longer sustained him, but choked him – twelve hours of torture. Until a year ago.

From darkness comes light, so they said. Amid his father's appalling new instruction to inject Trident blood into their veins, something happened that no one had foreseen: the Trident blood kept his siren at bay.

Roman had never grown in strength or malice from the blood, like his family and peers had. Instead his body utilised the blood in a different way. It used it to absorb the mutation. No more being tied to the ocean bed. No more spasming muscles and gasping for air. Once a month, he injected the blood and he could live as any other man.

His father had smiled at the discovery. Then, he'd proceded to lock the blood away. Roman had no access to it. It was kept out of his reach through protection and boundary spells. He had to beg for it every month.

Seven months ago – five months after this discovery – their father had finally died, thank the gods. No one missed the cruel bastard. But Bab had become an ogre in his place. Roman had almost left – sod family oaths, sod any inheritance, sod the sanctuary of the damned blood, sod it all. He'd been chafing at the bit to leave for years, his fear for his worsening mutation the only thing keeping him close to his family and the Trident blood they kept, and how he'd detested his cowardice for that.

His mind came back to the present as the wolf's eyes passed over his, skittering around the room. She was looking for escape, and he damned well knew that feeling. His cunt of a brother was forcing her to smell her mate's scent in his veins, and it made Roman sick with anger – not just at Bab's actions, but at his own utter failure to extricate himself from his family's dark web.

She gave in and leaned into Bab's neck, smelling him, then scooted back in horror, shock and repulsion – and worse – defeat, written all over her face. Her arousal was plain to see, but it was manipulated; planted there by a twisted mind. She had to know that.

Bab laid his hand on her abdomen ... lower ... and Roman was glad the wolf's mate growled in warning because it masked the sound of his own protest he didn't quite manage to contain.

With Bab caught off-guard, consumed by his own lust and power, Roman did what he almost never dared do. It was one of the rare gifts of the siren, and one so elusive, he didn't really have a handle on it: he weaved his way into his brother's emotions, hooked himself into them, and altered them with his own, directing Bab away from the wolf.

His brother halted all movement, then slowly retreated, stood, gave his shoulders and neck a stretch, and then looked at his watch.

Roman released himself from Bab; withdrew before his brother could sense he'd been there. He glanced at the wolf, willing her to understand he only wanted to protect her, knowing she'd never hear him, nor understand.

Her mate, Gabriel, bristled; he was close to cracking. Bab would only enjoy antagonising him further.

Roman stepped forward, ready to throw himself across the she-wolf if he had to. Gabriel's reaction had reignited Bab's need to best the Alpha, he could feel it. He was already turning towards the she-wolf again, his need to have her rising.

"...we'll catch up tomorrow night, Selena," Bab was saying, his words dripping poison, "when the moon is fully round and you're the last of your kind left on the planet...."

Roman blocked out Bab's voice as he tried to recall other words – ones from his childhood – ones his father would often use that Bab listened to.

That was it – he remembered. Roman cleared his throat, hoping he was pronouncing the family tongue correctly since he hardly ever spoke it. "Bab, you're weak. You're led by your feelings.

You master nothing if you don't master your emotions."

It worked.

There was a pause, the silence heavy, and then Bab's smile widened mechanically, and Roman knew he'd gotten through.

"Of course. You may leave now," Bab directed at the wolf.

Roman let out a silent sigh of relief. It was short-lived when everyone moved to leave ... except for the she-wolf.

Jennifer – known as Selena back then – stared right at him, remaining on the couch as Bab and his goon ushered everyone out. Their gazes locked.

On the floor of the Travelodge, Roman whimpered and shook himself, trying to wake from the trance. He couldn't. What the hell...? He'd never been unable to pull himself free of a trance.

Jennifer stood, still as naked as she'd been brought in, her eyes never leaving his. She was frowning as if trying to piece something together, and he suddenly knew exactly what that something was.

He was fucked. This wasn't how it was supposed to go.

He tried again to wake. No such luck. *She* kept him there. Her siren demanded he stay, and he couldn't resist her call. Surely she wasn't doing this consciously.

No – she must be dreaming.

Their surroundings faded as she walked towards him, raking her gaze over him in puzzlement like he was some kind of specimen in a museum she was seeing for the first time.

He tried to speak, but words failed him.

She was right in front of him now. He was surprised to find himself caught in the rush of her nearness. He could smell her natural perfume and feel the warmth from her skin. He hadn't been this close to her since he'd pulled her from the ocean, but then, her eyes had been closed, and she'd been cold. Really cold.

Her eyes were stunning this close. They gleamed copper as she studied him. Her gaze fell to his neck mostly hidden by the collar of his shirt.

He finally found his voice when her hands reached for the buttons. "Wait."

But he couldn't move. It was no longer his trance, but her dream, and somewhere between the two they'd connected. This wasn't how he wanted her to find out.

She predictably ignored him, her fingers deftly undoing his shirt, one button at a time, until he stood there, helpless as she parted the lapels and pulled the shirt right off his shoulders.

Her eyes went immediately to his scales. They covered a large area now the moon was near its peak, running all the way down his torso.

He heard her small gasp. She hadn't quite connected the dots yet. Instead, she seemed entranced by the shimmering across his skin; pearlescent rainbows of colour that caught the light in bewitching ways.

She tentatively raised her hand towards them.

"Don't," he whispered. But it was no use. This was her dream, and her siren was strong.

Her fingertips stroked his scales. He couldn't help the small moan that left his parted lips. No one had ever touched his scales. As a child, everyone in his family had been repulsed by them, and fearful of becoming somehow infected if they made contact with him. He'd learnt quickly to hide his deformity from them under polo necks, scarves, and shirt collars, and as time went on, it had become easier to show no one. No one ever had to see him naked; sex could be carried out clothed.

She pressed her whole palm against his scales – a gentle touch, almost feather-like. It had him reacting in ways he never thought he could to such an action.

Of course, the moment was short-lived. He'd known it would be, even as he'd carelessly allowed himself seconds falling into the warmth of her caress.

She looked up; met his eyes once more, and there it was.

Realisation dawned.

Her chin trembled, her frame shook, horror – no, terror – turned her irises almost gold, the warmth gone as she snapped her hand back.

"Please don't," he stuttered, though he was saying the wrong words. He wanted to eloquently and calmly explain he wasn't her enemy, he wasn't her past, that she had no need to be frightened. But eloquence and calm seemed to have deserted him.

A door closed.

They both flinched, and Jennifer turned towards the sound, the scene around them reappearing – the coffee table, the couch above the butcher's shop, and...

She started to cry.

Bab, unaware of their presence in this dreamscape of the past, walked back into the room now everyone had left.

Jennifer's head snapped back to Roman, her face contorting into disgust as the realisation of his deceit – for five years – coloured her tear-streaked countenance.

Bab walked towards the sofa, knelt, and stroked the leather exactly where she'd been sitting.

Roman shook his head, unable to stop the nightmare playing out. "I'm not your enem—"

He never finished the sentence. Jennifer finally cracked, opened her mouth, and let out a blood-curdling scream that ended everything.

Roman fell onto his back, the walls of the Travelodge taking place of the walls of the living room above the butcher's shop, a cry of 'no' on his lips. He flipped onto his front, then to his feet and lunged for the phone on his bedside table. "*No.* No, no, no. *Please no.*"

Chapter Twelve

She leapt from the bed, not that she knew that's what she was doing. In her mind, she was still back there, the smell of raw meat faintly permeating everything; the distant sound of a gunshot and the feel of her brother slumping into her arms – always with her whenever she conjured that butcher's shop in her mind; the smell of her future in Bab's veins ... and *him*. HIM.

She only understood she was screaming when her breath ran out. Her next understanding brought her attention to the floor where she'd landed, her back to the wardrobe. She'd splintered the wood of it with the force of her body.

She was awake. She'd dreamt. But like fuck had that been a dream. *He'd* been there.

She was sure she had fresh bruises on her from her lunge into the wardrobe, but it wasn't bruises she was feeling. It was...

Hurt. Deep hurt.

Her rescuer was Bab's *brother*. Over fifty notes across five years... She'd depended on them, needed them... *She'd trusted him.*

Her stomach cramped. The force of it rolled her onto her hands and knees and she heaved. Spittle streamed from her mouth in a long string, landing on the carpet amid two drops of tears. No vomit rose from her empty stomach.

She'd been lying in his bed. *She'd been lying in his scent.*

A wretched sound left her; it became a furious wail of rage and loss. Forcing her shaking legs to work, she stood and finally found her momentum. It led her straight to her rucksack and overnight bag. She was already clothed.

She grabbed her jacket from the floor where it had fallen at some point and shoved her arms into the sleeves.

Her phone sounded.

She froze.

Another scream crawled up her throat; her head was ringing with it. She was shaking so much, she could barely pick up the device.

I'M NOT YOUR ENEMY.

The phone then beeped again in her hand and another message came in. Her grip tightened around its frame.

PLEASE. DON'T RUN. TALK.

Another beep; another text.

YOU CAN TRUST ME.

Bab's brother.

His fucking *brother*. He'd seen her abused, seen her held hostage, partaken in her imprisonment, had laughed along with the others, had stared along with the others...

The phone beeped.

She howled her fury and threw the handset across the room. It hit the wall and smashed, plastic flying off it.

She picked her rucksack up and slung it over her back.

Her hood went up next over her hair and as much of her face as possible. With her overnight bag in the other hand, she fled the apartment, with no idea which way to go.

~*~

Hai sat at the foot of his stairs turning the handset of his landline telephone in his hands. His heart was heavy. That was one of the most difficult phone calls he'd ever received, and knowing this day would come – was perhaps even overdue – didn't make it any easier.

It was about one in the morning in Binhai, a town southeast of Beijing overlooking the Bohai Sea, where his father was taking his last breaths.

Other than his aunt, his father had no one. Hai had been his only child – a small miracle his infertile sperm had created at the age of fifty, surprising everyone – and Hai's mother had died a long time ago. His aunt had been the one to call him. *"Not long left now. Come home, Hai."*

He'd wanted to return home two months ago, but his father had insisted he stay; that his visit would not make any difference.

Hai could have felt hurt over that, but he understood his father's meaning: his visit wouldn't make any difference because his health could not be cured. He was old – older than most – it was his time to go.

The phone in his hand rang loud and shrill. It made him flinch. "Hello?" he answered.

"Hai, it's me."

"Roman." When he'd taken Roman on as his protégé at the age of six, thereby sealing the deal with his own immigration into Great Britain, his father had understood. He had even encouraged it. "What's wrong?" He wasn't going to be catching his rest today, then.

Roman's voice came out in short, sharp bursts. "She found out – pieced it together. I wasn't there, and now she's gone."

Hai breathed in ... and breathed out. Caught between his father and the one he considered his son was an uncomfortable place to be.

"I'm going to the flat now. Can you meet me there?"

He hoped his father could wait until beyond the full moon; just a few more days... "I have the spare car. Let's hope it starts."

Roman hung up leaving Hai trying to remain calm against the panic he'd heard in his voice. The boy – or man, as he had been for many years now – was so caught up in the wolf, he hoped it wouldn't be his undoing. This whole thing was so much more to him than saving her life, or saving his own. He was seeking his atonement through her, and that was a lot for anyone's shoulders to bear. The she-wolf had carried enough.

Nevertheless, she was as entwined with him as he with her. For the first time in a long while, Hai found himself unable to partake in the events before him. He could physically be there for Roman, of course – for them both – but their journey forked into a different path he could not travel. And it seemed he had an alternate path appear before him, leading home.

He just hoped tomorrow's moon would show mercy to everyone he loved.

Roman was already there when he arrived. He'd found himself a green Toyota to replace the Volvo. *Let's see how long this one lasts.*

The man sat on the end of his bed looking crushed. Hai's

eyes travelled to the corner of the bedroom where he spied remnants of Jennifer's mobile phone scattered across the floor. "Aah."

"I've fucked up," he whispered. Anger and desperation swam under the quietness of his words. "I should never have brought her here. I should have known my scent would lead her wolf to the right conclusion before I got the chance to."

"Where else could she have gone? My flat is too far from the city for her needs, and my neighbours are nosy – this was the best and safest place for her."

Roman's eyes darkened as he stared at the broken phone on the floor, then he stood. "I can track her. I can zone in on her feelings – they're screaming right now. I'll find her that way."

"Are you sure you should?"

"I can't leave her. At least not before tomorrow's moon. Trident blood no longer protects hers from the siren. If the siren does to her what it does to me on the full moon..."

Hai looked away.

"It could kill her." Roman sighed. "You were right. I should have told her much earlier. I should have shown my face last night and laid it all on the table. I didn't want to scare her more than I had to."

Hai approached him and patted him on the arm. "It's not over. Come on. Let's go find her."

"And then what? She won't listen to me."

"She's terrified. She feels cornered, and everything she's known the last five years – things she used to try and fix herself – has just fallen apart. She'll come around."

"I think her fear's too great; I think her self-loathing is too strong."

"You'll know how to help her then, won't you?"

Roman met his gaze in silence, held it for a good few

seconds, then finally looked away.

Hai led him to the door and cracked a smile. "It's not over 'til the siren sings."

"Jokes, Hai?" Roman threw at him, incredulously.

"Always. There is always time for jokes. As my father would say, humour is the spark that lights every dark."

~*~

On the third ring, someone answered. "Hello?"

Just 'hello'. This was an inside number. MI6 didn't 'announce' themselves. Her heart was hammering against her ribs. "Hello, I'd like to speak to Officer Coney, please. This is Prisha Patel and it is a matter of some urgency."

"Is he expecting your call?"

"No, he isn't."

"One moment, please."

She waited. He probably didn't even remember who she was. She remembered him – he'd wandered in on her interview. She had actually been introduced to him by her interviewer – he hadn't taken much notice, though. But she'd taken notice of him because he'd mentioned the name of a decryption code sequence that had only just been retrieved from computer cryptographers in Russia.

She'd wanted to jump in on the conversation, but she'd wanted the job more, and hadn't wanted to come across as someone who couldn't be managed, so she'd said nothing, but had successfully sneaked it into the conversation very briefly with her interviewer later on. It might even have earned her the job.

Her palms were sweaty against her phone.

There was a crinkle on the line. "Ms Patel?"

"Yes?"

"I'm afraid he can't be reached right now. May I take a message?"

Damn it. It wasn't a message she wanted to leave. She glanced at the screen of her laptop, and took a chance, hoping it was the right one. "It's about the Bosley Farmhouse in Kent."

The line went quiet. A good five seconds passed, and then, "Can you hold a moment longer, Ms Patel?"

"Yes, I can." She smiled.

As she waited, she took in the image on the screen. Revulsion curdled in her gut. She was sure what she'd found shouldn't be floating around on the world wide web; people didn't realise how easy it was to break into cloud storage. No one would know what it meant, though – nor did she to an extent – but she knew it meant *something*, because the only reason she'd found it at all was because 'Jennifer Warren' had led to 'Selena Smith'. Selena Smith had turned up nothing – nada. A birth certificate dated twenty-nine years ago, and that was it. She'd thought it had been another fake ID, until a random 'Selena' search had thrown up this. *This*. It made her stomach turn. She had no doubt there were more of these images hidden in some vault somewhere Secret Intelligence Services were privy to, and she wasn't.

Someone picked up the phone again from the other end, though there was no answer right away. She heard a tap, and a slight buzz, and suspected they'd put a tracker on the line, perhaps a block on it, too, so it couldn't be tapped into at her end. That was fine. It was why she'd called from the landline. "Prisha Patel."

"Yes."

"This is Brian Coney. I've been told you have a position here from next week. Congratulations."

"Thank you, sir."

"How may I help you today?"

"Thank you for speaking to me. The incident at Bosley Farm in Kent five years ago..." Her voice caught. She was a bundle of nerves. This was huge. What she'd seen on her screen was *huge*.

"What about it?"

She hoped to god she wouldn't lose her new job over this, but she'd made up her mind she had to do this for David. She had to keep him safe. "Selena Smith," she said.

The silence at the other end spoke volumes. There might be no further data on Selena beyond her birth certificate, but they damn well knew who she was referring to, and it was confidential information she shouldn't know because all the shit she'd uncovered was not on public record anywhere.

"I'm of the understanding she's been missing since the shootings took place there." And what a wealth of information she'd discovered about that. Not just shootings, but cages in some sick cellar used to enslave and torture women. Then, there was the matter of what was on the screen right in front of her. There was no doubt that 'Selena' was 'Jennifer'. What the hell she'd been involved with while at the farm, though... Jesus.

The paused video on her laptop burned into her brain. She felt repulsed. It was vile. That woman was never laying a hand on David again.

She continued. "The five men in the news that died in the Yorkshire Dales this morning, their deaths were unexplained – that was her doing. She was at The Olde Shippe pub last night, too, in York City, at the exact point all hell broke loose. Two men ended up in hospital, one died – the death also unexplained. She goes by the name of Jennifer Warren. I can help you catch her."

"Why?"

"I ... beg your pardon?" She hadn't expected that question.

"What's your interest in Selena Smith?"

Her mouth went dry. She could lie, but he'd find out anyway... "She's dating a man called David. He's my best friend."

"Ah. If you're personally involved, I'm not sure I—"

"I have a video," she cut in.

"A video?"

"I found it online – on a private cloud. I ... I know what I'm seeing, but ... I'm having a hard time ... getting my head around it."

Another pause on the line told her she had his attention. She just hoped it wouldn't be to her detriment.

"Ms Patel, I have your interview file here in front of me. I have to say it's beyond impressive. Your skills are ones that are highly sought around the globe. However..."

Oh, no. Her heart sank. He was going to dismiss her. She almost didn't catch his next words, but when they finally registered, she rose up in her seat.

"...there are areas of the globe most have never even heard of, let alone set foot in. The world is much bigger than most believe. I'd like you to meet me in our offices tomorrow at midday."

He *wasn't* dismissing her.

Midday? She'd have to leave soon. She'd be driving all night. "Yes, sir."

"Bring the video, and everything you know about Selena Smith. We have a lot to discuss."

~*~

Jennifer was heading east, or maybe south-east. She knew this because she was walking in the opposite direction to the sun, now low in the sky, but still a couple of hours from setting. It was also a fact that north, east, south and west *smelled* different at different times of the day. Beyond her acute sense of direction though, she had no plan.

Despite how warm she felt, she kept her hood up, and her jacket zipped as high as it would go, which took the collar right over the bottom half of her nose. Only her eyes and some strands of hair were visible from the opening of her hood, and she hoped it wasn't enough to identify her.

She felt the gun she'd stolen against her breast as she walked. It calmed her as she followed the quiet, winding B-road. There wasn't another human being in sight. Nor any cars. The only life forms sharing in her misery were some sheep in the field on her left, and crickets.

At least this gave her time to think, and as much as she didn't want to, she needed to come up with a plan. None came to mind. She felt royally fucked over. Her identity – whether her old one or new one – was shot to pieces. She couldn't go back to being Jennifer. Were people still looking for Selena? She doubted she could go back to being Selena either.

Getting out the country's not happening then.

She wondered if Bab's brother could conjure up a new identity for her, and then immediately regretted the thought. She didn't want to think about him *at all*. Ever again.

What an idiot she'd been.

She'd have to lie low. The beggar she'd spoken too on the street in Canterbury five years ago came to mind – no money, no friends, no family, no home. She should have known that's how she'd end up.

She blinked back tears, annoyed they kept springing up. Crying would get her nowhere. She had under £25 in her wallet, and she'd have to ditch her bank cards and her driver's licence. She needed to figure out how she was going to survive.

Unbidden, her mind went back to Bab's brother as she continued down the road. She couldn't recall his name, even though she was sure she must have heard it at some point during her imprisonment. He was the boy in Hai's story. Was he really a good guy? Could anyone coming out of that family be good? It made no difference – she couldn't be affiliated with him in any way, not after everything. God, all the things he'd given her over the years – her first flat, her name and bank account, a monthly income into that account as she'd gotten herself on her feet...

Blood money.

She felt sick again, then realised she'd never eaten. Great. She wouldn't be having a feast. That £25 had to last for god knew how long, and she couldn't sing for her supper unless she wanted to leave a trail of dead bodies in her wake.

She heard a car approach from behind her.

Fuck. She made sure she was as over to the side of the road as she could be. *Just keep going,* she willed the unknown driver.

The car slowed down.

That too-familiar sense of danger snaked over her skin. *What now?*

The vehicle reached her, then slowed down further, cruising along by her side.

Giving in, and needing to know what she was potentially up against, she looked over at the driver. Her walking slowed to a stop, and so did the car. Right in front of her.

She didn't know who or what she'd been expecting – perhaps Hai, or Bab's brother – worst case scenario, the police. She hadn't been expecting the creepy blond man from the beauty spa.

He leaned out his open window, smiling at her. "I thought it was you."

He'd recognised her all rugged up like this? From behind?

The wolf in her paced restlessly. Something wasn't right.

"You remember me?" he asked.

She decided to play dumb. "Um ... no, I'm sorry, I don't."

"You work at the beauty spa. I was there with my girl-friend yesterday afternoon."

It felt like forever ago. "Oh, right. Yes, I think I remember now." She disliked him just as much now as she had then. His stare raked her up and down, and she was acutely aware she was completely alone on a road that stretched on for god knew how long. She had no idea where the nearest village was. She was also starting to think she attracted this kind of shit – a wolf-siren thing perhaps. But something was still off. He hadn't just 'happened' upon her, surely, which would mean he'd been following her. Had he seen her face on the news? Did he know she was wanted?

This probably wasn't going to end well.

She considered opening her mouth right now and belting out a tune. She could see how it could become addictive: just *sing* whenever she was in danger – talk about an easy way out of any threatening situation. She'd get so used to it, she'd sing at the drop of a hat whenever anyone fucked her off. Killing had never been so easy.

Despite the urge to do so, she didn't want another dead body on her hands. That would also lead the police to her whereabouts. The easy way out wasn't always as easy as it seemed. "Your girlfriend not with you?"

"No." He kept that smile on his face.

Wonderful. "So, do you live around here?"

"Nope." He turned his engine off.

Here we go. Running was futile. There was only one road, the verge, and open fields beyond a barbed wired fence. She thought of the gun in her inside pocket, but it would take far too long to unzip her jacket to get to it. He'd then know about the gun; he could use it against her.

She took a step back when he got out of the car.

"Saw you on the news."

Her heart leapt into her throat. He was done with the small talk then. "What do you want?"

He was still smiling. "You think I'm going to ask for something in exchange for my silence, right? Something to keep me from turning you in?"

And judging from his wandering eyes, she had an idea what that something might be. "Aren't you?"

"No. You probably think I'm looking at you because I find you attractive; because I want to fuck you."

What the hell... She wasn't sure where this was going.

"I guess that's what whores like you would think."

She stared at him, shocked. There was veiled hatred in his tone, but where had it come from? Who *was* this guy? She kept her mouth shut, suddenly confused as to his intentions.

"'Cause *that's* what you are, right? A whore. I know. I've seen it – seen the evidence."

"Evidence?"

"Yeah," he replied, friendlily, as if they were just having a jovial Saturday afternoon chat. "I'll show you." He pulled his phone from his coat pocket.

She warily stepped back, but it was pointless because he approached her with phone in hand until he was right in front of her.

A quick glance behind her told her she'd be falling into the verge if she wasn't careful, so she did her best to hold her ground.

He increased the volume on his phone and turned it so she could fully see the screen.

That ground she was holding might as well have fallen from beneath her feet. She gaped at the phone, stunned. She was *not* seeing this. She wasn't ... *she wasn't...*

Except she was. The sound of her voice through the speaker proved it.

"Oh, Edwin."

"Yes?"

"Why don't you find something to prop up the phone and come over here."

Blood drained from her face – she *felt* it drain. "Where did you ... how did you..."

On the small screen, she watched herself turn back to Gabriel. She sat, naked, astride his lap, holding a gun down his throat.

"You know what comes next, don't you."

This was Edwin's video. Edwin had captured the depraved moment, which, looking back on it now, seemed so... That didn't seem like her, but she knew it was. She knew what she was capable of. She'd been so fucking desperate, held captive by those repugnant beasts with no conscience. She'd wanted to escape; she'd had to play by their rules. She'd had to find a way to the top so they'd listen to her.

She forced her eyes away and stared at the man who held the phone. "Who are you?"

"Don't you know? Can't you guess?"

"Now, Gabriel, please bear in mind this is going to hurt me almost as much as it's going to hurt you. Edwin..."

She watched herself rise to her knees above Gabriel before throwing her next command at Edwin.

"Lick me."

On the screen, Edwin knelt behind her, between her legs and dutifully obeyed.

She closed her eyes; found it hard to breathe. Shame swept through her, but so did old anger and its long-time friend, resilience. Five years must have done something to her; she must have moved on somehow because watching it now was like watching a stranger. But a stranger she felt for, none-etheless. She hadn't forgotten the despair, the desolation, the sheer *hopelessness* she'd fought against every day she'd been cap-tured. "You don't know what you're seeing," she said through gritted teeth.

He moved fast. Her head was snapped back as he grabbed her hair and yanked.

She shrieked.

"*I* know what I'm seeing!" He spat in her face. "I'm seeing a *whore* who ruined my brother."

Brother? The blond hair and youthful look... *Oh, god. Oh, no.*

Before she could reply, she was hurtling through air, palms out in an attempt to shield her from wherever she landed.

Where she landed was on the barbed wire fence. She screamed when it pierced her hands and her cheek. There was no time to check her wounds or wipe the blood. She was grabbed again by the hair, and this time, he didn't let go of it when he sent her head flying towards the wooden pole that held the wire up.

Her scream ended when her head hit the pole. The pain was blinding. She'd bitten her tongue on impact, and blood filled her mouth. She heard a faint groan – it was hers.

"Still awake?"

She looked at him – *Edwin's brother* – but he was spinning and fuzzy. She tried to speak, but couldn't think, let alone form words.

Something came at her. Too late, she realised it was his fist. It must have connected with her face, but all the different types of pain blurred into one, and she wasn't sure. But she didn't need to know. Darkness called to her, louder than pain, and then, there was nothing.

~*~

Roman slammed on the brakes of the Toyota he'd acquired.

Hai yelled as they were both lurched forward against their seatbelts.

It took a moment to catch their breaths. "That was bracing," gasped Hai.

"Something's wrong," Roman mumbled.

"Perhaps driving in a more—"

"Sshhhh ... wait." He closed his eyes and concentrated, but it was no use. "She's gone."

"What do you mean?"

It had taken Roman bloody near twenty minutes to finally home in on Jennifer. She'd been too damned angry and scared. Those frenzied emotions had acted like spiked armour around her, knocking his senses into orbit when he tried to get a reading on her location – even just a vague idea of it.

Eventually, her anger and fear had dissipated a little, and he was finally able to sense the truth at the core of her emotions. Those were more akin to her *real* feelings, and he'd latched on to them. They had provided him with a direction: east-south-east. According to his SatNav, that direction led to one B-road, that road stretching all the way to the coast near-as-dammit, not too far from where they'd taken her last night.

But not five minutes had passed when he suddenly felt like he'd been drenched in ice water – so icy it hurt, like a brain-freeze – then it was gone, and so was she.

"I had her, Hai. I could feel her as clearly as I can see you, and now there's nothing."

"Nothing?"

"Nothing."

"If you can't track her emotions, it means—"

"It means she's not experiencing them. I feel them only because she can."

"Even in sleep, one still has feelings."

"Which means she's unconscious." His mood darkened. "Or worse."

"Do you think she's been found by the police?"

"Why would they need her unconscious?"

"Maybe she struggled."

"Or it's something else ... or someone else." Roman put the car into gear. "I'll keep driving ahead. She was about twenty minutes in front of us I think."

"Could it be the wolf hunters?"

His whole body went tight with pent up fury. If it was, the police would have more dead bodies on their hands once he was through with them.

Chapter Thirteen

He'd woken up into some kind of nightmare, surely. David blinked, then blinked again. But no matter how many times he blinked, Jennifer's face remained, right there, on the hospital's television as the news reporter relayed what had happened that morning near their home village.

His head ached. His stomach felt weak from hunger, even though he'd been fed intravenously. Or maybe the weak feeling in his stomach was disbelief.

Someone moved across the archway that led into the ward. He turned towards the shadow, and almost cried. He was so relieved to see a friendly face. "Prisha."

"Hey." She smiled. "You're awake." She made her way over to him and took his hand in hers.

"I think I wish I wasn't." He nodded at the TV.

Prisha's gaze followed his. "I was hoping to make it back here before you found out."

"What the hell's going on, Prish?"

"You need to stay away from her."

"Are you kidding me? This is a mistake. They've got it all wrong."

"You don't know that."

"Of course I bloody do. Jen's not a murderer, for god's

sake."

"She was seen running away, covered in blood, and it seems like she had help from someone."

"No."

"David—"

"*No*, Prish."

She started at the tone of his voice. He rarely raised it, but he was beyond pissed off. It didn't help that he was trussed up to this bed unable to do a damned thing.

"Jesus, you really think she's capable of that? Killing five men – *five*? What with? The report was sketchy."

"I don't know any more than what's been reported."

"Pull the other one. A crime's taken place potentially involving a person we know, and you haven't gone snooping?"

"Look, I don't know what's going on, not really, but what the police have ... the reporter's not lying. She was seen fleeing the village with a man in a dark blue Volvo."

"A ... who? What man?"

"I don't know. No one seems to have got a good look at him."

"If they didn't get a good look at him, what makes you think they got a good look at her?"

"David, the whole village said they saw her. That's not a sketchy witness report, that's the *whole damned village*."

"Whatever's going on, it's not what we think, I guarantee it. I want to get out of here, but the doctor said he's not releasing me for another day to be sure the swelling's gone down."

"Sounds sensible."

"I need to find her, Prish."

"David, no. Listen, whatever's going on, stay out of it."

"You know that's not going to happen."

"It was *your* home that got trashed, too. Don't you think it's wise to make sure *you're* not some kind of target before taking off after her? You'd put her in danger."

He paused, confused. He hadn't thought of that, but honest-to-god, he had no idea who would be gunning for him or why. He had no enemies. But Jennifer did. "Prish, what if it's the same people from her past, people who did awful things to her. You said she escaped in a car, but what if it wasn't escape? What if she was taken? *They* might have killed the men and however she's involved, she might have had no choice."

Prisha took in a breath, seemingly contemplating his words. "You might be right."

"So I *need* to find her."

"You won't be doing anything for at least twenty-four hours – doctor's orders."

"Which is why I need you to help me."

She looked away, nervously. Prish was never nervous. "I can't. The new job I've got that I told you about? They want me to start early – tomorrow in fact – so I've got to drive down to London tonight."

"Tomorrow? Tomorrow's Sunday."

"Do you think the Secret Intelligence Service has weekends off?"

"You're leaving?" He hadn't meant it to come out quite like that. It was just that with Jennifer gone, and Prisha going, too, he felt... Damn it. No. He'd figure it out. He wasn't going to abandon the woman he loved. He'd have to be patient. No matter how much the long, slow wait for everything was killing him right now, he *was* a patient guy – he could do this. He was going to get answers one way or another.

"I have to go. I'm so sorry. But I wasn't going to go without seeing you first, and I really am glad you're awake. I was so worried." She squeezed his hand.

He squeezed hers back, then removed his from under it.

She looked hurt for a moment, and then took a step back.

"There's one more thing – it's a confession, and I'm dreading telling you because it was wrong of me. I have no excuse other than being so angry to find out you'd been brought here and—"

"Prish, spit it out." Although he wasn't sure he wanted to know. He was still replaying the news reporter's voice in his head.

"I showed Jennifer the ring you bought her and told her you were going to propose."

He was shocked. And more than hurt. That was... "I can't believe you did that."

"I know. I—"

"Jesus Christ, Prish, that was for *me* to tell her. It was going to be a surprise. I was planning how to do it and—"

"I *know*." Her eyes shimmered. "I wasn't thinking straight. After knowing you'd been hurt, I just wanted to make sure she wouldn't hurt you further. I showed her the ring and told her not to say yes unless she meant it one hundred percent."

"You told her ... god, I can't believe I'm hearing this."

"David, I'm so—"

"Leave."

Prisha shook her head by way of apology; her tears fell, but he wasn't buying it.

"*Leave.* I don't want to see or talk to you again. Not until I've had time to think – there's too much to... You've made everything worse. Just go." He knew his words speared her, and maybe he'd feel guilty about it tomorrow. Right now, he was furious, and he didn't do 'furious' very well – it wasn't in his nature. He took most things others found offensive with a pinch of salt, but *this*... "I mean it. Please go."

He thought she was going to say something else. In the end, she didn't. She turned, and left, leaving him to figure out when exactly everything had fallen apart, and more importantly, *why*.

He turned back to the TV. The news had ended, but they were summarising the day's events once more, and there she was again – his Jennifer's face filling the screen as if she were a criminal.

They thought she was, though, didn't they. He suddenly realised he'd be questioned, and sooner rather than later.

Determination simmered beneath the battering fatigue he felt from his injury and his medications. "Hang in there, darling. I'll find you ... I'll find you."

~*~

Not since waking up in the hospital five years ago had she felt the brunt of pain as a human, but even then, it had been somewhat dulled by medicine and painkillers. That wasn't the case right now.

Jennifer came to wishing she hadn't. When she tried to move, she couldn't. When she tried to speak, she couldn't. Duct tape sealed her mouth; her hands were tied in front of her; her ankles were also bound.

If she could laugh, she thought she might actually have done so. Twice in twenty-four hours – she had the best luck. Last time she was tied up though, there'd been no bruises, and no pain.

It seemed her left eye was swollen shut. Her face smarted in more than one place, and her head was throbbing so much, she wondered if the damage was permanent. Without the wolf's strength, could she even heal?

"I'll start by saying you should be grateful you're still alive." He was sitting in front of her and off to the left just a little. It was a bit hard to see him because of her eye. From what she *could* see, it looked like they were in the middle of a thicket or something, surrounded by countryside, and she guessed probably not too far from where he'd attacked her.

It felt like the gun was still in her inside pocket judging by the weight she could feel there. He hadn't noticed it, luck-ily, but the zip of her jacket had slipped down more than half way – probably through his dragging her body by the look of the grass stains and mud on her clothes.

Her own voice sounded, stark amongst the trees, though it did not come from her sealed mouth. He was watching that damned video again.

"Ed loved his photographs ... is that something you knew about him?" He looked at her, and the look was nothing short of menacing.

She attempted a nod, and winced. Everything hurt.

"When we were teens, he'd let me go out on a shoot with him. How many fifteen-year-old boys do you know who'd let their twelve-year-old brother hang around with him?"

Her own brother never minded her hanging around too much. It crossed her mind this might be fate's idea of payback. By her own hand, she'd killed her flesh and blood – now, she was intrinsically tied to Bab's brother, and Edwin's brother was a fucking nutcase who, by all accounts, was going to make sure she suffered. Maybe this was her own brother's revenge from beyond the grave.

"He did though. He showed me all the photos he took; showed me how to work a camera, too. Can't say it became a passion of mine the way it was his, but I enjoyed the time we spent on his projects. And when he left home to go to univer-sity, he kept me in the loop. He started to store his photos on a cloud server, and gave me the password so I could see them and give him my opinion. That all ended eight years ago when he went missing. I had contact with him once a week at least, and suddenly, all contact ended. He went MIA. Our mum was distraught; I spent so much fucking time and money searching for him. I stopped after two years. Fell into depression; couldn't stand looking at anything that reminded me of him... Do you know how difficult it is to get on with your life never knowing for sure what happened to someone you love? If they're dead or alive?" He looked at her, as if waiting for her answer.

She didn't know what it should be, so she didn't move.

For a minute, she thought that angered him further, but he looked back at his phone and carried on. "Then, five years ago, all those missing people started showing up again. It made me think about Ed, and on a whim, I decided to see if I could still access his cloud storage." He smiled a grim smile and held up the phone. "I could. And it turned out, he'd been busy. Five years ago, from June to August, he uploaded a whole load of shit you would not believe – although, maybe you would, since you have a starring role in that shit."

Edwin ... fucking hell. If Gabriel or Bab had caught him out he'd have been tortured and killed. He'd died anyway. What the hell had he been thinking? He must have known his brother would eventually see those photos. Maybe he'd been thinking of escape, too.

"He took photographs of the farm he was at, so I know he was involved in the whole mess that went down there; only, when all those missing people showed up – some of them stating that's where they'd been held – he wasn't among them. I didn't go to the police with this. I didn't go because I knew they'd take it all away from me and make sure I didn't have any copies – these photos are all I have left of Edwin; I couldn't let them take them. And they *would*, because the stuff he photographed," his voice lowered; took on a threatening tone, "and the stuff he *recorded* ... well, that's not stuff you let the public know about."

Her insides felt like ice. If Edwin had recorded half of what went on at the farm, she was in the biggest of all trouble. For a period of time, no matter how short, she'd led the Tridents. If this guy knew that, she wouldn't last the night.

"*This* footage, I particularly like." He pressed a button, then held the phone in front of her face.

She tried to turn away – memories were one thing, but to see it all played out like this...

He wasn't having that. He slapped her hard across the face, making her cry out behind her gag, then grabbed her cheeks and forced her to look at the screen. "You're going to fucking watch this, bitch, then we're going to have some fun of our own."

She blinked the tears out of her eyes until the screen was no longer a blur.

God ... no.

Gabriel was fucking her on his bed. He'd done that a hundred times, but she knew exactly when *this* moment was because she wasn't bound to the headboard; she wasn't bound at all. This was hours after she'd shot her brother. Edwin had been in the room – she'd let him watch. She hadn't known he'd been bloody filming it.

Gabriel rutted into her from behind, both of them on all fours; then, he suddenly stopped. She saw him lean into her ear. The phone hadn't picked up what he'd said, but she heard it anyway like it was yesterday. *'You're a little deranged, my love. Are you addicted to pain?'*

On reflex more than anything else, she tried to turn her head away once more, realising her mistake too late.

Edwin's brother growled his rage and hit her again, a hell of a lot harder this time, his hand a fist against her jaw.

She starting sobbing into the tape; didn't want to, but couldn't help it.

Her face was turned back around and held still in a grip that might break bones. "*Watch*," he yelled.

She did as he ordered, and saw it happen – saw Gabriel still, stiffen, then change into the beast he was whilst embedded inside her.

Fuck it, she hoped that was it. If that's what he wanted her to see, she'd seen it. She moaned in protest, needing the mental torture to stop.

He ignored her and kept the phone right there in front of her goddamned face, making her watch it all – the completion of his change, and every damned thrust until the moment they both climaxed. The phone picked up some sound. She heard herself come; she heard Gabriel roar, grunt and howl in conquest.

Finally, he threw the phone to the ground in a fit of rage. *Disgusted* rage. Both his hands went around her neck and he pulled her to her feet, not an ounce of care in the act. Her back was slammed against something – a tree trunk at a guess, given the roughness cutting through her top – and she yelled as he pulled the duct tape off her mouth, ripping skin. The yell was more of a choking sound. Both his hands were back around her neck, squeezing.

"Now you're going to tell me what the *hell* I just saw, and then you're going to tell me what happened to my brother."

She opened her mouth, but nothing came out.

"Do you know how long it took me to find you? So many times I almost gave up. I didn't though, and I need to send Google a fucking thank you note, 'cause in the end, all it took was the best facial image Edwin had of you uploaded onto Google's image recognition search. Bingo: Jennifer – an office manager at a health and beauty spa fifteen miles outside York, according to the headshot on the spa's website. It took half a year for me to relocate so I could be near you. I found a job up here, rented a flat; met a nice girl a couple of months ago who was a regular at the spa."

Jesus Christ. If she hadn't thought her life was in peril up until this point, she was left in no doubt now. He'd been tracking her for half a *year*. He wasn't a nutcase, he was a psychopath with a premeditated plan.

"And yesterday, I finally got to meet you. I have to admit, it threw me, seeing you in the flesh. I looked at you and I doubted myself. You didn't look like you were capable of the filth I saw on that video. I held back; I had to be sure. After all the time I spent looking for you, it would ruin me if you'd turned out to be the wrong person."

God, he needed to stop squeezing her neck; she could barely breathe...

"But then I heard about what happened at the pub last night – two men taken to hospital, one now dead – and you were there. Coincidence perhaps. Surely not after this morning though, right? Five more deaths, and lo and behold, *you* were there."

Finally she spoke, hoarsely, barely a whisper against the force of his grip, choking her. "It's ... it's not what you think."

He released her, she gasped for air, but any relief was short-lived. He punched her in the diaphragm. It was so winding, she thought she'd puke. The ground rushed towards her, but before she hit it, he yanked her up again by her hair. "No complaining, whore. I know you like it rough. Tell me what the fuck you did to my brother."

How could he be such a shit? Edwin hadn't been a shit, not really. He'd been nice – for a Trident, anyway. "Have ... you always ... been a cunt?" she croaked out, knowing she damned well shouldn't, but if this was her end, she'd make sure it was a miserable experience for him. She'd cheated death enough times. She knew she was all out of chances.

He laughed.

No – it wasn't a laugh. It was some passive-aggressive noise meant to sound like a laugh. "You really *do* like it rough."

He threw her.

It was her shoulder that hit the ground first – with her wrists and ankles tied, she couldn't brace herself for the fall. If she cried out in pain, she couldn't really hear herself – her voice was nearly gone, her throat likely damaged beyond repair. That ruled out a jaunty sing-along. *Sorry, siren.*

New pain jarred her whole body, and she realised she'd been kicked in the stomach, the force of it so hard, she was rolled along the grass. The zip on her jacket ripped loose and her gun fell out. If she'd had any hope for her life left, she would have cried. Luckily, she didn't. Game over.

A *real* laugh sounded now. "Well, looky here!" The loon picked up the gun. "It's like you're making this easy for me on purpose."

She heard him release the safety.

"What happened to my brother?"

His brother... How could two brothers be so different? How could the same blood tell two stories?

His name was Roman.

Odd timing, but she remembered it now. She'd heard it mentioned in passing once or twice.

I'M NOT YOUR ENEMY. YOU CAN TRUST ME.

Running away from him had been a mistake – the clarity of that realisation was startling. She'd made many mistakes, hadn't she? She was about to make another, not that it mattered anymore. "Edwin's dead," she whispered, whispering all she could manage.

He stilled. Red crept up his neck, anger taking hold of his

face.

Yeah, at least she'd go to her grave knowing she'd hurt him just as much, and the crushing desolation of losing a brother was something she was well versed with. Hoping he could hear her words, she gathered her strength and drove them as hard as she could into him. "He was forcibly turned into one of those monsters you saw in the video. He died in a pool of blood from a poison which melted his insides. It was a painful death."

The guy's eyes teared up, he was that enraged. He looked like he might combust.

Good. I'll drag you to hell, you sick fuck. "And I never knew he had a brother. He never mentioned you once."

Everything went deathly quiet. She was ready for another kick, and she wasn't disappointed. He aimed at her ribs. Fresh tears stung her blood-crusted eyes as she heard them crack, then he drove his fist into her face again, not once, but twice, growling in pain as he did so.

This was it. Blackness lurked, threatening to take her and she wished it would. She willed him to hit her again. *Make it quick, you shit.*

Instead, he lowered himself to the ground and straddled her, then undid her jeans.

Some witty retort was on the tip of her tongue – *thought you didn't like fucking whores* – but it slipped from her mind as she slipped in and out of consciousness. Unfortunately, the bliss of passing out was just beyond her reach.

She grunted as her body shook with the force of his yanking her trousers and knickers down. They stopped and bunched where the ropes met her ankles.

"Remember how you face-fucked that man in the video with your gun? Did you do that to Edwin, too? Looked to me you were treating him like shit on your shoe."

She really hadn't treated him that badly. And the times she had, she recalled he'd quite liked it. She didn't voice her thoughts – her voice had gone. She was just about gone, too.

"Payback's a bitch, honey. You're the one who's going to get fucked with a gun now, and I'm not going to be so careful with the trigger. In fact, when the bullet tears up your insides, I want the last thing you think to be how fucking painful it is to die in a pool of your blood."

She waited for it: violation, pain, death. Somewhere in the depths of her mind, she heard herself laugh. This place she found herself in – it was kind of like an old friend. She'd been here quite a few times before. *Hi, me again. How have you been?*

She'd lost her mind – knew she had. These were the ridiculous musings of a dead woman.

She heard a yell from somewhere; echoey; distant, like it had travelled vast oceans just to reach her. Other strange sounds followed – grunts and thuds – but she couldn't create a picture from them.

The gun fired.

She must be dead – the bullet must have hit her – because she no longer felt anything; she was just floating...

But her vision from between her nearly swollen shut eyelids hadn't quite faded, and she was grateful, actually, that the last thing she saw before her death had nothing to do with dying in a pool of her blood, but were very dark brown eyes that met her own. They held a fierce regret that rocked her soul, and it was comforting in some ways to realise she still had a soul – it hadn't turned to ash after she'd killed her brother. Only eyes that carried an understanding of such darkness could look at her like that. And there she was in the rich brown irises of that understanding, staring back.

"I'm sorry," she said in a broken hush. It was for Maggie, and for Edwin, and for her brother and father; it was for

David. It was for the she-wolf in her she'd betrayed. "I'm sorry."

Chapter Fourteen

Roman had zoned in on Jennifer ten minutes ago when he'd gone from feeling nothing at all from her, to sheer terror. His own fears hadn't been allayed when they'd pulled up by a car on the side of the winding lane. He wished he had wolf senses, but his senses were mostly human – his gift of vision and empathy, and his emotional connection with Jennifer were the only things that set him apart from the rest of the world. That, and the scales trailing down his torso.

It was turning dark. The sun had set, and the moon had risen, a low, huge orb which would bring him to his knees tomorrow night.

Standing on the other side of the barbed wire fence they'd just leapt over, Roman held a hand out to hush Hai, whose footsteps rustled the grass.

He got the message and stilled.

Roman concentrated on nothing but the intensity of Jennifer's fear. It almost swamped him, but he suddenly saw the core of it behind his closed eyes, the image her fear created like a red ball of dread. He pointed to a small thicket of bushes and trees. "There."

They ran. At some point, he gave up trying to be quiet, the need to reach her too great. This was the kind of fear found only at the point of no return. His only solace was that she'd been at this point before, and lived.

He was so focused on her overwhelming waves of terror, he didn't see the flash of movement through the trees.

Hai did, though. He sprinted into the thicket, and everything that happened next was a bit of a blur. Hai attacked the man who leant over Jennifer on the ground.

Hai's safety in a fight was not something Roman needed to worry about – the man was like an aged Bruce Lee. He was unrivalled in his art. What did worry him was the female at his feet. Her blonde hair caught the light of the moon.

A gun fired amid Hai's grapple with the man, the bullet whizzing past Roman, taking a sliver of his jacket with it. He didn't flinch. He was transfixed by the heart wrenching sight in front of him.

Dear god...

Her bruises... Not an inch of her cream-coloured skin showed through the blue and black. Her face was swollen, her nose and cheek bleeding, and when he leaned over her to check her breathing, it was clear she'd been choked. Her throat was an angry purple. Looking further down to where her top rode up her stomach, he could see she'd been kicked – more than once.

'Seeing red' wasn't a euphemism. Cold rage ran through him, with it the deepest of regrets: he'd let this happen. He'd kept things from her, and she'd run. He should have told her everything months ago; years ago.

She gurgled, trying to speak. He just about made out she was looking at him through her pummelled eyes. Who the fuck *did* this to a woman? To *anyone*?

Your dad did; your brother did...

And for too long he'd turned a blind eye. His body hardened with ice-cold steel, his own frenzy rising. *You're not bound to the bastards anymore.*

"I'm sorry," she said, at least he thought that's what she'd said. He couldn't really hear the words, but the sentiment was clear. "I'm sorry."

She should be the last person apologising – for *this.*

"Roman," Hai called, his voice strained.

Roman turned.

The man Hai held in an arm lock on the ground went still on seeing his face. If it showed an ounce of what he was feeling this second, he should be pissing himself.

"What do we do with him?"

The man's face all at once contorted in fury. "You've got the wrong person. It's *her* that's evil. I can prove it – acts of depravity. She's *sick.*"

Roman approached him, then knelt down in front of him, ignoring Hai's questioning gaze. He pushed his face into the man's, nose to nose and eye to eye.

The man didn't shy away, but held his ground and jutted his chin in stubborn defiance. "She's not human," he spat out. "She's a monster."

He undid the top two buttons of his shirt and pulled the collar open.

The man's eyes fell to his scales. His face went pale.

"A monster like this?"

Speechless, his eyes only widened in fear.

"Put him to sleep," said Roman.

Hai did as requested, forcing his head forward into the arm that gripped him around his neck until his struggles ceased, and his gasping breath became silence. The man slumped in his hold.

Hai dropped him to the grass. "He'll wake in minutes. We need to secure him."

Roman gripped the man's hair in his left hand and pulled

his head back; held it as still as possible, then drove his right fist into his neck as hard as he could. His trachea cracked and crumbled.

"Jesus," Hai swore under his breath.

Roman didn't reply.

"He could have had information."

Roman picked up the phone, which he assumed was the man's, lying three feet from him. "We have this."

"And the trail of dead bodies we're trying to avoid? If you didn't want to leave him, we could have taken him with us."

He didn't want to hear it, not now. He wasn't going to put this cunt in the same car as Jennifer – end of. "Get the gun."

Hai did as instructed in silence. Roman knew he'd get an earful from him later. Murder was to be used only as the last resort. As far as he was concerned, he'd reached the last resort.

He hurried back to Jennifer and knelt by her head, putting his ear to her mouth. "She's still breathing – just about. Help me get her up; I don't want to make her injuries worse."

"Roman, look." Hai pocketed the gun and knelt down by her legs.

He looked to where Hai was pointing; his breath caught when he saw it. Beneath the cuts and bruises, and under the light of the moon, her thighs shimmered with scales. So, it *was* true. Without the Trident blood, she was as vulnerable to the siren as he. He'd hoped to have been proven wrong. His heart twisted in regret. "We need to get her to the ocean."

"We'll need to treat her injuries."

"The wolf's already trying – see how these bruises are yellowing? The sea will do the rest."

Hai glanced at the moon. "Let's hope she can hold out one more night."

~*~

It was dark, then light, then dark again. Hours were passing – she knew this; had a sense of it – but she had no idea how many hours, or what time of day it was in the brief moments she rose to consciousness. In the past, she'd gained some comfort from pain; moments of security. Even power could be found in pain. Not this time. *This* pain had stripped her into complete powerlessness. And without the wolf's strength, she was as defenceless as any human could be. It beggared belief exactly how a human with their thin skin and fragile bones could survive such brutality, but Maggie had; those other women in Gabriel's cages had; those women in the counselling session she'd fled from five years ago had. She'd had no idea.

She did now.

Hai's voice drifted in, there was a laugh on it; dry humour, though she hadn't a clue what about. She smiled inside, then drifted off again.

On her next rousing, she heard Roman's voice – at least, she assumed it was his; she could feel his presence; feel his heart and what stirred him, and it was more than mesmerising. There was a rare valiance to his nature that warmed her to her core, and belied the coward she'd believed him to be. It didn't warm her enough though, for pain assailed her again, a strange heat to it this time, as if her legs were on fire. Breathing became a chore, and she drifted off once more, unconsciousness able to soothe her in ways the world of the living could not.

Darkness kept her wrapped in its safe embrace for what seemed like an age – no dreams, no thoughts, no musings, no doubts, no regrets...

When it finally released her, she woke to darkness still, both inside and out. The fire in her legs had increased tenfold; her chest was the tightest she had ever known it – far beyond the tightness of the mating pains she used to get.

The giant, full Supermoon to her left illuminated everything as it kissed Earth's basin of water – the ocean. They'd brought her to the ocean.

A shadow crept across the moon, darkening a fraction of the silver globe. The eclipse – it was tonight. It was happening now.

She was on a rowing boat.

And she was tied to Roman with rope, her chest against his, both of them naked.

It should have alarmed her. She should be screaming and trying to break free, but her sheer exhaustion brought instinct – not logic – to the fore of her being. Instinct took over all, and her instinct told her she was safe.

She couldn't open her eyes all the way. Every bruise throbbed angrily; her head hurt so much; stabs of pain across her ribs took her prisoner – they must be broken from the kicking they'd gotten. Her throat felt marginally better, but she knew it would hurt if she tried to speak.

There was nothing wrong with her sense of smell though, and she would surely lose herself in the exquisiteness that was Roman's scent. It sent a bolt of arousal to her sex, suddenly and sharply, and she moaned a sound from her parched throat.

He'd been speaking to Hai as the older man knotted the ropes that held them bound to each other. He stopped on her moan, and looked down, seemingly glad to see her awake.

She couldn't say she felt the same way. Smells like that – like the way he smelled – those were smells she had to escape. Smells that made her *want* only ever led to desolation and ruination.

"Don't be scared," he whispered. Then he brushed her hair with his fingers before cupping his hand behind her hanging neck and bringing her head in to his chest. "I'm not going to hurt you. I'll never hurt you, I swear it. No one's going to hurt

218 | Blood Shadow

you again."

She believed him, she did. But that explained nothing of what was happening or why she was tied to him with ropes, and she didn't have the strength to ask; barely had the voice to speak.

They were standing on the boat. She was literally held up by the uncompromising tightness of the ropes around their trunks. Her arms were free, as were his, but she couldn't really feel her feet – in fact, she couldn't feel her legs beyond the un-bearable burning that ran up and down them.

Her moan this time, was one of agony. It was too much. Whatever this was, she couldn't do it. She welcomed the black-ness that crept into her vision, beckoning her once more into a peaceful lull, but this time, she was dragged back into stark reality, Roman's hands either side of her face, shaking her gently awake. "Stay with me. This will be easier if you're awake."

She sounded her protest.

"Please try."

She didn't have to – he wasn't going to let her slip into blissful slumber. Between the ropes fastening them together, she felt his fingers graze the skin of her back in purposeful strokes. The arousal she'd felt earlier bloomed again. He was aware of it, she was sure. He was doing this to keep her awake and it was working. The stimulation the simple movements caused was enough to battle with the sleep she craved. "How long..." was all she could get out.

He understood her meaning. "Almost twenty-four hours. You've been in and out of consciousness; I've been monitoring your recovery. The wolf has healed you a little, but not enough. You *will* heal, though – don't worry. The man who did this to you is dead."

She felt every muscle in him tense on that last sentence.

Roman looked nothing like Bab, she could see this now, though it was in the *sensing* of it through their odd connection that she could see it best. His eyes were dark brown where Bab's were a pale green; Bab had been wiry and on the thin side – Roman was more filled out and muscular. His dark brown hair hung to his shoulders; Bab's had been short. And now, she spotted his scales. She tried to focus on them, even though her vision was fuzzy with trying to stay awake. They ran from his neck, all the way down his front to beyond where she could see, her own body covering the rest.

"Hai, we need to go down now. Her breathing's getting worse; so is mine."

He was right, she realised with a strange detachment. She was rasping every breath in and out as if the next might be her last. Her chest was getting tighter by the minute.

"We're here," said Hai. He pulled the boat up against a small jutting rock and reached out to attach a mooring rope to it. After knotting that, too, he turned to Roman. "You have the knife?"

"I do – against my hip."

"And the key?"

"Around my wrist. Don't worry, I'll make sure we find our way back."

She felt Hai lay a hand on her shoulder, and squeeze it in a show of care. "You're strong, Jennifer. Just hold on. I'll see you when you come back up."

She had no idea what they were talking about, but all of a sudden, she bucked and gasped on reflex, her body following its own orders. She couldn't breathe *enough* – there was no air.

"Now, Hai!"

"The boat's secure – we're ready."

Hai pulled and tugged at the ropes to her right. She managed to glance down and saw him attach something to them: a weight. It was a weight with a lock on it, and it must have held at least a ton.

Roman grunted with the effort of carrying the extra load; then, she was lifted against him as he used the rock for leverage and took them both off the side of the boat and into the sea.

She cried out when the water met her legs. Like ice to a burn, they stung like nothing she'd ever known. She imagined her skin peeling off.

"It's okay. Trust me." His voice was strained. He was taking all their weight against the rock, struggling to breathe himself.

It didn't matter if she trusted him. This was like no pain she'd ever felt, and she couldn't do it anymore. Her whole life had been pain of some kind or another; five years ago saw the worst of it and she feared she might not live through it. But she had, and after that there had been relative peace – sometimes anxious peace, sometimes dull peace – but peace nonetheless. To go back to this...

"It's the siren, Jen, that's why it hurts. We're going under the water. It'll be agony for a few seconds, but I need you to be brave. I need you to fight your instinct to survive – breathe *in* the water; let yourself drown. I promise you won't. You'll live. There'll be no pain after that."

She was sobbing. She didn't care; she couldn't do it. "Let me die ... let me die ... please."

He lowered them further. The water wet her chin. "I can't do that. Sorry."

"Death is my redemption," she whispered, her tears falling on his chest before rolling into the lapping ocean.

He stilled for a moment, and she felt something warm and wet slide down her right temple and past her ear. *His* tear.

His nose brushed against her forehead, before his lips

pressed a kiss to it. "It seems we're at a bit of an impasse, then. Because your survival is mine."

He let go of the rock, and before she could attempt another breath, they went under.

~*~

Fuck all the gods – that had been one of the hardest things he'd ever done. Her desperation damn near killed him, but he'd been here before, drowning in his own desperation. It was the end game he focused on. He knew the way out of this dark tunnel; he wasn't about to leave her in it.

Roman fought every natural urge in him to kick and pull his way back to the surface. The pain would be acute, but quick.

Jennifer did kick though – or tried. This was why the ropes had been necessary. She bucked against him, trying to break free, her face contorted in fear and anguish, and he knew in this second he'd spend the rest of his life begging her forgiveness for putting her in this position.

He pressed his forehead to hers. *Relax*, he said with his mind, and she would have heard him if she hadn't been so terrified. Her struggles were lessening; she was still so weak from her injuries.

Breathe, Jen.

She wasn't listening. He couldn't blame her her fight. He'd done exactly the same the first time. His brother and father had been far less caring though. Not in a million years would he have bound her down here alone.

His air was almost gone. Closing his eyes, he forced every muscle in him to loosen; ignored Jennifer's thrashing against his frame; and breathed the water in.

The liquid filled his lungs, the freezing cold of it adding

to its heaviness as it seeped the vastness of the sea into his being, every tide of every year since the beginning of time defin-
ing his existence. Every muscle in him spasmed; he held fast
against the onslaught. It lasted only a few seconds; his next
breath was a *real* breath. His diaphragm expanded to open the
gills between his ribs, and he took in everything the ocean had
to offer.

This was as far as his transformation went, and by all accounts, he should be dead. No male siren had ever existed as
far as he was aware.

With Jennifer, he wasn't altogether sure how the siren
would manifest itself.

He watched her as her eyes widened with a final silent
plea for life, and then her body did what nature bade it do,
despite the water surrounding her: she opened her mouth and
gasped for air.

Water poured into her mouth, down her throat; she con-
vulsed in his arms.

He held her as best he could.

All at once, she grew rigid, then flopped, falling against
him, unmoving.

For a few dreadful seconds that seemed to stretch forever,
he thought he'd gotten this all wrong – she'd died after all. But
then, her head lifted.

If he'd had access to air, it would have lodged in his
throat. Her eyes were black, even the whites of them, just like
the first and only siren he'd ever seen all those years ago. And
just like then, he found himself drawn to them; drowning in
them.

She no longer struggled, but breathed as he did through
gills between her ribs, no longer broken. The transformation
would have sealed the fractures.

Her hair billowed around her. Something twined around

his legs.

He looked down and saw her tail. It shimmered blue.

Awed, he could do nothing but stare at it. He wasn't sure she'd change *fully*, not least because she also housed a wolf inside her.

His gaze landed back on her eyes. *Can you hear me?* he asked.

He wasn't sure of the answer. She didn't reply, but then, she might not know she could. He couldn't read her black eyes as easily as he could read her human ones. There was less expression – very little, actually.

Her hand found his face, and her thumb stroked his lips, then pressed against them, demanding he part them. Her intention was clear: she wanted to mate.

No. Not that he wasn't aroused and hard against her – he was – and his body ached at the mere thought of the siren's intimate kiss. But he had no idea if she was really in there; if her thoughts were conscious ones or driven by a sea creature's basic impulse. *I swore I'd never hurt you and I won't.*

He pulled her head against his chest, just like he had on the boat, and to his relief, she didn't fight him, but let it nestle there. He felt her relax into his frame. An amount of peace passed between them – true contentment – and he hoped it would be enough to take them through 'til dawn. Every month, he had to restrain himself from untying the ropes and swimming off – he could end up anywhere, halfway across the world before he broke the surface again. But he had the human will to resist freedom's call. He suspected Jennifer might not have – at least, not yet.

Her breathing against his was steady. She was calm. He wondered if she'd fallen asleep – she still had a lot of healing to do. The siren and the saltwater would take care of her wounds.

Above him, just visible beyond the surface of the water,

the moon turned red as the earth's shadow eclipsed it fully.

Something inside him released – finally. Something he couldn't name, but that he'd been holding onto for an aeon.

He sighed as gratitude washed over him. He pressed Jennifer closer to him, protectiveness for her rising.

She accepted his lead and let out her own sigh of bubbles which drifted past his face as her tail brushed his legs.

And there they waited, two silhouettes in the Atlantic under the Blood Moon, for dawn to come.

Chapter Fifteen

S he opened her eyes to the sound of gently lapping waves and chattering people. It was warm. She expected the sun when she blinked her eyes open, but wherever she was, it was mostly dark – a room of some kind. It was clearly day outside, though.

Outside?

Jennifer pushed herself up to sitting. She was in what looked like a small, wooden cabin – smaller than that: a shed. She suddenly realised it was a beach hut. She was at the beach, though she had no idea whereabouts.

A lamp was lit in one corner of the hut, and she was lying on a blow-up mattress on the floor.

Events came rushing back – most of them, anyway.

Looking down, she saw herself naked. She pushed that alarming fact out of her mind and checked her body for injuries. There were none. She couldn't see bruises; her ribs felt fine. In fact, she felt like she'd been given a brand new body. She couldn't detect any aches or pains at all.

A white, cotton bathrobe lay at the foot of the blow-up bed. She reached for it, and slipped it on, kneeling up to tie the belt.

The door of the hut swung open, and she scooted back, ready to bolt. Or pounce if she had to.

"Easy," he said, slowing his movements, and raising his hand in a show of amity. In his other hand, he carried what looked like clothes.

Roman.

He practically filled the small hut, though he couldn't have been more than six foot tall. "These are yours." He held up the clothes; then, with deliberate slowness, stepped forward and placed them at the end of the bed. "They were caked in mud and blood. Hai took them to the launderette. They've just come out the dryer."

She watched every flick of his hand and click of his heel.

He watched her watch him.

They said nothing for a while, then he let out a breath and sat on the only stool in the hut. "It's nearly eleven in the morning; it's Monday. The full moon was last night. All your wounds have healed; there don't seem to be any repercussions from your attack." He studied her carefully. "We have a lot to talk about, but first, I must apologise to you, because we should have talked about it much sooner."

She didn't know what to say. In some ways, she didn't know if she could trust what she remembered. It seemed un-real: the full moon; sinking to the foot of the ocean ... and did she remember *breathing*? Underwater? Or had that been a crazy dream?

She'd been trussed to him with ropes. Her eyes went straight to his chest where she remembered seeing scales.

He followed her gaze, then brought his hand up to the top of his shirt and started undoing the buttons. His shirt came off.

He relaxed on the stool, and let her take him in. The scales were not all over his chest and abdomen like they had been (providing she hadn't dreamt it). Now, they made up a smaller patch, about the size of the palm of her hand, concentrated on the right side of his neck, just above his shoulder.

"The full moon makes it worse," he said, quietly. "It forces the mutation, a little like a she-wolf's first change I should imagine. I never fully change, though. It's as if my body wants to but can't. I'm male. I was never supposed to ... well, I'm not even sure I was supposed to have survived thirty years ago. I probably shouldn't even have survived my own birth."

She tore her gaze from the scales; his muscled chest... She looked up to meet his eyes. "Did we...?"

He didn't appear to get her unspoken question at first. Then, his eyes widened. "No. There was never ... I would never – without your... No."

She blinked, studying every contour of his face. She believed him. "What happened to me under the water?"

Regret flitted across his eyes. She remembered seeing that look when she'd been beaten on the ground wishing for death. "What do you remember?" he asked.

"Nothing after going under. I remember trying to break free; I remember ... I would say I remember drowning, but here I am."

"You didn't drown. You changed."

"Into ... a siren?"

"Yes."

"And then what?"

"And then, nothing. The siren would have raced through continents for her freedom had she not been secured."

"With ropes. To you."

"To the bottom of the sea, with a weight for an anchor. I have to secure myself also, every month, in the same way. I have some restraint, but if I'm not bound in some fashion, like with ropes, I'm certain the call of the ocean depths would be too great a lure for me to resist. Had we not been bound, we could have ended up anywhere, halfway across the world, and separated from each other."

She shivered. That sounded so ... desolate.

"Is that something I have to do every month now? Tie myself to the bottom on the sea?"

"Yes. Or any body of water – it doesn't have to be salt-water, although I do find the transition easier if it is. I'm sorry. I never intended for..." He sighed and looked down; gathered himself. "It was Trident blood that kept the siren at bay. When the last trace of it died in your system, the siren finally broke through."

"So ... the wolf *can't* keep her at bay?"

"Apparently not. I would hasten to add, though, that your wolf does not appear damaged in any way from the siren's presence."

He was right. She let her mind trail inwards, seeking her wolf. There she was, quite content, and as grateful as her human counterpart for the new energy her body seemed to have emerged with from her sleep. "Why don't I have my wolf's physical strength like I used to?"

"I don't know. I'm sorry."

She lowered her eyes. There were so many questions she had no idea which ones to ask. "What happens next?"

Roman leaned forward on the stool and laced his fingers together. He seemed to be thinking on his next words. His long, dark hair fell forward over his face. "That's up to you."

She raised her eyebrows, surprised. She'd half expected to learn she was now a prisoner of sorts, trapped by the siren.

"You can't be Jennifer any longer with the police looking for you quite literally everywhere. We have to be careful the moment we step out of this hut. You also can't go back to be-ing Selena because of all the images of you retrieved from the farmhouse five years ago – that case is not officially closed. We can set you up with a new identity, though – that won't be a problem. After that, the way I see it, you have some choices."

Another new identity. It had taken her years to get to grips with being called Jennifer – she was going to have to do it all again. "What are my choices?"

"One: go it alone. In this country, or another – up to you. Two: go back to your pack in Surrey."

Her heart leapt in her chest. She hadn't even considered she *could* go back. To have it laid out in front of her as an actual possibility... "They'll kill me. They'll put me on trial and kill me."

"Maybe, maybe not. I'm led to believe some things have changed. If they take you back, they'll protect you as their own, I have no doubt. But it might be an idea to come clean about the siren because every full moon you'll have to submerge yourself in water if you want to survive."

"Come clean the way *you* did?"

He dropped his head.

It was a dig, she knew it was. But she was still smarting over the secret he'd kept all these years.

"All I can do is keep apologising, and mean it. I can't change the bad decisions I've made."

She bit her tongue. She knew he genuinely regretted it because she could feel that regret in him – something else she'd have to talk to him about at some point; the weird emotional connection thing – but she didn't want to start an argument right now. "Is there a third option?"

"Yes." He brought his head back up and stared at her. "I'm going to Santorini, in Greece. My flight leaves in two days. I've been informed there are monks on Mount Athos who hold information about sirens; important information that dates back to their creation by Demeter herself. I'm hoping to gain more understanding on how a human male and a female werewolf can carry the siren gene, and what exactly we're supposed to do about it. You can come with me." He paused, then added. "I'd very much like you to come with me. But I'll respect whichever decision you make."

Greece. Wow...

But the chance to go home to her pack...

She was no longer just a wolf though...

Her mind was jumbled. So many years wishing for choice, and there suddenly seemed too many.

"There's one more thing you should know before you decide. Hai and I are still digging around for more information, but we suspect someone higher up the chain is pulling some strings; setting things in motion."

"What do you mean?"

"The way you all but walked into a wolf hunter's lair; the way this guy found you last night..."

"He said he'd been tracking me for half a year. He found me online."

"But *how*? Google searches and luck? Something doesn't add up. The way it all happened at once, and the fact I was blindsided... I've been looking out for you for five years, I up-turned every stone before any huge decision you made like a new job, a new address, a new boyfriend—"

"David?" she interrupted, sharply. "You *vetted* David?"

"Of course I did. What if he'd meant you harm?"

She wasn't sure whether to feel angry or pleased. She'd known he'd looked out for her because of all the notes, but the levels to which he'd gone; the invasion of privacy... It was starting to become clear.

"My point is, I should have seen a village of fucking *wolf* hunters from a mile away, and I didn't. I've been going over it in my mind, trying to understand why."

"And?"

"I've got no answers yet, but you've been living in Summerbridge a whole year without a peep from the villagers, then suddenly they strike. I believe someone tipped them off about you being a wolf, and I suspect the man last night had some help finding you, even if the help was anonymous. Someone, somewhere, knows who you are and is trying to get at you – for what reason, I don't know. But whatever choice you make, you've got to be careful."

"Why did you do it?" she asked, suddenly. "Why have you spent five years watching my back? Saving my life? You thought I was human; you'd done your job making sure I'd survived – you could have left me at that point to lead my human life in peace and not looked back."

"Except for every nightmare you suffer and every emotion you scream."

She blinked, understanding slowly seeping in.

"I tried. Three years ago, I tried. I cut contact with you; I left the country for the best part of a year."

She knew exactly when that had been. She'd received no notes for months and months. She'd felt their loss, much to her chagrin. It was at that point she'd begun to realise she'd depended on them; needed them. His notes had touched a part of her David never could.

"But every time you were upset, angry, scared—"

"You felt it."

He stood up and crossed his arms.

"You told me you can show me that night you pulled me out of the sea; that I can see it how you saw it."

He nodded, though he looked reluctant. "I can. If you ask, I will."

"Would it mean I … would feel what you felt that night?"

"Yes."

She fell silent. She knew he hadn't meant to hurt her –

she knew that now. But the fact remained that in 'siren world', he'd essentially raped her. She wasn't ready to know what that was like from his angle. "Not now," she whispered. "But one day, I might ask."

"Whenever you ask, I'll show you," he said quietly.

More silence.

Her future had changed drastically in a matter of days – less than days. "What if I decide to go back to my pack? Won't you still feel all my feelings?"

"I'll deal with it," he replied flatly. "I'm not about to trade your freedom for my weakness."

She flinched. That had sounded ... harsh.

Roman's shoulders sagged, and he shook his head. "I sound like my fucking father. Look, I'll be fine. I'm not someone you ever need worry about. I brought you into this mess, and I'll help you fix it as much as I can, but only for as long as you want me to. And if you *don't* want me to, that's fine, too. You'll be safe with your pack. I would seriously consider that as an option. You might have to prove your loyalty to them, but I doubt they'd sentence you to death, not after everything."

She went silent again. Silence seemed to be the fallback mode for them both. She had no idea what to do. Most of it hadn't even sunk in yet. And this man ... *this man* ... was the one daring to give her hope. "You left me at that farmhouse." Her voice broke, the accusation coming out much more furiously than she'd intended, but history never faded that fast. She couldn't brush it under the carpet.

He froze on the spot. All she could see was the profile of his straight nose for the hair draped across his face.

"Were we never going to talk about it? You *watched* as they violated me over and over again, and you did *nothing*. You were there. *You were there.* You watched me shoot my brother.

Could you have saved him? *Could* you?"

No reply.

"Do you think anything that's happened over the past two days makes all of that just go away?" Hot tears filled her eyes – of fury; of shame.

He said nothing, and the silence seemed to stretch out forever. He finally spoke. "I'm going to leave you to get changed."

Bastard. She brushed her tears away, furiously, angry he'd seen them; angry she'd fallen prey to a moment of weakness. He wasn't going to acknowledge his part in her imprisonment and her brother's murder. He wasn't going to talk about it.

"This beach hut," he continued. "It's our motel for now. The police have been scouting all the B&Bs and hotels in the area for you, so this was our best bet until my flight."

Fine. He could bury his head in the sand. Let him be an arsehole about it if he wanted. She didn't need him; she *couldn't* allow herself to need him. She had her pack. That's where she was going. She'd made her choice. She gritted her teeth. "I'm going home to Surrey."

His frame stiffened, then relaxed. "All right, then."

She hated herself for feeling disappointed he put up no argument against her decision. "What about my house?"

"You can't go back to it. The police restricted access to it for the first twenty-four hours after the murders, but they're done with it now. David left the hospital last night. He's most probably at the house now."

"The hunters…"

"They won't touch him. They must know he's human. They might question and prod him on the sly for information on your whereabouts, but that'll likely be it. I should imagine David will grieve, then move out of the house. He's still got his old flat, hasn't he?"

"Yes, he rents it out."

"That's where he'll go. He's not stranded. But you *need* to sever all contact with him. You know that, right?"

Reluctantly, she nodded.

"It's for his own safety."

"I know. My heart aches for him, though."

"Better your heart aching, than his not beating."

"I almost killed him."

"But you didn't."

"No – him, I lied to for two years. It was six others I killed." *And your brother makes seven; Gabriel makes eight.*

"It's not a good idea to count your conquests or your kills."

She looked at him, startled he could tell what she was thinking.

He stared back at her, grimly; darkly; warring with some secret part of himself she couldn't quite see. Maybe her questioning his part in the brutal treatment she'd suffered at the hands of his brother had gotten to him.

Good.

He spoke quietly. "I was a coward. I've *been* a coward. So have you. We've both got blood on our hands. We're not the heroes who saved the world, we're the villains who survived it. I've made my peace with that. You should, too, because guilt is a weight you'll never swim away from."

He walked out of the beach hut and shut the door behind him.

~*~

His insides churned over the conversation he'd just had, although, all in all, it had probably gone better than he could have hoped. Even if it had opened him to his own darkness. He fought it every goddamned day.

But he'd lost her. She was going to go back to her pack.

Which is where she belongs.

Maybe it was. It didn't matter – he couldn't force her to stay with him.

Hai called his name from a few feet away as he walked down from the car park.

Slipping back into his shirt, Roman made his way over to him.

"Is she awake?" asked Hai.

"She is."

"You've spoken to her?"

"I have."

"Am I going to get more than monosyllabic answers from you?"

He shot his mentor a look. "I laid out her options for her."

"Options? What options?"

"You know – her options: stay with me, go at it alone, or go back to her pack."

"Back to her *pack*? Are you a fool? She needs to be with you."

"She's not my prisoner, nor do I intend to make her one."

Hai gestured at the sky in a show of despair. "Does she even remember the change?"

Roman looked away and rammed his hands into his trousers. "No."

"And you're sending her away."

"I'm sending her nowhere. She's *choosing*."

"Of course she is! Because she doesn't know any better! Everything I said before still stands: her wolf seeks your dominance."

"I'm not the man for that. Her siren—"

"Her siren seeks *you*."

He shut up and stared out at the horizon, where sea met sky.

"She just can't remember it."

"Then she'll find me when she's ready, but I'm not taking her by force."

Hai rolled his eyes. "You're being very dramatic. It's not 'by force' – you're not your family. It would be by assertion; persuasion; even by reason—"

"Hai, enough. There's no tie here, bar the emotional one, which I can withstand if I have to. This was never a mating; it was never a bonding – not in that way. She's free to go, and she should if her instincts tell her to. I have enough challenges waiting for me in Greece – perhaps it's best she's not a part of that."

"She's the reason you're going there at all." But Hai sighed, and shrugged. "It's your life. Unfortunately ... mine is also beckoning me away."

Roman frowned and turned to face him "What do you mean?"

The older man swallowed hard. "My father is dying. Days left, if that."

"Hai ... I'm so sorry."

He nodded. "I've been called back home to China. I must go."

"You won't be coming to Greece?"

He looked at him apologetically.

"No, no," said Roman, "it's fine – of course you must go home." He ignored the sinking feeling he'd be going to Greece alone. He had no idea what he was walking into out there. Never mind. Needs must. "When do you leave?"

"My flight is tonight. They wanted me sooner, but ... I couldn't leave you until after the full moon, given the circumstances."

Warmth filled him. This man had always put him first. Roman stepped in and gave him a hug. "I'm indebted to you for all your help the past few years."

"Hey ... come now. I plan to return in two weeks. Preparations for the funeral have already been made – it's a waiting game from here."

"I'll be in Santorini."

"I'll meet you out there. I promise. Here..." He pulled an envelope from his inside coat pocket. "I have her new documents."

"You're fabulous." He took the envelope. "Is everything here? Passport, driver's licence, birth certificate—"

"Everything's there. It wasn't a problem at all."

"Any more news on who might be watching her?" If they didn't find out who was behind the organisation of the attacks the past few days, he feared leaving her behind, though he'd certainly feel better if she was back home with her pack.

"No. Every lead takes me down a dead end."

"All right. Safe journey home, Hai."

"And you. Be careful in Santorini."

"I will be."

A noise to his right had them both looking that way. Jennifer walked out of the beach hut, dressed. She spotted them, and tentatively waved.

Hai waved back, enthusiastically, like a big kid, and Roman saw her smile at that.

Hai laughed. "She looks well. I'm going over to say goodbye."

"Let her know I'll drive her to Surrey. If we leave soon, we can be there before nightfall."

Hai nodded and made his way to the she-wolf.

Roman caught her looking at him, past Hai, but she swiftly averted her eyes, and threw Hai a big grin. The old guy wasted no time enveloping her in a hug. Hai's fondness for her had grown rapidly since Roman had unwittingly pulled her into his mess five years ago, and interacting with her, face-to-face, the past two days had only cemented Hai's adoration.

Roman shook away the feeling that *this* felt like his pack; his family. That would do no good and likely was nothing more than the wish of a boy who had never felt part of his own.

He turned away from them both and headed to his car. He had phone calls to make.

Chapter Sixteen

Roman pulled the green Toyota over along the side of the lane as she took in her surroundings. The smell of 'home' carried in through the crack in her window.

Home. She blinked back tears – of loss more than anything else. She daren't hope they'd take her back. The hope felt far too fragile.

"Are you sure you want me to stop here?"

"Yeah. There's a back way in almost no one knows about. Stephen and I used to use it as kids when we snuck out. I saw three security cameras when we drove along the outside of the land, but there won't be any here. I want to go in unannounced."

He parked the car and switched off the engine. "All right, then."

There was an awkward pause. She turned to look at him and found him looking back. He cleared his throat. "I have your new ID for you – all the paperwork." He leaned over and opened the glove box.

Her stomach clenched at his aroma; at his nearness.

If he sensed her reaction, he ignored it. He handed her an envelope. "I apologise in advance for the fact that you're married to me."

"What?" she said, taking it. She opened the flap at the top – it had never been sealed.

"Hai sorted out the documents. At the time, he believed you'd be coming with me to Greece, so he arranged for you and I to be married. The authorities aren't looking for a 'mrs' – it would buy us time to leave the country."

She pulled out the papers. "Laura Dalton. That's my name?"

"It is."

"Dalton's your surname?"

"Yes."

"It was Bab's surname?"

She felt him tense. "Yes."

How weird that she'd never known that. All that time in the farmhouse, and she'd never known. Knowing Bab's surname – Bab Dalton – somehow made him a little less scary.

"I realise you want as little to do with my family as possible – as do I, believe me – but there was no time to change my identity, too. So, Dalton it is. I'm sorry." His voice softened on his apology.

She pulled her gaze from his face and looked at the paperwork. She saw a driver's licence, birth certificate, a new address even though she wasn't going there, a passport, bank cards for a new account, a new phone with a bill detailing her new number, and... "A plane ticket?"

"Like I said, he arranged it all thinking you were coming. You can tear it up. If anyone questions you in the future about your husband, say I left you. Say you don't know where I am. My existence makes no difference to your identity."

She slid everything back inside the envelope and placed it in her bag. "Thank you. And thank Hai, too."

"I will."

"Laura ... I think I can do Laura. Rolls off my tongue

more easily than Jennifer, anyway."

"You didn't like Jennifer?"

"I've just never felt like a Jennifer."

There was another awkward pause. She decided she needed to go. She opened the car door and stepped out with both her rucksack, and the overnight bag she'd stuffed in the footwell. She dropped both at her feet. "Good luck in Greece."

"Thank you. Please remember what needs to be done next full moon."

"Like I could forget."

He looked away. "Goodbye, Laura."

"Goodbye." She shut the door.

Goodbyes were always so clumsy, and she didn't even know this guy – not really.

Nevertheless, after he'd started the engine and pulled away, a pang of remorse made itself known. She clenched her toes in her shoes to stop herself from chasing after the Toyota.

She was home. *This is home.*

She turned to the trees that towered above her and closed her eyes to hear the birds better. She felt oddly trapped. She should be sprinting in; she should be happy, despite the hard work ahead of her making amends with everyone.

Her wolf was strangely silent inside her. Not unhappy; just silent.

The siren, however, seemed to fidget. She wanted the expanse of the sea before her, not the expanse of the land, no matter how fresh and fertile it was.

Gingerly, she walked towards where the hidden entrance used to be, hoping it was still there. It was, though somewhat overgrown. Memories flooded back, mainly of Stephen and days playing on the grounds. So much had happened since then.

Ten metres into the property, she stopped, uncertain.

Everything felt so *uncertain*, and she'd never felt that way before – not here.

She'd killed Stephen. There was no coming back from that. She'd changed in so many ways, the siren only a tiny part of the overall picture. When she'd left here, she'd been twenty-four and angry. She was verging on thirty now, and she didn't know what she was – not just angry. And any anger still lingering was different from the anger that had been.

The faint sound of laughter carried towards her through the trees. She looked towards it.

The second reason she'd chosen this spot – the first being the hidden entrance – was that it was high up. If you stood in the correct place beyond the army of trees, managing not to slip where they dipped and hurtle into the quarry fifty feet below, you caught a glimpse of the main house and its grounds.

She placed her bags on the ground by a holly tree and made her way to that exact spot. She remembered it like the back of her hand. Slowing where she knew the ground would give way beneath her feet, she stopped by a tall beech tree – another old friend – and looked through the gap to its right.

There it was. There was home.

The laughter had come from a child – two children – with light blond hair. They were specks in the distance, but she was sure they were boys. Another speck sprinted towards them, this one with longer, dark hair. A girl.

They collided ... more laughter – it was some kind of game. A large, grey wolf emerged from the woods behind them, stalking them, and she caught her breath. Even from here she recognised him.

At a speed less quick than she knew he could muster, her father charged at the kids. He seemed to be limping, though she wasn't certain of that from this far away. If he was, it didn't break his stride.

One of the boys spotted him and screamed; then all the children joined in with the screaming as they jumped him.

He shifted into his human form, howling a laugh that dwarfed all their screams of delight, and she found herself laughing with him. She knew he'd lived – Roman had told her as much in notes. Now, she knew he was happy.

Her smile slowly faded as the stark reality of what she was seeing hit her: a grandfather with his grandchildren. Without a doubt they meant a lot to him; she couldn't ever re-call him playing with her like that. Almost thirty years on, she still wasn't a part of ... *this*.

The grief and regret that hollered in her chest was an abrupt contrast to the happiness she was witnessing.

You'll taint it.

She stepped back. She *would* taint it. If she went down there with her baggage and her brokenness, trailing the past behind her ... she'd ruin it all. She'd already ruined it once. She couldn't do it again.

Roughly wiping her wayward tears with her jacket sleeve, she turned to leave and almost jumped out of her skin when she nearly collided with a figure – a tiny one.

Battling down her yelp of surprise, she took in the child in front of her (this place was filled to the brim with children, it seemed). She couldn't have been more than five or six. She had dark brown hair and dark brown eyes, although ... she didn't mean to stare, but one of her eyes was green. Heterochromia iridis; rare in humans. It was beautiful – so was she – but it was startling. Almost as startling as the way the kid stared at her.

She'd only been here five minutes and she'd already fucked up. She hadn't wanted to be spotted. "Hey," she said, her voice hushed. She looked around for others. She didn't want to attract any wolf within ear shot, but she saw and smelled no one else. "Do you ... live here?" Perhaps the question was too direct, but she wanted to get some idea of what she was dealing with and how to get out of it.

Slowly, the girl shook her head, but then, she stopped, and started nodding instead. "I moved in today."

She didn't smell like a wolf, but there was scent of wolf around her. She wasn't alone.

The girl pointedly looked at Jennifer's rucksack and overnight bag on the ground a few feet away. "Are you moving in, too?"

Jennifer decided to stick with the direct approach and knelt down to meet her at eye level. "No. I'm just leaving actually. And if you don't mind, I don't want anyone to know I was here."

"Why not?"

She stalled. She didn't have an answer for that.

The girl had one for her. "Is it because you're a monster, too?"

That shocked her. She shivered. "What do you mean?"

The girl dropped her eyes. When she looked at her again, they were filled with sadness and pain. It got to her – a lot. This kid should be running around laughing with the others; like she and Stephen had done before the world went to shit. Instead, she was burdened and sullen. The girl's voice fell to a whisper. "I have a monster in me. It's my fault we came here."

Jesus Christ. "Who's 'we'?"

"Mummy, Daddy, and me. They're talking to the wolves that live here. They told me to play with the others while they talked."

So she *did* know about werewolves. But what *was* she if not a wolf? She didn't smell altogether human. "But you found your way here, instead?" How, exactly, Jennifer didn't know. The main house was half a mile away. The girl had just *walked* here? Up the steepest slopes? By herself?

She nodded. "I'm scared to play. The monster inside me killed a boy, and I'm not supposed to tell anyone."

Hell, she felt like she'd been slapped. What a tragedy, and the girl had said that desolately – almost without expression – but that wasn't so because her eyes shimmered with hurt.

The memory of Stephen's head snapping back from the bullet she'd fired slipped into her mind. It hurt as much today as it did five years ago. There was one thing she knew about people, whether human or wolf: if you kept beating their natural optimism with sticks and stones, they'd give in to the monster eventually. Everyone had a breaking point. Everyone.

Jennifer sat down on the grass, carefully, not wanting to scare the girl away, but needing to keep an ear out for anyone approaching. She'd made the decision to leave; she didn't want to be found. "We're even then. I know something about you I'm not supposed to, and you know I was here even though you're not supposed to."

The girl shrugged, still sullen. "I guess."

"I'm going to tell you one more secret, though. If you want me to, that is. But you can't tell anyone – ever."

She cocked her head in interest. "I won't tell, I promise."

"You were right: I have a monster in me, too. It's also killed people – the bad feeling from that never really goes away, but … that's not my secret. This is." She reached into the pocket of her jacket and brought out the velvet ring box. She hadn't wanted it in her rucksack, but on her person where she knew it was safe, and she was glad for that now. She suddenly felt a bit lighter. Jennifer opened the box and showed the girl the ring. The setting sun that peeked through the trees caught the diamond.

The girl's eyes lit up. "Wow," she said.

"Yeah. This was given to me by a very special man who

loved me *in spite* of the monster in me. He didn't care, you see. The monster couldn't make me ugly to him; he just saw all the good stuff inside me, and the way he loved me was like ... *real* love, you know? Like people *should* be loved. He loved me so much, he asked me to marry him.

"Well, I *can't* marry him, but that's not the point. The point is that no matter how big, bad, and scary that monster in you gets, someone out there will still love you. I'm going to give you this ring because I want you to remember that."

She audibly gasped, her odd-coloured eyes widening. "You're going to give me the ring?"

Jennifer took it out of the box and held it for her to take. "Yes. But you have to keep it a secret, and you have to *promise* that every time you look at it, you'll remember the story, and that there are people in the world who will love you no matter how big that monster gets. Do you promise?"

She took the ring, handling it like she might handle Cinderella's glass slipper. "I promise."

"Good."

"But I have nothing to give you in return." She looked worried about that. "Mummy says when someone gives you a gift, you should give them something back if you can."

"There's no need to give me anything. But there *is* something you can do for me," she added as an afterthought.

"There is?"

"It's just a little thing, but ... since you're going to be living here... There's an old wolf who also lives here called Richard." Her throat suddenly constricted, and she had to pause and take a breath, blinking fresh tears away as her father's face filled her mind. "Look out for him, please? As best you can? But don't *tell* him you're looking out for him, because he always likes to think he can look after himself, even when he can't."

She smiled, and nodded enthusiastically. "I'll look after him, I promise."

"Thank you." She stood up. She had to get out of here.

"You're going now?"

"I have to."

"What's your name?"

"It's Je—er ... Laura. My name's Laura. What's yours?"

"Jasmine."

"That's a pretty name – one of my favourite flowers."

She beamed with pride, and Jennifer felt better than she had in a long time. A really fucking long time.

"Will you be okay finding your way back to the house?"

"Yes."

"It's a long way – are you sure you can walk it?"

She was still smiling, and clutching the ring like it meant the world to her. Maybe it did. "I didn't walk."

"Oh." If she didn't walk, then... No. She didn't have time to get into it. She had to go. "As long as you're careful along the steep bits, okay?"

She nodded again, fervently. "Bye-bye, Laura."

She placed the rucksack on her back and grabbed her overnight bag. "'Bye, Jasmine." She headed for the hidden entrance that would lead back to the lane, but couldn't resist a look back to make sure the girl was heeding her warning about the steep bits above the quarry.

She wasn't there.

Jennifer froze, then scanned her surroundings – left, right... She couldn't make out the girl's tracks either; tracks she should have left since it was muddy enough. Even her scent was fainter, almost as if she hadn't been there at all. But she had. She *definitely* had. And Jennifer had only turned her back for ... god, no more than three seconds, surely.

The girl had completely disappeared.

Suppressing a shiver, she left the shelter of the trees, turning the strange encounter over in her mind as she walked down the lane. Five minutes later and she still hadn't made sense of it, but something else caught her eye now, bringing her to a stop, and stirring both her relief, and her annoyance.

The green Toyota was parked in a bay on the right.

Unbelievable.

She strode up to it and leaned down to look through the window.

Yep, sure enough, there was Roman, munching on a packet of crisps. He turned towards her and smiled.

She banged on the window, indulging her annoyance and ignoring the relief, stubbornly refusing to admit she felt glad for his presence.

With a bemused expression, he rolled down his window, and held out the packet in his hand. "Crisp?"

"You *knew* I'd change my mind?"

"Oh, you've changed your mind?"

Git.

"I just fancied a bite to eat. Didn't want to drive and snack."

She narrowed her eyes.

"You getting in?"

With a low growl, she stomped to the passenger side and opened the door, ignoring the slight smile he wore on his face. She threw her bags in the back. Getting into her seat, she shut the door and grabbed her seatbelt. "So, what exactly is the perk of having you as my husband? If I have to put up with you, you're going to have to do a better job in selling me the concept."

He started the engine, folding the empty crisp packet into the groove of his car door's panel. "Well," he began as he pulled away from the verge, "there's less chance of dying."

"Pfft," she replied. "Living is overrated."

"The possibility of your capture and torture are greatly reduced."

"You mean like they have been the past few days, what with the wolf hunters and the maniac with a grudge and th—"

"You can sing in the shower without my brain exploding."

She threw him the mother of all looks.

He grinned.

She hid hers by turning her head and staring out the window. "What happens when *you* sing?"

"People tend to leave the building. Other than that, not a lot."

They fell into a silence which was ... uncomfortably comfortable. Uncomfortable because the last male she'd been this easy with – had *ever* been this easy with – had been her brother. Even with David, she'd been guarded to an extent. Walls didn't exist with Roman due to their sirens, and she wasn't ready for what that might mean. The bruises on her body had healed; her heart still carried every one.

"There's another packet of crisps in the glove box if you're hungry."

She wasn't particularly, but for the sake of something to do to keep her confusing thoughts at bay, she opened the glove box to get it out, and paused when she spied the gun nestled in there next to a chamois cloth, the car's manual, some gum, and a packet of tissues.

We're not the heroes who saved the world, we're the villains who survived it.

Roman was right – she had yet to make her peace with that. This wasn't exactly how she thought her life would end up when she used to dream of the future as a child.

She pulled the crisps out and closed the glove box.

~*~

Prisha had never felt so uncomfortable. It was hot in the room anyway, but she was feeling more and more sweaty by the second, wanting nothing more than to strip off the suit jacket she'd decided to wear for a more professional look. It didn't help, she supposed, that the only other person in the impersonable interview room – Brian Coney – was a male who was watching the same video she was watching on a whiteboard screen fixed to the wall. Talk about seeing every fucking detail – 'fucking' being the operative word.

On the screen, the woman she knew as Jennifer was on all fours on a bed, moaning in what might be ecstasy or pain – it was hard to tell which – as a black-haired man fucked her from behind like it was the first time he'd gotten his dick wet in years.

She'd seen this before, of course. This was some of the footage she'd hacked into on that personal cloud storage she'd told Brian Coney about; this was what she'd brought in with her as evidence. But watching it all play out on the big screen was...

She pressed her palms against the side of her pant suit's trousers hoping its fabric would absorb some of the sweat. She couldn't take her jacket off now, because she was sure she'd leaked a wet patch under each armpit.

Jennifer – or whoever the hell she was – gasped loudly, then reached a hand out and gripped the side of the man's thigh.

Mr Coney turned the volume up, and her voice boomed around the small room. "Change."

The man fucking her stilled. He looked crazed – from the little she could see of his face, anyway. "What?"

"*Change.* No more games, no pretence, show me the

monster in the man. Take me as you really are."

Prisha shuffled on her feet and was aware her breathing had changed. She'd seen what happened next. She felt Mr Coney's stare burn into her. She forced herself to calm and kept her eyes glued on the screen, even though half of her wanted to rip her eyeballs from her head.

It happened. The man stiffened, his muscled twitched, he growled, then ... he changed. Into ... *that*.

Jennifer was gasping and whining, in obvious pain, but also in obvious arousal. At some point, she started to protest, but it was too late because his transformation was complete. He howled and resumed the fucking, this time driving her mercilessly into the sheets as she cried out.

The image froze, Mr Coney holding the remote out in front of him, and Prisha realised she'd stopped breathing. With effort, she drew air into her lungs, trying not to acknowledge the fact she was uncomfortably warm between her legs. It was all kinds of wrong. It was sick.

"Ms Patel..." Mr Coney's voice made her jump; she hoped he hadn't noticed. She needed more air – *outside* this room – but he didn't seem to be in any hurry to go anywhere.

Prisha turned her gaze away from the image on the paused screen, though it remained branded in her mind.

"This is valuable information – two videos and," he peered at her laptop screen on the desk, "forty-eight photographs, all from this private storage account, you say."

"Yes, sir." Her voice sounded throaty because of her parched mouth. She blushed, hoping he wouldn't mistake it for any kind of desire after what they'd just watched. She felt repulsed.

"So, tell me, Ms Patel, what it is we just saw?"

She blinked, then blinked again. It was a question she'd asked herself many times, and though only one answer came to mind, she sounded ridiculous saying it out loud. "I realise it's impossible, sir, but it looked like ... like he changed into an animal of some kind ... erm..." She swallowed, not knowing what more to add. What the hell was there to say?

Mr Coney smiled. "The word you're looking for is werewolf."

She balked, her eyes widening, her brain not quite registering what she was hearing. "A..."

"Werewolf, Ms Patel. If you're going to work for me, you should know I'm not keen on repeating myself."

"Work for ... *you*?"

He stood from the desk he was half sitting on, pressed a button on her laptop, and the screen and whiteboard finally went black, thank god. "Technically, he was *more* than a werewolf, but for our purposes the term will do. Come with me, Ms Patel." Not waiting for an answer, he strode out of the room.

Not wanting to lose her new job, and dying to leave the confines of that room, she followed.

He led her to the elevator in the hallway. When it opened, and he signalled for her to step in before him, she risked a look down to make sure she was about to step onto an actual floor rather than nothingness.

Mr Coney chuckled, noticing her actions. "Don't worry, Ms Patel, it's not me you need to be worried about."

Lifting her chin, adamant to show a bit of grit and hating herself for doing otherwise, she stepped into the elevator.

Mr Coney stepped in behind her and pressed the blank button at the bottom of the column of buttons. The doors closed.

"Where are we going, sir?"

"To a place few dare to tread."

She said nothing else, and they travelled in silence, going

downwards, to wherever the hell the blank button was taking the elevator.

It finally stopped, bouncing gently and making her stomach rise and fall. *Don't throw up.*

The doors opened into a brightly lit hallway. Mr Coney stepped out. "Follow me."

She did as instructed.

He turned towards the second door on the left, which said FIRE EXIT on it (it didn't look like a fire exit), took a card out from his shirt pocket and slid it into the identifier on the wall. It clunked and unlocked. They walked through it, but he turned straight away to the first door on the right. He didn't use his card for this one, but pressed his thumb on the black pad on the wall. The pad beeped, then shone a red light from the top. He leaned down, placed his left eye in line with the light and waited for it to pass over his retina.

Prisha waited. Her gaze hovered over the door they were about to enter. This one didn't say 'fire exit' on it, but MI99.

MI99?

She'd heard that at one point in time – before the Second World War – there had been a few divisions to the Secret Intelligence Service. MI1, all the way through to MI20, though she wasn't privy to the ins and outs of it. But MI99?

There was a click, and the door opened. Mr Coney walked through. After she'd followed him in, he secured it shut behind her. If at any point she'd felt the urge to run away, that opportunity had well and truly gone now. Luckily, no such urge had overcome her.

Prisha blinked at what lay in front of her, and her mouth dropped. The room was *huge*. They'd gone downwards in the elevator, so she'd assumed they were heading towards some kind of basement, but it was more than a basement – its area clearly took up the *entire* bottom level of the building. It had the floor space of twenty houses at least, and it was segregated into sections: one looked like a library housing ancient, hardbound books; another looked like it housed office cubicles filled with computers and other sorts of ... telecommunications machines? A door towards the bottom of the massive area opened, and a man in a white coat, holding a clipboard, walked out – he looked like a doctor or scientist.

"That's the ward through there," clarified Mr Coney. "Complete with operating room and morgue."

Morgue?

She made some kind of noise, not quite able to get words out. There was so much to take in. Her eyes finally landed on large airtight jars filling rows and rows of heavy duty metal shelves along part of the left wall. Inching closer towards them, surprised her legs were working at all, she noticed the jars on the top row were filled with liquid and contained what looked like human foetuses. On the next row down, the jars were occupied with yet more of the same, but the foetuses looked different – their heads were larger as were their eyes, their skin a slightly different colour.

The third row down was where her gaze remained, glued to the contents of the glass jars from one end of the wall to the other. Some held paws, some held tails, the furs all different colours; the ones that transfixed her carried entire heads – heads of wolves. Some of them looked like your average wild wolf, and others looked like mutant wolves – beasts like she'd seen on that video.

"Werewolves," she whispered. And finally, *finally*, something clicked into place. It all made a strange kind of sense. Realisation filled her mind the same time its glint filled her eye. She turned to her new boss in wonder.

He smiled, widely, in complete understanding of her reaction. "Welcome, Ms Patel, to MI99."

~*~

David sat in a stupor, his eyes tired and gritty from exhaustion and grief. He'd cried more the past twenty-four hours than he had his entire life.

He'd been sitting here, like this, in Jen's house. It was still overturned. He hadn't been able to bring himself to tidy the evidence of her abduction.

He stared at the two laptops he'd set up next to his desktop PC. He'd wired everything right, but hadn't been able to take the next step.

His heart hurt; he hurt everywhere, but his chest felt like someone had taken a metal spoon, dug their way into his beating organ and twisted the metal instrument; kept twisting it...

It *was* abduction. It had to be. Jennifer was many things, but she wasn't a quitter. She wouldn't flee. She was a fighter. She wouldn't run off if she could stand her ground, which clearly, she hadn't been able to because ... well, look at this place. What more proof did he need?

David glanced, dully, at the windows which had been smashed; the furniture, turned over; the drawers, emptied; her personals strewn everywhere. It was like witnessing a part of her violation, and his imagination took care of the parts he couldn't see.

Her toothbrush was gone, as were some of her clothes. The police were mostly convinced she'd run of her own free will. If she had, her hand had been forced, which as far as he was concerned, still constituted abduction. At least, it was no better or safer than abduction. If someone didn't have her, someone was after her.

He sat up in the wooden chair. His spine clicked. He ran his tongue over his dry lips, and his right hand over his five o'clock shadow. He hadn't shaved in three days and didn't have the will to do it now.

Coffee. You need coffee for this.

Robotically, he finally got up from his chair, went into the kitchen, and put the coffee machine on. His eyes brimmed with tears again as he took in the mugs they'd used for their last morning coffee, still unwashed by the sink.

He felt a little stronger when the beautiful, bitter aroma of the brew hit his senses. He took his mug and went back to his chair, and woke up his laptops and PC. He knew how to do this, he just had to get on and do it. He knew it would take time, especially because Prisha always covered her tracks. Still, she was human. He was bound to find a weak spot in her system at some point. And there was always a chance he'd find Jennifer first if he scoured enough systems up and down the country hard enough.

He hadn't believed Prish when she'd said she didn't know what happened to Jennifer. She was the first who would have snooped given his relationship to Jen. If she was hiding something, he'd find it. He didn't quite have Prisha's skill, but he had patience and determination. And now, he had time. Shit-loads of time he had to occupy so he didn't go insane.

He sipped his coffee, ignoring the sound of a couple of the villagers walking past the living room outside, staring at him through the broken window as they did so. They'd been acting fucking odd since he'd come home, but they'd left him mostly alone. It was a pain having to deal with their glances and whispers, but it added a layer of anger to his determination, which he needed. *They'd* done this to Jen's home, believing her to have murdered those men. How they could even think that was beyond him. The lot of them could fuck off. He'd clean this place up, then he'd have a think about where to go. He had a flat in York he rented out, and the current occupier's lease expired in a couple of weeks. He could give them their month's notice from then.

The screens on the laptops fired up at last, taking him to the command page he needed on one of them. He'd find a way to tap Prisha's ISP and her mobile phone, then he'd search databases in the country, starting with the NHS, and moving on to the police, hotel chains, airports, shipping harbours... "I'll find you, Jen," he muttered as he typed in command after command, watching each one fail, and knowing this could take hours if not days. "I'm coming for you."

Epilogue

The scent of incense, moth balls, and Jasmine leaf tea always took him aback a little every time he came home. It was nostalgia, of course, but with that nostalgia was a sense of peace and warmth.

Unlike Roman, Hai had been cherished as a child, and had wanted for nothing. But he'd also been taught humility, particularly towards those less fortunate than he.

"Nín hǎo," said Hai, greeting his father's carer, Chanming – the long-time family doctor – as they both bent at the waist in a show of respect. The formal greeting seemed strange in a way given they knew each other well, but suited the sombreness of the moment.

"Hai, welcome home."

Hai nodded with a smile. It had taken him a few hours since landing in Beijing Capital Airport to come to grips with his mother tongue having not had to speak it daily in years, but having known no other language well into adulthood, it was like riding a bicycle. "How is he?"

"Any breath might be his last. He has been waiting for you."

Hai put his luggage down. Two housemaids came out of seemingly nowhere and hurried to take it. The doctor instructed them to place it in the guest room.

This house he'd grown up in hadn't really changed at all, from its dark mahogany wood to its grand staircase. "I shall keep him no longer."

"Would you like us to bring you tea?"

"That would be very much appreciated, thank you."

Chanming led Hai to the door that in turn led into one of the reception rooms. "He has been sleeping in here for months, far too weak to take the stairs like he used to."

"Thank you for looking after him the way you have."

"It has been both my duty and my pleasure," he smiled. "I shall leave you both in peace now, but will be in the gardens if you need me."

"Xiè xie." They both bowed once more, and then Chanming left, and Hai found himself a little lost. His father had been – still was – the most respected man in his field in China. That his field was steeped in mysticism and the supernatural made him invaluable for his knowledge and skill. He loved his father greatly, but had always been overwhelmed at the thought of stepping into his shoes when the time came. He was also filled with trepidation at how it would work. He did not wish to move back home – much of his heart was in Great Britain, and with Roman, but he could not counsel Roman forever. This past moon saw a definite shift in dynamics. He was both proud and afraid that the time had come for the student to become the master.

He eased himself into the room. His gaze immediately went to the man lying on the bed, both indomitable and painfully fragile. At one hundred and twenty years old, his father had defied time as well as anything else. He was skin and bones now, yet, on hearing Hai's footsteps, he opened his eyes and with very little movement, laid them on him.

"Father," said Hai, softly. He approached him and took his hand in his as he sat on the edge of his bed.

His voice was barely audible, and he had trouble both breathing and speaking. "My ... son. You're ... here."

"I am."

"Good. Time to ... go."

He was talking about himself, not Hai. Tears surfaced at the understanding he'd been holding on just for him.

The old man pulled his hand out from under Hai's with very little strength in him.

Hai quickly withdrew his hold on him so he wouldn't find the action painful.

His hand disappeared under the sheet. After a few seconds, he slowly brought it back out, something clasped in his fist. "Your ... destiny." He pressed the object into Hai's palm, but kept his hand closed around both the object and Hai, gripping him in a handshake; not yet ready to let go.

"Father ... I am afraid. I'm afraid I will not know how to accept my destiny, or how to fill your shoes."

His father's mouth turned up a fraction at the corners. "Destiny will ... find you. You need do ... nothing." He gasped for air, but didn't let go of his hand. "My shoes won't fit."

Hai laughed.

"Wear your ... own."

His laugh died down, and his tears spilled at last. "I will miss you greatly, for you are a great man."

"All of us ... great ... my son. There is ... there is..."

"Yes, father?"

"A ... boy."

"A boy?"

He pressed the metal object into his hand harder.

Hai found himself surprised at his grip. Perhaps it was something close to the fabled 'death grip' now he was so close to the end. A last show of strength before his muscles seized for good. He waited patiently for him to continue.

"Borne of ... magic. Bound ... to dragons."

Hai raised a brow. *Dragons*? He knew his father's work had involved the magnificent beasts thought long dead. But he, himself, knew very little about them. If he was thinking of the correct time period, he had long left China and had been travelling the world when his father had been working on 'the dragon project' – about nine years ago. Yes, that was right; and three or four years after that, Roman had contacted him (having not done so for a decade) after his brother had died and Jennifer had been 'sirened'.

"Everything ... coming ... together. Help the ... boy. You ... must."

"How do I find the boy, father?"

"He will ... find you. Protected ... he ... is ... protec...."

His father stilled, then relaxed. His hand slipped from his.

"Father?" whispered Hai. But he already knew he'd gone.

The tears fell harder. He leaned forward, and rested his head on his father's chest, wanting to absorb his warmth before it left him completely. "Thank you," he said through his tears. "Thank you for all you have done for me."

With a shaking hand, he reached up, and closed the man's eyelids. He couldn't quite bring himself to do much else straight away. He just stood there, basking in memories decades old of the strongest, most loving man he'd ever known.

Minutes passed.

He had to tell the others, and then tell the village; the town; the country: the great Ri Tian was dead.

Standing, he remembered the object his father had pressed into his hand, its edges digging into his skin because his fist was closed around it so tightly.

Heavy with grief, he opened his hand and looked down at the silver pendant on a thin, silver chain. The metal glinted in the nearly dark room, almost unnaturally, and had been melded to form two Chinese symbols. It had been a long time since he'd seen them, but he knew them. His father had shown them to him as a child, and he remembered their meaning.

Primeval Chaos.

.

ALSO AVAILABLE

Aftershock

Blood Never Lies, #2
An Eye of the Storm Companion Novel

This is the story of Jasmine's first five years.

~*~

Further details can be found on Dianna's website.

To keep up with all new releases, works in progress, and general writing updates, please join Dianna on:

Facebook.com/AuthorDiannaHardy
X.com/TheWitchingPen
Website: DiannaHardy.com

Acknowledgements / Author's Note

SPOILER ALERT! Please don't read the acknowledgements before you've read the book!

Dum-de-dum ... have you looked away yet? Seriously, come back here when you've finished the book, 'cause this is a MA-JOR spoiler.

This is your last warning.

Okay, good. If you're reading this far, I'm not to blame – it's not my fault. Here we go: I want to talk a little bit about that ending – the epilogue. Hai's father. Yes, you read that right, Witching Pen fans: *Primeval Chaos*. There's a boy. Yes, it's who you're thinking. Yes, in the future The Witching Pen world and the Eye of the Storm world will cross, though they will no longer be called those things. (And don't worry if you haven't read The Witching Pen series – you don't need to.) The two new series will have new titles and new characters, new adventures and new romances, new mythologies and new threats.

This likely won't happen until 2019 / 2020, but I will make it worth the wait.

I loved writing *Blood Shadow*, I really did. Finally, I feel I have done Selena justice – I put her through shit in *Eye of the Storm*. She needed a voice, so I gave her a BIG one. That kills people. (Sorry, Selena.)

Now, she's Laura. Laura suits her, actually. She and Roman are going to go ahead into a brand new series of their own that in the series timeline will begin two weeks after *Blood Shadow* ends (though I can't write the first book until 2019 as I have to write a couple of others first). There's a thing there between Laura and Roman. I don't fully know what that thing is yet, just as they don't. We'll have to wait and see how it develops, if at all. They both have quite a bit of healing to do and we'll get to see that. We'll also get to see the (fictitious, of course) monks of Mount Athos, and immerse ourselves in whatever they'll discover in Greece. And Prisha and David – oh, my! What will they do? (I have no idea yet.)

Thank you a million to my Beta Readers (Maureen, Pam, Elizabeth, and Alastair), to my invaluable ARC Readers, to both Lynn Worton and Elizabeth Morgan for all the support they give me; to my always-fabulous editor, Amanda Pederick; thank you to all my readers wanting to read *Blood Shadow*, even though *Eye of the Storm* has now ended. I know this book isn't Lydia, Lawrence, Taylor, and Ryan (everyone's favs, I know), but it heralds the start of new relationships that will prove to be just as fulfilling in the long run. I'm excited to take my time a bit to build new worlds; to create a really good story. Thanks for taking this new adventure with me.

Lastly, I just want to say thank you to everyone who has tweeted my books, and shared them across Facebook, Instagram, and social media sites, and to everyone who TALKS about my books, face-to-face, with their friends and other readers. It's all appreciated more than you could know.

I can't wait to bring you *Aftershock*.

Dianna Hardy
March, 2018

Addendum, October 2025: Due to personal upheaval, Dianna had to take time out from writing. Fathoms Deep (the novel that comes after Blood Shadow) will now be released in April 2026 and is likely to be a standalone rather than a series.

Also by Dianna Hardy

The Witching Pen series

Plus the companion novel, *Saving Eve*.
This is a complete, finished series.

Witches, angels, demons, Heaven and Hell all come together
in a dizzying story of friendship, love and forgiveness. A
titillating mix of paranormal romance and urban fantasy
brings you a sensational series you won't forget.

Blood Surge
A Vampiric Urban Fantasy Novel

A beautiful library in a sleepy town in Hampshire is the
perfect place for Sophia to escape a fraught childhood and
forgotten past until an old lover borrows a book, a woman
dies, a ridiculously gorgeous man keeps turning up around
every corner, and a stately home party goes awry. It turns out
Sophia's life (and past) isn't what she thought it was at all.
Passionate vampiric urban fantasy.

Once Times Thrice

Practical Magic meets *Serendipity* in a beautiful, fun, and
magical series about love, family, and second chances, set in
Cornwall, England. Follow Merri, Jamie, Pippa, Jimmy and
Candy as summer turns to autumn.

Contemporary romance with a touch of magic.

Broken Lights

One gunshot, one scramble for life, one unlikely couple, one very long night ... can one damaged woman and one ordinary man, find the extraordinary in the very last second they're given?

Broken Lights is a standalone short novel of what's really worth fighting for, when one second is all you have left.

About The Author

Dianna Hardy is an international bestselling author of (cross-genre) fantasy fiction, most notable for her dark (often explicit) paranormal fantasy and the raw, intense *Eye of the Storm* series. But her heart-warming *Once Times Thrice* series proves she thrives in the light as much as the dark. Whatever your poison, what she loves most is to bring you stories that are action-packed, fast-paced and not short of heat, with the focus on character development, relationship dynamics, and the plot. She writes full-length novels and short fiction.

In December 2012, *Releasing The Wolf* hit the Kindle Paranormal Fantasy charts in both the US and the UK, where it stayed for three months, enjoying a highest ranking of #20. Both books in the *Eye Of The Storm* series have enjoyed success in the top 100 of Fantasy charts on Kindle US, Kindle UK, and iTunes (Australia, top 40). *The Witching Pen* series, *'Til Death Do Us Part* and *A Silver Kiss*, have also hit the top 100 of iBooks (Apple Books) charts in Fantasy, Romance and Horror in ten different countries worldwide.

Although quite active online, Dianna prefers the quiet company of nature and animals to the hustle and bustle of people. She loves anything paranormal (she doesn't really consider it "para"), organic food, walking barefoot, the smell of the woods after rain, and summer days.

However, she is also sustained by coffee, chocolate and the occasional vodka.

Having graduated from Richmond Drama School (London) in '98, she spent the next few years in a multitude of jobs (both acting and non-acting), studying anything that fascinated her, searching her soul, and finally found her passion where it had always been: at the end of a pen.

She currently lives on the south coast in England with her

partner and their daughter, where she writes full time.

Official site:
www.diannahardy.com

Facebook:
www.facebook.com/authordiannahardy

X:
www.x.com/thewitchingpen

www.ingramcontent.com/pod-product-compliance
Lightning Source LLC
Chambersburg PA
CBHW022151170626
46807CB00005B/2167